Totally Bound Publishing books by Elle Q. Sabine:

The Misbegotten Misses
The Outcast Earl
The Rusticated Duchess
The Troubled Knight

I0674973

The Misbegotten Misses

THE TROUBLED KNIGHT

ELLE Q. SABINE

The Troubled Knight
ISBN # 978-1-78651-958-0
©Copyright Elle Q. Sabine 2016
Cover Art by Posh Gosh ©Copyright May 2016
Interior text design by Claire Siemaszkiewicz
Totally Bound Publishing

THE TROUBLED KNIGHT

Dedication

"[A] beautiful woman without a mind of her own leaves her lover with no resource after he had physically enjoyed her charms." ~ Casanova

Dear Mr. Sabine, thank you for encouraging this mind of mine. I hope you benefit from it as much as I do.

Author's Historical Note

The Peninsular War was fought between Napoleon's French Empire and the allied powers of Spain, Portugal and Great Britain from 1807 to 1814. Beginning in 1809, the Marquess of Wellesley—later the First Duke of Wellington—commanded the British forces in Portugal. He arrived in Lisbon in April, 1809. In April, 1814, the allies defeated the French at the Battle of Toulouse, mostly because the news of Napoleon's abdication and surrender arrived in the middle of the battle. Among Wellesley's forces was the Second Division, commanded by Lieutenant General Sir Rowland Hill. The Second Division, consisting of twelve regiments of English and Portuguese infantrymen, was actively involved in many battles as the allies pushed the French army out of Portugal, across Spain and back into France. In 1828, Sir Rowland Hill succeeded the Duke of Wellington as commander-in-chief of the forces and held the post until 1842.

Chapter One

"Happy May Day, angel." Peter's words reached Genevieve's ears, but she didn't respond immediately. Peter was half reclining on the divan in her studio, thoroughly distracting her from the afternoon of painting she'd planned. Instead, she was completely nude, stretched out comfortably over Peter's thigh, her upper body tucked against his so comfortably that he might have been a silk-covered pillow. Given the cool rain falling outside since luncheon, she could have been cold, but Peter had built the fire high before tempting her away from the easel with hot chocolate and delicious biscuits. While she'd nibbled on the mid-afternoon snack, he'd stripped her of her smock and the simple gown beneath it.

Not that she'd objected. No, when he stroked her skin and his admiring gaze scanned the curves of her form, Genevieve felt the urge to preen, not to pretend any sort of false modesty. But quite soon she'd found herself lying on her side, her plump thighs between his hard ones. Peter was an expert at fondling her bottom, and if he'd lightly smacked it a few times as he rubbed away the stiffness in the muscles of her hips and upper thighs, she'd only arched and tried to open her thighs to invite him to explore much more intimately.

Peter had, eventually. And here she was, his fingers still inside her from behind, bliss-filled and completely at ease.

At least the babe was quiet, perhaps worn out by the morning dancing in the village square and their afternoon antics. Genevieve spread her hand over her abdomen, the curve of her swollen body evidence of the change in their marriage in the last year. He followed her movement, clasping her hand in place against her skin.

"All the village women say that I need to slow down and rest more. How could I possibly do that, unless I'm to lie flat on my back all day?" Genevieve finally asked. But resting did sound awfully enticing. She didn't want to move. She wanted to dwell happily in this warm, bliss-filled cocoon of Peter's embrace. "No one will let me do anything except walk in the gardens and paint."

He chuckled. "I am quite fond of you lying flat on your back. Should I demonstrate?" he suggested wickedly.

"I should let you demonstrate how to do such a thing, then bring my brushes over here and paint it," Genevieve threatened.

Around her, Peter shuddered. It was such an unexpected reaction that Genevieve was immediately intrigued. He was aroused by the idea. Peter couldn't hide the jumping of his cock, even though it remained inside his trousers. Her outer thigh had been pressed up against his groin, and erections didn't lie.

"Would you like me to paint you, Peter?" she purred, turning her head to look at him. "Strip off your shirt, run my brushes over your chest, your hips, your upper thighs?" She hummed happily at the thought, her imagination wild with a thousand possibilities representing the plethora of emotions and dreams she'd experienced with him. "And, of course, your cock."

He grunted, not a particularly eloquent reaction. Peter was usually articulate when it came to intimacy, so she forgave him the momentary inability to speak. She, on the other hand, had at first been unable to express herself in any sort of intelligible language. But slowly, as the months had passed, Genevieve had been able to spell out what she was imagining and experiencing. Peter enjoyed that too.

"Though you'd have to remain still — very still — or it would just be messy. Not a proper piece of art at all." She permitted herself the luxury of envisioning it — Peter spread out on the divan, his arms and legs spread apart. "Perhaps I'd have to tie you in place, to make sure you didn't try to stop me halfway through."

Peter began to shake his head, widening his eyes, but Genevieve put out a hand to his chest. "You've said that turnabout was fair." Both of them suddenly jerked as she remembered the day months earlier when she had been tied down to her bed for hours while Peter had driven her nearly to the brink of unconsciousness through repeated orgasms. Genevieve could tell from Peter's face that he was remembering the same afternoon. She liked to think it was then that she'd conceived the wee babe inside her. "You like it when I'm astride you. You like it when I take you in my mouth. You'll like this too. You find being the focus of my attention, my imagination, extremely pleasurable."

He gasped, but he didn't deny being intrigued by her words. "And how exactly will I explain it to Grady?"

Genevieve smiled, raising her eyebrows and admiring the hard muscles before her, even if they were still covered by his shirt and waistcoat. Inwardly she was amused by the thought of Peter's two devoted servants—his fastidious gentleman's gentleman, Robin, and strictly reserved majordomo, Grady— trying to help Peter remove the paint from his body, but she'd never admit to that. She'd probably enjoy removing it herself anyway. "You will admit that you cannot deny me anything or that I'm fascinated by your beautiful skin. Or that you can't stand it when I cry and I seem to all the time now that I'm in this delicate condition. Or that we were drunk and it seemed like a good idea at the time."

Peter humphed, but his fingers were tangled at the buttons of his waistcoat. Genevieve sat up and kissed his jaw, her fingers slipping the buttons open and pulling up his shirt. He grunted. "I'll undress. You get your paints."

Not bothering to hide her smile, Genevieve stood, grabbing her smock from the floor as she did. With some three months to go, she could still bend, but the maneuver was more difficult.

"Don't you dare put your gown back on or I'll take it right back off." He paused. "And no tying me down. What if you fell or the coals in the fire needed tending or someone came to the door?"

Genevieve frowned, but Peter's fussy protectiveness was a natural outcome of his love and affection. He'd always been protective, but since he'd deduced she was expecting, he truly hovered. "I'd ring for help," she returned serenely, slipping the smock over her shoulders. "The object is to paint you, not me. I need to wear something."

Behind her, Peter grumbled, but she heard him moving, so she found a dry palette and considered what she might do with the opportunity. It took her only a few minutes to retrieve the paints she wanted, then she turned back to Peter.

He waited obligingly on his back on the divan, completely nude with his erect staff displayed proudly. Perhaps it was obscene for it to be that blatantly erect, but Genevieve had long since lost any inhibitions when it came to admiring Peter's body. He lusted for her touch, and she loved pandering to his cravings.

Genevieve licked her lips. He'd spread his arms out wide, gripping the legs of the divan on each side. His feet rested against one end, since he'd chosen the piece to suit his height, and he'd spread his legs so that there was enough space between his knees for her to kneel, should she so wish.

She grinned at him, and he fidgeted slightly.

Nevertheless, he was as still as a church mouse as she positioned her supplies alongside the daybed and joined him, her finger reaching out to trace his hip then over the front of his pelvis. She found the edge of the scar that marked his damaged skin and followed the edges of it up to his shoulder. Unable to resist, she bent forward and used her tongue to follow the path her fingers had made.

All of Peter's muscles hardened, which she rewarded by pressing her lips tenderly to the nipple closest to her. "Thank you for letting me indulge my fantasies, husband," she whispered.

"As long as they have to do with me, you're welcome to use my body any way you see fit, angel," Peter allowed. His voice was already low and strained, so she straightened and took up her brush and palette.

It was careful work, and she put all thoughts of intimacy out of her mind to concentrate. Keeping in mind his masculine pride, she kept to the red and orange hues, mixing the paints and gradually adding darker tints.

She'd never done anything like this before, and she loved it. She wanted to keep him there longer, but sitting for a portrait was fatiguing, so she knew this enforced stillness that Peter was enduring would exhaust him. She used a very narrow brush, blowing on the black lines, and wound the image around his nipples, leaving them clear, working her way down and using his muscles to define the shape of the animal she was constructing.

"I've always wanted to paint you, as you very well know," she said. "I didn't imagine this. I rather thought a more traditional portrait. Someday I will paint you on a canvas. You know I've sketched you. You've seen several of those early attempts. And I've done detailed studies of your hands and your face. I'd do a complete study of your full body if you could be still for that long, though you know I've sketched you nude as well. But this...this is something different entirely. And you're being so patient for me. Thank you, Peter."

He moaned, and Genevieve looked up in surprise. She'd thought the sensuality from earlier was lost as she painted, but Peter apparently had the opposite reaction. He was stretched to utter stillness, but he was still wildly aroused. She glanced beside her, noting his stiff member. She remembered her hands, brushing over his skin and resting on his bare torso as she worked. She wondered how the tiny brush strokes on his skin and the drying paint felt.

Suddenly she very much wanted him inside her — not that she could paint that way, not that she wanted to hurry, not that she wanted the fantasy on his chest damaged before it dried and he could see it.

"How long until it dries?" he asked.

Genevieve swallowed heavily, using a finger to smudge a bit of the feather. "You're fucking beautiful," she whispered, watching the visceral reaction of his cock to the profanity he'd taught her to use. "And I'm going to drive you to utter madness when I sit astride you, but not before it's perfectly dry."

"Wash the damn brushes out before I cannot wait," he ordered.

Genevieve ignored him and continued to use her hand to add a few final touches to her project.

"Genevieve." Peter's voice cracked at the end, and she knew she had to be satisfied. She drew back, staring, breathing deeply. "It damn well better not be a picture of a naked woman or a card game," he said.

"A little late for such restrictions, isn't it?" she asked, raising an eyebrow to him. "It's all done but" — she paused dramatically — "I would like to sign it, if you don't mind." He groaned but nodded, so Genevieve took the fine brush she'd used to give line and definition, added a bit of black and carefully added her signature to the edge along the fantastical tail feathers. "Can you stay still while I clean up?"

Peter gave an infinitesimal nod so Genevieve gathered her things and moved around the room, setting the brushes to soak and covering the canvas she'd worked on earlier. The late afternoon sun would quickly dim the room, and she would paint no more today. Like Peter, she was certain she'd be exhausted this evening.

She wondered if he would keep it as long as possible or if he would scrub it off at the first possible opportunity, so that his chest was again smooth and bare pink when he next came to her bed. Only time would tell.

As she closed the paint jars, she noticed Peter's head. It had turned just slightly, so he could follow her movements.

She obligingly stripped off the smock and left it on its hook, so that she was again unclothed. She'd felt awkward at first, being nude in front of him, especially as her stomach extended, but Peter had insisted and his behavior had clearly demonstrated his enthrallment with her body, even if she was too short, too buxom and breeding.

Genevieve returned to his side soon after, letting her gaze roam his body. "It's not dry, not yet," she told him. "But put your legs together, slowly. Keep your chest still, and don't move your hips if you can help it. Yes, like that." She breathed deeply, gathering herself. "If you can be absolutely motionless," she whispered, kneeling on the divan and swinging one knee over his, straddling him. "I have a suggestion, for something we might try while it finishes drying."

Peter's eyes glinted from beneath half-closed lids, but he was silent as she moved up his body, careful to keep her hands away from him. When she sank down, his cock sliding up inside her welcoming sheath, he couldn't stop from clenching his abdomen and thrusting inside her. Her eyes flew open. Despite that movement, her art was intact.

"Let *me* move. Stay still," she ordered, knowing Peter could not have much stamina, patience or tolerance remaining. To give him surcease, she cupped her breasts with her hands, squeezing them together, and shifted her hips, pushing out and back down. The babe moved, so she released her breasts and cupped the mound at her belly. She didn't want her swollen stomach bouncing against the paint. His lips pressed together tightly, holding back, but Genevieve could feel his engorged rod within her. She pumped again and pinched her nipples. Peter watched intently, his hips and buttocks clenched tightly beneath her. She supposed asking him to relax was laughable. He couldn't come inside her if he was relaxed.

She breathed shallowly, her eyes half closing as she watched him. He caught her rhythm and found a way to urge them both along, using his thighs to guide her withdrawal and forward thrust. Balancing on her knees, she crawled forward an inch and rode him faster, thanking whatever deity that was listening for this man who was so much more than she had ever dreamed he would be. "Peter," she moaned, desperate.

"Yes, angel, come now. Show me heaven." Peter thrust upward, hard, with his hips, but this time Genevieve didn't object. Instead, she screamed as the pleasure she found in his company spiraled into the climax he always gave her.

Tears were running down her cheeks when she managed to climb off of him. "Good tears," she whispered, catching Peter's anxious look.

"I'm going to stand now," he announced. "I'll be as careful as I can, but I need to take care of you."

"Go look first," she whispered, reaching for his hand.

He came off the divan in nearly one motion, still making an effort not to twist his chest. Keeping her hand, he brought her along, through the sitting room of their apartment suite and into her boudoir where a tall cheval mirror waited. He paused in front of it and stared.

"The legendary phoenix," he whispered.

"Resurrected from the fire for a new purpose, a new life," she whispered.

"I have loved every canvas I've ever seen you paint," he murmured, still absorbing the long bird, which was rising from the faint scars along his side. "But this is the most magnificent thing I have ever seen, outside of our bed."

"So now you want Grady and Robin to see it," she teased softly.

"Hell, I'd let the world see it. I *want* the world to see it."

"I don't." He glanced down at her sharply, but Genevieve shrugged. "I don't want any other woman admiring your chest except me."

He bent his head and pressed his lips to hers, until her mouth opened and she stretched onto her toes, kissing back. Even so, they both remembered and held each other a foot apart.

"Thank you. For the painting, of course, but also for my new life, for giving me a new purpose."

"Thank you," she whispered. "You may be a phoenix, but I'm the one who has benefited. Think of where I would be without you."

Peter's lips twisted. "Your sisters would have found some way to save you, if I hadn't reassured Fiona of your safety."

"But you are the one who rescued me, Peter. You were my hero. You still are."

He nodded, and finally unable to bear being apart from her, pulled her close to his opposite side, away from the painting. He led her to a chair then brought her to sit carefully on his knees. There, together, they both remembered all that had happened to bring about their wedding—and later, their marriage.

Chapter Two

Three years earlier...

Peter watched, his façade of sophisticated boredom rigidly in place, as the earl's heir threw out on his third cast. As the years had passed, it had become harder to see these youngbloods lose everything to dice, whether it had been hazard or the newer games that favored the hell house over the individual bettors. Still, Peter thought it better this buck should lose to him than to the other sharps who hung back in the corners of these smoky London rooms. Peter knew this one's father, and they would reach some accommodation over the vowels. The hothead wouldn't be forced to sell the family lands to meet his obligations, but he would spend a number of years rusticating in the country learning to make money, instead of in London, hazarding it away.

He slid the mark across, watched the boy's hand shake as he signed the vowel, but Peter contained any expression of sympathy or denigration. "I expect you'll be speaking about this to your pater tomorrow," he finally suggested when the boy, perhaps only twenty-two or twenty-three years of age, swallowed.

Peter had been even younger when he had brazenly purchased colors with his newfound fortune and gambled his life on the Marquess of Wellesley and Lieutenant General Sir Rowland Hill. Despite their exceptional leadership and Peter's decorated departure, he'd spent a half-dozen years trying to recover from those glorious campaigns in Portugal and Spain. Indeed, most gentlemen of the *haut ton* would see his semi-residence in this hell as a signal of Peter's failure to become the proper gentleman expected of a well-bred Englishman.

Perhaps it was better that this one learn the painful lessons of prudence and discretion at the hands of debt, rather than at war.

"It seems I will," the boy finally agreed, sobering up rapidly as Peter folded the document and secured it inside his jacket. "I should go."

"Yes," Peter agreed, standing. He followed the young man from the table but remained inside when the young lord escaped the den, satisfied to see the boy head into the street and not immediately into more trouble. Peter had no reason to leave, though. His small townhouse in Clarges Street was blessedly empty, except for his slumbering majordomo and gentleman's gentleman. Even so, Peter never slept during the night in London. The noise of men and carriages on the cobblestones in the darkness disturbed him, and the constant odor of smoke in the air kept his mind running constantly. He evaluated the possible dangers—how to escape from the bedchamber alive, how to save his servants, the routes by which he could reach his mother at Fielding House and defend her from —

Peter cut off the swirling thoughts, viciously swearing under his breath. London in 1822 was relatively safe from any imminent uprising by the masses, and Fielding House was a proper brick mansion set apart from the houses on each side of it, lowering the danger from fire. In any event, his stepfather would have any threat dealt with and annihilated before Peter could even make it the few blocks from Clarges Street to Fielding House.

Peter might be overly sensitive to the crowded conditions and atmosphere in London, but his stepfather was ruthless about protecting his wife from danger. Peter honestly hoped Sir John Fielding never had reason to suspect the madness that sometimes ruled Peter's life, but even that was preferable to having it whispered about among his mother's friends.

Peter shuddered at the thought.

A loud voice in the corner had Peter turning instinctively, the awareness he'd been suppressing leaping to life again. It was a familiar voice but attached to a man Peter had hoped to never see again in this lifetime. General Malone — a colonel with a temporary command of brigadier general at Waterloo — was standing with two others, each with a glass of whiskey in hand as they watched a serious game of piquet.

The general apparently thought he was a better piquet player than the sharp and the three peers at the table, even if the sharp was drunk. Peter considered leaving, but Malone was not known to frequent this particular den. His unusual presence sparked Peter's suspicions. Almost against his will, he crept closer from behind, tipping his head to better pick up the banter.

"Lord knows she's a pretty thing, but hell, the chit's not old enough to tap properly," the stranger to the right of Malone said disparagingly.

"The general's not tapping her. He's marrying her," the other stranger reminded the trio, tipping back at least a finger of whiskey in one gulp.

Peter held his breath, but Malone only laughed and tossed back his own drink. "Of course I'm marrying Winchester's little princess. It's the only way I can get my hands on that perfect young ass. And her tits? Christ, I'm going to keep that girl on her back for a month."

"Better take advantage of the chance," one of the others admitted. "You'll knock her up. Won't be able to enjoy her then."

Malone laughed, but it wasn't a pleasant sound. "She's only sixteen, damn it. I know what to do with girls who are knocked up. She won't ever know there is one on the way. For the amount I'm paying Winchester for her, I'm going to enjoy every goddamned minute, whether she wants it or not. If she's not underneath me, she's going to know who owns her cunt every fucking second of the day. I'll keep her on her knees if I fucking choose."

Unbidden, Peter's brain presented him with a memory of Winchester's youngest daughter. The earl had four, and Peter had seen them all with their mother at Fielding House on several occasions. Once, he'd appeared in the middle of an informal afternoon tea to inform his mother he was leaving London for his Scottish lodge, and he had been bombarded by a crowd of silk gowns and dainty laughs. Lady Fielding had insisted on introducing him to every young lady in the room — fifteen in all — and their mothers. Most had still been in the schoolroom and enjoying the novelty of such an innocent event in the Season prior to their come-outs, when Peter, the known rake and card sharp, had shown up to add excitement to the outing. The giggling had almost felled him, but he remembered the girl Malone was discussing.

Lady Genevieve de Rothesay. She had been memorable because she hadn't giggled. Instead, she'd held out her hand and properly greeted him, kindly informing him that she thought it was considerate to call on his mother prior to traveling. Then she'd wished him well on his journey. Afterward, she'd turned to the side and engaged another young lady in conversation, allowing him to move on.

In his memory, her eyes were a glittering hazel—not memorable for their hue, perhaps, but for the intense focus in them. Beyond that, he could recall few details of her face beyond an impression of blonde hair. He did remember that she'd had to look up at him when they'd spoken, and that she'd worn an ice-blue gown that wasn't quite the right hue for her complexion.

Nausea rose as he thought of Malone's hands on her.

Peter truly would be damned if he could do something to stop that twisted maniac from this madness but chose to step aside instead.

Swallowing down his reaction, Peter thought rapidly, replaying Malone's words. A half-baked plan came to mind. Malone would be a much harder mark than that poor sop from Derbyshire, but it might just be the most important game Peter had ever played. Casually, consciously readjusting his face to look slightly hammered, Peter snagged a glass of whiskey from a passing server, dumped half of it, spraying a few drops on his jacket and pants, then swirled the amber liquid in the glass and sloshed it against his lips. Hidden by the dark fabric of his clothing, the stench of the spilled liquor would sour as the hours passed, preserving the illusion of Peter's drunkenness.

He stepped forward and bumped into Malone's companions, looking up in surprise. Peter's eyes opened wide as he straightened with a brief apology, as though he'd just recognized that Malone was in the house. "General" — he proffered his hand for a shake — "haven't seen you in years. Toulouse, I think."

Malone's eyes narrowed. In Toulouse, Peter hadn't been a drunken sot in a gambling den. He'd been a decorated colonel, a war hero, a sober and well-loved regiment commander admired by his soldiers and his commanders alike. Malone had hated his successes. But after, Malone had been hale and whole, and Peter had been broken, a casualty of the battle, both in mind and body. Malone hadn't known that. He'd departed for England in the company of the other celebrating officers. Peter had remained behind, confined to a field hospital, then recuperated in Spain for several months. He hadn't gone to Waterloo.

"Peter Devon? Quite a surprise, seeing you here. Heard you were an expert at this sort of thing, but still surprised, I suppose."

"You've been well?" Peter asked, slapping him heartily on the shoulder, his touch a bit too hard.

Malone's companion guffawed. "He's having a bit of an evening. Just signed a marriage settlement, you see. Came here directly from meeting the lucky father-in-law."

"Never!" Peter looked appropriately horrified at the thought of being leg-shackled. "No wonder you've come here, then — a final hurrah before the *grande dames* of the *ton* demand you appear to be feted for hours on end. What's your game? Piquet? Interested in playing?" He moved the glass to his mouth and splashed more of the whiskey against his lips, noting that Malone's companions did the same.

Malone's eyes narrowed and Peter felt a sick sense of triumph. He truly wanted this prick's fortune, and piquet was not a high enough stakes game to accomplish that in one night. "Dice seems more like my game than cards," Malone demurred.

Peter hemmed and hawed, apparently thinking it over. "Don't play hazard all that often," he lied. "We need a third and fourth to make the table complete." He eyed Malone's companions, narrowing his eyes to improve his focus.

One elbowed the other. "George is here. He's got the funds to throw."

"Would give us time to catch up," Peter taunted. "Always wanted to beat you fair and square."

"Ass," Malone muttered. "Haven't changed a bit, have you?"

Peter offered him a happy grin. "Let me go refill my glass and find a fourth. Looks like we can try that table." He gestured to an empty table off to the side.

Malone nodded, flagging down a server. "Get the man a drink, on me," he instructed.

Peter waited until all three had turned away and taken a few steps, out of reach of his low voice. "Jim, keep topping me up, but make it mostly water. I need to stay sober. And where's Lockley?"

"Right then. Stepped out into the back, sir. Want me to fetch him for you?" The servant boys all knew Peter was good for his tab and extra, and treated him accordingly.

"I'll go myself. Tell the gentlemen I stepped out for a piss, and give them full rounds of whiskey—the most potent you have."

Jim nodded briskly and edged away.

Peter took the side door out of the room. Lockley was always ripe for an adventure, and this surely counted as one.

He wasn't surprised to find Lockley in the back courtyard. Only the den's staff and a few of the hard-core regulars were allowed to use the space, though few others would ever wish to spend time there. Aside from the filth that most would find hard to ignore, the narrow, enclosed area was too cold and foggy right now for his taste.

Lockley was sitting casually on a bench, shielded by shadows. The girl on her knees between his thighs wasn't even a surprise.

Bemused at his appearance, Lockley waved one hand in a negligent greeting and tightened his other hand in the skirt's hair. "Come to enjoy her too?" he asked, reaching down.

Peter's eyes followed Lockley's hand to where the chit's breasts were spilling out of the loosened bodice. Lockley twisted the girl's nipple, and she moaned, a sound that clearly pleased his friend, who grunted appreciatively and adjusted his position, sinking farther into her throat. She sucked happily, almost purring as Lockley handled her.

"Not tonight," Peter declined. He wasn't innocent and he'd even enjoyed himself on that same bench a few times with one or more of the maids, but this woman didn't interest him. Maybe he was aging, but he also liked to take his time, which required a comfortable piece of furniture—and Malone waited inside. "I came out to offer you something of an opportunity. There's some risk as it is hazard, but the man's already half drunk."

Lockley grinned in the darkness. "Give me five minutes to pleasure this lusty lass and clean up."

Peter nodded and leaned against a nearby tree to watch. Malone would be encouraged by his delay, presuming Peter was reluctant. Lockley wouldn't mind, and clearly the girl didn't object to the show. She slid her hands up Lockley's thighs and clutched his waistcoat inside his jacket. The man hadn't done more than flip open the placket of buttons that held his trousers closed and pull his shirt out of the way enough for the woman to perform her magic.

Lockley was quite happy with her performance. He grunted as he spewed in her mouth, then lifted her to his lap and pushed his hands up under her skirts.

She gave a performance for that, too, arching backward and moaning rather loudly as he stimulated her. Peter guessed the climax was at least real, if somewhat exaggerated. The woman was practiced at her role.

As they walked inside, Peter explained his plan. But in the back of his mind was the realization that he hadn't felt a bit of interest or desire, nor a moment of regret, that he couldn't take his turn with Lockley's tumble.

* * * *

Peter met Lockley's eyes across the table. George had long since withdrawn from the game and on the winning side, but neither Lockley nor Peter had given Malone any indication that he might be playing too deep or exactly how much he'd lost. Peter had promised that Lockley might have the bulk of Malone's cash funds. He'd explained that his primary objective was the marriage settlement contract that Malone had signed earlier in the evening. He'd heard Malone's comment that he'd need to lay out a good deal of cash to make the marriage happen, so Peter planned to interfere by being sure Malone didn't have the ready funds.

"I've got one more in me," Lockley sighed as he finished his third cast.

Malone grunted, swallowed back another finger of whiskey and took the dice. He narrowed his eyes at the chips and coins on the table, the quantity of which Peter and Lockley had been concealing for hours by the simple and long-practiced expedient of stacking their whiskey glasses and snack bowls in front of them, and waited. The three played the round. Peter laughed under his breath when Lockley deliberately threw out the first two casts. Peter bet on both, but small amounts, telling that he wasn't willing to risk any additional blunt, and Lockley lost both. Malone fell for the ploy and bet large on the last cast, which Peter fully expected Lockley to win. Peter shook his head and declined then restrained his smile when Lockley took Malone's tokens. Malone, who had been hearing stories for the last two hours about Lockley's legendary losses at dice, frowned, but bet again. Lockley threw out the cast, ending the round and sent a much smaller token back across the table to Malone.

Peter tossed the first die and waited for Malone and Lockley to make a side bet. To his surprise, Malone actually bet on Peter throwing in, so Peter took his time and let fate have her way. Malone won the bet, so Peter hid his smile and tossed again. The two bet back and forth as Peter lost two more rounds, until Malone's confidence grew. All three knew that Peter had one last throw to finish the night. He threw the first die and waited until Malone and Lockley bet, then reached down and tossed down half of the tokens at his elbow to the setters.

Lockley could barely restrain his grin.

Peter tossed the die and sighed, while beside him Malone uttered a string of curses. He collected his winnings from Malone as Lockley produced his stack of tokens and markers and started calculating. Peter waved Jim over and quietly asked for a round of watered wine. Malone held his liquor well, but he wanted Malone sober enough to think realistically.

Lockley had done Malone up well. By the time the two had traded out the markers, it was clear that Lockley held a fortune in Malone's vowels. The general looked to Peter, swallowed, and without writing out an IOU to Lockley, asked bluntly, "Settle up with me first."

Peter presented his pile of markers. It was much smaller, but with Malone's debt to Lockley, even the three thousand more pounds must have seemed overwhelming. But Peter had no desire to be sympathetic. "Horses, real estate, a warehouse full of salable goods if you've exhausted your cash reserves?" Peter suggested.

"Damn it, I have the money in the bank for the Lockley vowel," Malone claimed. He shifted, rubbing his jacket lapel. "He'll have it tomorrow. I just didn't want to use it. Had other plans for the blunt."

Peter raised an eyebrow. "An investment?" Then he braved a wide grin. "Ah! The marriage. You have to pay for it?"

Malone grunted.

"Must be a love match." Lockley smirked. "So what's it going to be then, Malone? Your house or your bank account?"

"Damn you, Lockley. I thought Peter would be the one to try to fleece me."

Peter laughed. "If you like, I'll do you a damn favor and act as your agent. Paying to marry any damn girl is a wrong deal. Hand over that contract. I'll get you a dowry that will get you out of the mire, instead of a damn debt."

Malone grimaced. Lockley smacked his hand down on the table to get his attention. He leaned toward Malone and said clearly, "Are you saying you can't meet your debt?"

"Not what I said," Malone demurred. He put his hand up and shoved it into his hair. Peter leaned back in his chair and waited.

Five minutes later and Malone was sweating. He'd already signed the vowel for the balance he owed Lockley and another he owed Peter. But Lockley wasn't satisfied. He wanted his blunt immediately. Malone was starting to look for Peter to help, as it seemed clear that Malone's two companions from earlier in the evening had slipped out of the den. Lockley, however, had two bruisers edging closer, watching to see if Malone reneged on his debt.

As if tired by Malone's predicament, Peter finally intervened and revealed his terms. "What the hell. You want to cancel my vowel? This marriage of yours is arranged. There will be other girls. Give me that damn marriage contract and you'll only have Lockley to satisfy when the bank opens tomorrow. Keep your house, your stables, your honor. Otherwise, all of London is going to know tonight's outcome."

His face red, Malone reached inside his jacket, withdrew a set of folded papers and threw them on the table. Peter opened them and quickly read through, then picked up his vowel for Malone and marked it paid. "I'll leave you two gentlemen to resolve the rest, eh?" he asked, tucking the precious papers into the pocket inside his waistcoat.

Lockley, to whom Peter had already revealed the age of Malone's prospective bride, was determined to make an example of Malone to the rest of London. "Next time I let you winkle me into a damn hazard game at midnight, Devon, the beggar had better have fucking sovereigns on his person."

"Yes, next time I'll molest the man's pockets myself to see what he has on hand," Peter returned sarcastically. He stood and left the table without another word for Malone but did make sure to say farewell to Jim and the den's master to clear his tab. They knew he'd be back within a few nights, but periodically he made unexpected starts out of the City, and he didn't like leaving an account open. Jim, at least, deserved better.

Chapter Three

"Malone's voiding this embarrassment." Peter broke the news bluntly, tossing the signed contract onto Winchester's desk. "He's found himself in a bit of a bind and can't meet the payments you specified. She must be some chit, to pay that amount of cash for a girl who's still in the schoolroom."

A tic at Winchester's left eyebrow gave evidence of his irritation. "The man can't back out," he returned bitingly.

Peter gave a hollow bark of laughter as he realized the earl was angry over the cancellation, not over the implied disrespect Peter had just offered the earl's daughter. "Oh yes, he can and he has. The contract's not legally effective until the first half of the cash amount is delivered. As of ten o'clock this morning, Malone's bank accounts are empty. It seems Malone was a bit too cocky at hazard last night."

"My daughter still needs a husband. If not Malone, it will be someone else. If you're friends with Malone, I assume you have the same taste." Winchester sneered a bit. "Too young, too virginal—untouched in any way."

Peter restrained his urge to pummel the man. "What are you suggesting?" he returned. "That I'd marry the lass?"

Winchester leaned forward. "Would you?" he asked.

"Not for that outrageous price," Peter mocked. "She may not have a dowry, but neither am I a fool. I'd have to support her."

"She'd be inexpensive. Keep her locked up in the country, even Scotland," Winchester offered.

Fury rammed through Peter. Winchester was a cold fish and something more. Something unnatural was in his head, and Peter honestly worried about leaving the girl with him. What if he found a husband even less suitable than Malone? Peter could refuse to marry the girl, but who would look out for her if he did? If they were married, at least he could provide a twisted version of guardianship for her. She'd be safe, even if she was trapped in a life to which she hadn't agreed.

He had once gone to Portugal and Spain with the naive view that his actions would keep England safe, that the women and children of England needed to be protected from the mad Napoleonic version of government France had suffered through. He'd returned with a more jaundiced view of England's monarchy and military, but his ideals were the same at heart. He wasn't in Spain now, but Winchester was blathering about a husband for his too-young daughter—again. He'd fight to defend this innocent, just as he'd fought in Spain.

"Perhaps Malone has another friend who might be interested?"

Peter sighed. He knew the tactic, appreciated it, had used it the night before to draw Malone deeper into their game. But there was no help for it. *Bollocks.* This rescue mission was going completely off course, and after it had started so well.

"My mother has been pressuring me to marry and set up my nursery," he mused. "But my earlier statement stands. I won't pay you a fortune for the privilege, as I'll be paying all my life for her upkeep and that of the babes to come as well. Three thousand pounds sterling, and you will use that to prepare her trousseau and any other necessities – and host the wedding."

The offer was less than a quarter of what Malone had promised. Winchester scowled, but Peter held firmly silent. Instinctively he knew that if he gave Winchester even a bit of an edge, the earl would push for more. "Fine. But I want it finished, announced and the wedding breakfast held by the end of the month."

Peter smirked. "Better get your people to work then. Your man of affairs and solicitor should be in touch with mine. I'll give them their directions later today." He raised an eyebrow. "Don't fuck around with me, Winchester. You won't get a dime from me until the wedding is done, and if I find you haven't prepared the girl with a proper wardrobe and other essentials, I'll deduct the cost of providing for her, and you won't come around begging next time you get yourself into hot water. I'm taking the girl off your hands and after that, she's mine. You don't have a goddamn thing to say to her or about her, not without my permission – not even if I do lock her up in Scotland and use her for nothing but breeding."

Winchester looked too ridiculously pleased by the crudity for Peter's comfort, but all he said was, "It will be precisely as you say."

Peter sighed. He was going to have the devil of a time explaining this to his mother.

* * * *

Genevieve was shaking, but who could blame her? At least this debacle in which she found herself was not a church wedding. Her sister Abigail had had one of those two days ago in Warwickshire. And yesterday, her sister Gloria had married in St. George Church, of course, to the Duke of Lennox's eldest son, the Earl of March. Gloria had heard March described by every vile epithet in the book by her sisters Fiona and Abigail. Lennox House was only a few doors away, and the servants had whispered stories of his tirades and tantrums in her ears for years, so the thought of Gloria marrying him was nauseating.

She'd grieved for Gloria and worried about Abigail, until her father, the Earl of Winchester, announced that Genevieve, too, would be married. Now she was terrified. He'd told London—and Genevieve and her mother—by putting it in *The Times*. They'd found out by reading the paper at breakfast.

She'd cried. She'd begged. She'd slammed doors. Her mother had rushed out of the breakfast chamber, furious. Genevieve had found her mother later on the floor of her bedchamber, sobbing. Fiona had disappeared with old Frenchie, the maid who had been with them since before Fiona had been born, even though she was unmarried too. Genevieve didn't blame Fiona for running away, since Fiona was at risk of being sold off for a profit in the same way their father had disposed of Abigail, Gloria and Genevieve. If Fiona had offered to take Genevieve with her, Genevieve would have jumped in the carriage and run as far as possible.

So now she was about to be married to a stranger. Her sisters were gone, and Genevieve was sitting alone in her room at Winchester House, wondering what she had done to deserve the last eleven days of her life.

Sir Peter Devon hadn't seemed like an ogre when she'd been introduced to him at Fielding House all those months ago in the springtime. His mother, Lady Fielding, was one of the kindest ladies that Genevieve knew. Granted, she didn't know many of the popular London matrons, but Lady Fielding had definitely been one of her favorites. Even so, Lady Fielding had been unusually reserved, more formal than was typical, since she had shown up at Winchester House, as outraged as Fiona had been regarding the engagement. Lady Fielding had taken one stern look at Genevieve and Lady Winchester, whisked Genevieve's mother into the library for a private discussion and had returned to the drawing room, with Lady Winchester wiping away tears. Nevertheless, Lady Fielding had stood beside Genevieve and headed off the catty and snide remarks from the hordes of society's women who had called at Winchester House after seeing the engagement announcement. The experience had completely unnerved Genevieve, but when the room had finally emptied of callers, Lady Fielding had examined Genevieve's face carefully and ordered her to go rest. Too exhausted and upset to even look to her mother for guidance, Genevieve had simply obeyed.

Genevieve had seen Sir Peter Devon once during their ten-day engagement and that was at a mockery of an engagement dinner at Fielding House. Her father, thank goodness, had not appeared, even though he was expected, leaving only Genevieve's mother, Genevieve and Gloria, as well as Gloria's fiancé Lord March and his father, the Duke of Lennox, to represent the family. Of Sir Peter Devon's family, only his mother, Lady Fielding, and his stepfather, Sir John Fielding, were present, but the small size had been a relief. Sir Peter had kept himself sternly apart from both Gloria and Genevieve, despite Gloria's attempt to converse with him. He'd spent virtually the entire evening in discussion with Sir John Fielding and the Duke of Lennox.

At least she had a new dress. For years she had worn gowns that were refashioned from Gloria's and Abigail's wardrobes. But the day after Lady Fielding had appeared at Winchester House to face London's *haut ton* at Lady Winchester and Genevieve's side, Gloria and their mother had taken Genevieve to Bruton Street to visit the salon of a famous *modiste*. The woman, who Fiona had always sworn had a false French accent, had clucked her tongue, taken Genevieve's measurements and told them to come back three days later for a fitting. As a result, Genevieve was attired in a soft white silk gown covered in white Valenciennes lace, shot with small blue threads. Despite being the daughter of an earl, it was the finest gown she'd ever worn, but Genevieve knew that was because she hadn't yet come out. The gown should have been her come-out gown, in perhaps any color other than white. Genevieve did not like how she looked in white, and it was even worse with the elegant white bonnet with its satin ribbons and lace trimmings covering her golden curls. The colors were all wrong.

She wondered if she ever would have a coming-out gown—or if young matrons could even be presented at Court. Maybe this wedding gown was the finest garment she would have.

Her hands shook. No one had told her what would happen after the wedding. Indeed, no one had told her much of anything. She'd asked her mother, but Lady Winchester had pinched her lips and said she didn't know. Genevieve had read in *Debrett's Peerage & Baronetage* that Sir Peter Devon was a baronet, so her name would change to Lady Devon. She knew he had a country house in Suffolk called Devon Place, and a townhouse in Clarges Street. Clarges Street was a fashionable gentleman's address, but it certainly wasn't a mansion on Grosvenor Square like Winchester House or one of the older, majestic homes on Park Lane like Fielding House. In fact, Gloria had told her it was not exactly suitable for a married couple, at least not if one was expected to entertain guests.

Even worse, Sir Peter Devon was, if not *old*, then certainly not *young*. She was almost seventeen, but he was thirty-three, had been to war and had lived in London society or among his soldiers for a dozen years. Heaven knew what he would expect her to know, to be able to do. Would he want her to manage his households? Would he expect her to raise a family, having no idea herself of how to care for them, let alone what would be required to conceive them—

Genevieve cut off her own thoughts, trying not to imagine what she thought might come that night. She held her arms in front of her and shuddered.

Lady Winchester slipped into the room and closed the door behind her. "Genevieve, my little girl," she said softly, her eyes filling with tears.

Genevieve blinked back her own, surprised when the countess came across the room. "Forgive me, my child. I tried to stop it, but Winchester had gone too far before I found out. I am so sorry."

"Mama, I know you did not want this for me. Is he really such a bad man?"

Her mother took a handkerchief out and carefully pressed it against Genevieve's watering eyes. "I don't know. Common belief would have it said that he is a debaucher and card sharp, interested in nothing but fleecing the young gentlemen of their wealth and the young ladies of their virtue, but Lady Fielding swears to me that his reputation is grossly exaggerated, that he can be a good man when it pleases him to be. No one I questioned was able to name any virtuous young lady who has been ruined by him, so perhaps that rumor, too, is exaggerated. Furthermore, both his superiors and regiment infantrymen say he was a nearly ideal commander—honorable, courageous and just. Others tell me that war reveals the true character of a man, so I pray it is so."

Genevieve swallowed. "Is it time?" she whispered.

Her mother blinked back another round of tears and smiled. "Yes, my darling."

Genevieve drew a deep breath. At least she would go no farther than the terrace at the back of the house. The wedding breakfast, small by necessity and the scandalous nature of the match, would follow in the large Winchester House dining room.

Her fingers clenched around the bunch of bluebells, white peonies, star lilies and sprigs of lavender. Again, not her favorite colors, but what did it matter? Who could carry vibrant green fields or rich wheat gold glimmering in the sunlight?

Curious despite her resentment, she barely looked at Winchester as he escorted her the five feet forward from the back of the terrace to the front.

She looked ahead to her bridegroom and immediately knew he was ill at ease too.

His physical features intrigued her, so Genevieve committed them to memory as she took the last steps through the small group of witnesses to the place where Sir Peter waited with the cleric. The opposite of her own gold locks, Sir Peter's mahogany hair glimmered in the late morning sun. He returned her gaze, dark-brown eyes set symmetrically on each side of a flat nose. He had thin lips, but Genevieve did not know if it was his natural mien or a product of the situation.

She had thought Sir Peter wanted the match. Instead, he took her gloved hands stiffly as the priest asked, "Who gives this woman to be married to this man?"

"I do," her father answered. Genevieve swallowed heavily and looked down at the space between them. That direction only focused her attention on Sir Peter's body. Looking straight ahead, she connected with his white waistcoat and the diamond pin winking from his cravat. The waistcoat was set off by a dark-green jacket and matching inexpressibles. Below that, white hose extended to his black shoes, ornamented simply with silver buckles. But the clothes framed a form that made her fingers twitch. She wanted to sketch him, to see if she could put to paper what she saw before her.

A proud man, he was. Genevieve raised her eyes and found his focused on her. She caught her breath and followed the tilt of his head to the priest, who was beginning to prompt them for their vows.

Genevieve blushed and turned her head slightly to pay attention. Sir Peter spoke and she caught her breath. He had a deep, gravelly voice, full of personality. It wasn't the smooth drawl she'd heard gentlemen speak in the streets or the quiet voice she'd dimly recalled from Lady Fielding's tea. She shivered and looked at the priest to break the odd moment, relieved to find he was just prompting her. She repeated the cleric's words carefully.

She stumbled over the word obey but when her stomach sank, Sir Peter simply shrugged his shoulders and nodded to the priest. Though the cleric glared indignantly at Genevieve, that poor man huffed out his breath and took Sir Peter's cue to move on with the ceremony. Genevieve's hand shook when Sir Peter stripped off her glove, but his gloves remained in place so they did not truly touch. She was almost afraid to look, but the ring Sir Peter slid onto her hand was a deep-green emerald with diamonds around the band. It was, she thought, perfect.

Maybe it was the first perfect thing that had ever belonged to her, and Peter Devon was giving it to her, because they were married. *Married.*

Almost before she realized what was happening, he bent forward and brushed a brief kiss at the corner of her mouth.

And it was over. Genevieve looked about quickly but averted her gaze from her family when she realized no one smiled. The earl, dressed in subdued gray, was the first to congratulate Sir Peter.

Genevieve stood quietly at his side while her father clapped him on the shoulder. "You'll enjoy her," he congratulated Sir Peter. "Let me know if she's any trouble."

The baronet frowned and stepped back, taking Genevieve with him. "No longer your concern," he said briefly, then looked past Winchester, who was forced aside so that Lady Fielding and Sir John Fielding could step forward. Sir Peter greeted his mother and stepfather with an affection that had never been visible in her own family, then Lady Fielding stepped forward and kissed both of Genevieve's cheeks, whispering, "Don't be terrified. We will explain. He won't hurt you."

Genevieve blinked but knew not to let her confusion show, especially when Lady Fielding gave the same farewell to her son and the couple stepped away.

She greeted the others mechanically. Her mother, who had clearly been crying, clung to her tightly. She curtsied to the Duke of Lennox as her mother formally introduced them. He was an older gentleman and he told her she was a lovely bride. Genevieve remembered he was now Gloria's father-in-law, so in the future he would be considered part of her family circle. Afterward her mother's brothers, Uncle Colby, Uncle Neil and their wives greeted the newlyweds cordially.

That was the end. Those few were her only wedding guests. Both Abigail and Gloria were newly wed, and while Gloria was in seclusion at Lennox House, Abigail was in Warwickshire. No one quite knew where Fiona had gone yet.

By the time a sober meal was consumed in the massive dining room, Genevieve felt ill at ease in the house where she ought to feel at home. Her father was oddly jubilant, but the Fieldings and Sir Peter were wary when they should have been celebrating. Her mother, her mother's brothers and her aunts seemed anxious. His Grace, seated between Genevieve and her mother at the foot of the table, was as sternly disapproving as anyone Genevieve had ever met.

It was a relief to see her mother stand and graciously indicate that the women should withdraw.

Genevieve excused herself and joined the young maid in her dressing room upstairs. She removed the bridal gown, handing the fragile garment with its lace overlay to the maid. She looked around, but the room was mostly bare, except for the gown and a last remaining trunk. None of her personal possessions remained, and her chest hurt for a moment.

"Do you want it now, miss, or shall I send it after I've freshened it?"

"Later will be fine." Genevieve didn't know if she would ever wear the gown again, but she was silent on the matter and instead dressed in the waiting traveling gown, even though she didn't know if she would be leaving London. Her belongings had departed earlier in the morning under the direction of an efficient servant from Lady Fielding's household. Once Gloria's, the traveling gown was a lovely pale blue that complemented Gloria's countenance perfectly. It was lovely on Genevieve too, though green or a darker shade of blue would have been better. As she had not been presented at St. James, the gown was plain, without lace, ribbon piping or other ornamentation that might give evidence of Genevieve's standing in society. In any event, Genevieve had a lovely blue-and-white cameo brooch pinned at her throat that Fiona had left for her, along with a short note to be brave. *All will be well*, the note had claimed, but Fiona had not come back for Genevieve or for the wedding. Abigail and Gloria were married. Genevieve didn't have the three people she needed the most today, the worst day —

No. Today was *her* worst day, but not her mother's worst day or her sisters'. She mustn't forget that, must not lose control of herself as Johnny had. She would not end up as her only brother had, dead because she'd done something reckless or because she'd tried to run away. She would be an adult — responsible, mature, an upstanding lady.

She breathed deeply, took a last critical look in the mirror and turned to her bedchamber as a crash sounded from beyond the door.

She rushed through the dressing room and bedchamber to the doors that led to the corridor, throwing them open.

Just outside the doorway, her father was engaged in fisticuffs with the duke. Sir Peter was attempting to separate the two men. She heard herself scream and choked off the noise, trying desperately to work out what had caused such a row.

From the other side of the brawl, Genevieve saw Sir John also trying to separate the two.

Lady Fielding hurried across to her, gripping her arm. "Don't," she said sharply as Genevieve made a move forward. "They might hurt you instead of each other."

Sir Peter wrapped his arms around Lennox and hauled him backward into the bedchamber, past Genevieve and Lady Fielding. Genevieve realized her mother and Lady Fielding must have been waiting for her in her bedchamber, because her mother was struggling off the chaise longue by the fireplace. Still in the corridor, though, Winchester was restrained by Genevieve's uncles and Sir John Fielding was straightening his sleeves.

"What is the meaning of this?" Sir Peter demanded, shoving Lennox into a chair and standing in front of him as Sir John forced Winchester down into the other one.

Genevieve straightened in response to the command in his voice. She'd never heard anything like that in her life, and it reminded her that Sir Peter was not just a half-drunk top o' the trees aristocrat sliding through life in cards and dice. He had been a decorated colonel in the Peninsular War, knighted for his remarkable service. He'd commanded men, been heard, expected to be obeyed.

"That bounder has been asking for this for eighteen years," Winchester raged. Compared to Sir Peter, Genevieve realized that Winchester sounded whiny, even petulant. He struggled to free himself but Genevieve's uncles held him firmly in place. Genevieve turned to hear what Lennox had to say but her mouth fell open when her mother threw herself on the floor beside the duke and knelt up beside him, pressing a rag to his bloody lip, ignoring her husband.

"Lady Genevieve isn't part of our disagreement and Winchester is a twisted soul to bring her into this," Lennox returned, his hand coming up to cup the back of her mother's head. "And you? If Sir John hadn't informed me of your plans, you'd be a dead man right now."

The duke's caress was affectionate. Intimate. Genevieve blinked, heat coalescing in the back of her head.

"What is going on?" Genevieve demanded, suddenly unable to stay silent.

The Duke of Lennox turned his gaze on her, the pain on his face evident. "Winchester is not your sire," he claimed. "I am."

"Genevieve—" Sir Peter began to turn toward her, but from across the room, Winchester interrupted.

"The devil take it, you bloody, dishonorable weasel!" Winchester raged. Even as Genevieve tried to take in his rage, Winchester broke free and leaped across the rug toward Lennox and her mother. He shoved Sir John out of the way, who knocked against Lady Fielding at Genevieve's side. Like a game of dominos, Lady Fielding fell against Genevieve, who stumbled backward.

She cried out as the back of her head knocked hard against one of the posters on her bed. Searing pain shot through her and the edges of her vision dimmed. Sir Peter roared, slamming into Winchester and sending the earl flying backward.

Nausea rushed over her.

"Don't touch them!" Peter roared. "Never!" His left fist connected with Winchester's stomach and his right hit her father's jaw.

No. Not her father. She shook her head and immediately felt her wedding breakfast come up her throat.

Genevieve retched all over her dress and moaned. She was never getting married again. Never.

* * * *

Peter carried Genevieve from the house. She was wrapped in her pelisse, a pillow protecting the tender place behind her head. Ahead of him, Sir John assisted

Peter's mother into the carriage and Peter waited for them to settle before following.

The carriage moved forward as soon as Sir John tapped on the roof.

"God willing, this child will never set foot in that house again." His mother's words were sharp enough that Peter winced. None of them had understood the extent of the problems at Winchester House, and Sir Peter ached to know if the girl in his arms had suffered Winchester's rages even during the last few days of their engagement. Guilt ate at his stomach. He should have removed her immediately to his mother's care once the engagement was in place.

His Grace, the Duke of Lennox, had explained the dramatics while Lady Winchester's trunks were prepared. Her daughters were already scattered, and with Genevieve leaving as well, she feared for her safety if she stayed. Lennox was taking Lady Winchester openly into his house, insisting she live under his protection.

"If he wants to take it to the magistrates, then he'll do so. In the meantime, you will be safe," he'd told Genevieve's mother. According to Lennox, he and Lady Winchester had been lovers for some eighteen years, since she'd been *enceinte* with Gloria. Later, he had sired Genevieve. Winchester had only discovered their long-term affair recently, in late September. Enraged, at once he began to suspect that the four girls he thought were his daughters were probably not. Fiona had escaped, partly because she had inherited. The other three had not been as lucky.

As for Genevieve, Peter knew Lady Fielding and Sir John Fielding had sworn to the duke that they would stand *in loco parentis*, which had been Peter's agreement with his mother and stepfather from the time his surprise engagement had appeared in *The Times*.

Genevieve was too young to be living with Peter. He'd known that the moment he'd agreed to marry her, but it was his mother's willingness to chaperone the girl that had turned the situation from unsalvageable scandal to barely tolerable. Genevieve would live under Lady Fielding's aegis and have her first Season the next spring. Sir Peter had vowed to the duke that he would look after her from afar, providing for her but keeping his distance until she'd had at least two Seasons and her nineteenth birthday.

Even then, the duke had insisted that Peter's only duty was to protect Genevieve. Peter wondered if the irascible duke would be a fixture of his future or if the man was primarily bluster. The next few years would demonstrate the duke's true colors. The duke had always known Genevieve was his daughter, and yet he had made no effort to keep watch over her until now.

"I can't believe Lady Winchester has been having an affair with Lennox for so many years and no one suspected." Sir John frowned as he spoke, looking at his wife.

She humphed and waved a dismissive hand between them. "Quite easy when a couple lives mostly apart, John. But quite impossible for us."

"As Winchester has had a mistress for years, he's not precisely been a model of fidelity himself," Peter pointed out drily, cradling the bundle in his arms.

"I thought you said she was to have a new wardrobe," his mother observed. She was examining the hem of Genevieve's dress critically. The gown reeked of vomit, but all of Genevieve's belongings — aside from her wedding dress — had already been moved, so Lady Fielding had pursed her lips and announced she would arrange for Genevieve's care, including the removal of the aromatic gown, at Fielding House.

Now Peter glanced down and saw what his mother had observed. The inside of the pastel gown clearly showed where it had been refitted and sewn again. "The maids unpacking her trunks this morning said that all of her wardrobe is the same as this—newly refashioned gowns for a schoolgirl, not new ones befitting her status as a baronet's wife, or even my ward. Good quality seamstress work, but made from previous Seasons' fashions."

Peter tried to hold back a growl. In his arms, Genevieve shifted. Her eyes still closed, she whispered, "I had a new dress for this morning. I'm sorry I was sick on this one."

"Shh," he whispered. "Your head will hurt more if you move about." Looking up at his mother, he asked, "You will take care of it?" At her nod, Peter frowned. "Winchester was to purchase an entire trousseau for her, but he's apparently decided to try to test me. Whatever she needs, I'll put up the blunt, and I'll make arrangements for her quarterly allowance to begin immediately."

Lady Fielding looked severe. "I'm happy to take the child shopping," she agreed. Looking up at Sir John, who was frowning fiercely as well, she added, "Perhaps, dear, you can go back and put another fist in that man's stomach for me."

"I know you think she should be in public tomorrow, in your presence with a smile on her face." Peter looked her over again, committing the lines of her face to memory so he could see if she improved on the morrow. "But what if her head is too sore?"

Lady Fielding sighed. "She can at least come and sit in the drawing room. No doubt I'll have callers. I can make it clear that she's been under my chaperonage since the vows were said, and you can make it clear that she's not under yours by being out and about tonight. You know, I would normally try to discourage you from making a spectacle of yourself at the gaming tables, but tonight's an exception, my son. Tell everyone you like that she's safely under my roof and that anyone who maligns her will answer to you and Sir John. You might also make it known that you married her because you feared for her safety, and it was the only way to remove her from Winchester's madness."

Peter's lips curved. His mother was endorsing a bit of gossip, was she? She was right. It was time to bend the ears of the gossips his way, for once.

Chapter Four

August 1824

Genevieve sat in the window of her studio in Fielding Manor and stared into the darkness. She'd extinguished the lanterns and candles that normally lit the room at night, drawn back the drapes and pushed open the windows to allow the late-night breeze to blow through.

She ought to be in bed, of course, and it was not far away. High on the second floor at the end of the manor, her suite was a generous bedchamber connected to a large dressing room and an even more generous corner room that had once been Sir Peter's childhood room. Not long after Lady Fielding had brought her to Suffolk, Peter had heard Genevieve's request for a painting space and volunteered the room for conversion to a large working studio. He had pointed out the generous natural light that came through the tall windows and the wide bay with its southern exposure. The Fieldings had graciously agreed, accepting that Peter was unlikely to return to residence in the house with Genevieve there, with a perfectly acceptable country estate of his own only a few miles away.

Genevieve had been so grateful once she'd seen the finished space that she'd rushed thoughtlessly into his arms and kissed his cheek when she'd next seen him, startling them both. Since then, she'd found herself regularly gifted with the best of materials, including a steady supply of canvases.

They'd left London in mid-November, less than a month after the wedding. Lady Fielding had required only a few weeks to understand Genevieve was wholly unprepared to be at the center of the *ton's* scrutiny. After some discussion with Sir Peter and Sir John, Lady Fielding had commissioned John Constable to come to Suffolk and paint two portraits. In Genevieve's opinion, Mr. Constable was a remarkable landscape artist, though English society barely looked at his work. Sitting for him had given her time to discuss art and engage him in her tutelage. She'd also been able to observe him paint Sir John and Lady Fielding, and shortly thereafter had expressed a desire for a proper studio in place of the single easel and canvas before the window in her bedchamber.

Peter had given her much over the previous two years, but this room, its contents and the intention behind it — to be a space where Genevieve could grow and mature in her skill and talent, in a way quite beyond the expected parameters of a gentleman's wife — was a treasure to Genevieve.

The baronet's own house, which Genevieve was determined to someday convince him to share with her, was a lovely stone structure with Elizabethan architecture. Genevieve absolutely itched to paint it and its owner in full sunlight, though Sir Peter refused her permission "for the nonce," as he'd said. She'd noticed he used the phrase in place of 'until you're older', which she considered quite sensitive of him. Genevieve had visited once in the company of Lady Fielding and her maid. A second time, Genevieve had gone there while riding, despite the company of the two older grooms who always trailed her, and she'd walked boldly up to the front door. Surprisingly, Sir Peter had not been at home, but the housekeeper, Mrs. Inglebright, had settled her cheerfully into a chair in the morning room, served her tea and sent for Lady Fielding.

That time, Lady Fielding had explained gently that it would be Sir Peter's reputation that would suffer if Genevieve were found alone with him. She'd been too young for marriage two years earlier, of course, but Genevieve hadn't realized that Sir Peter had been the one who was blamed for the debacle. The responsibility had been solely at the feet of the Earl of Winchester, who she had gradually come to realize was more of an enemy than a parent.

The Duke of Lennox, her sire, and even her half-brother, Lord Alden Swenson, were openly supportive of her art. She'd spent much time with her mother and the duke when in London the last two springs, and had met Lord Alden upon his return from Amsterdam in June. He and Lord Oliver had been a wonderful addition to His Grace's household.

Even so, Genevieve had wanted desperately to return to Suffolk—not because she wanted to paint, though she did, and not because she wished to avoid the difficulties of the Season. She'd wanted to return to Suffolk because when she was in Suffolk, so was Sir Peter. And in Suffolk, she could see him much more often than was possible in London.

Two springtimes before, he'd spent the Season in London when she'd been there. He'd courted her very correctly, with a waltz at every ball and a strict twenty minute visit every day in the Fielding House drawing room. He'd sent her a come-out posy, attended the drawing room when she was presented to the princesses at St. James's Palace, and he'd watched over her from afar almost every evening as she'd chatted and danced away her first Season. He'd even chased away anyone he'd deemed inappropriate, even though he'd barely spoken to her in the ballrooms.

She ran the pads of her fingers over her bare arms and sighed. Perhaps, as His Grace and Lord Alden had suggested, she had been overstating the role of Sir Peter in her life, but he was something like a hero. He'd rescued her. He protected her and he continued to pamper her. Genevieve might have been a child when they'd married, but she was now almost to her nineteenth birthday, and she'd been trained by Lady Fielding in how to manage her personal finances and run a gentleman's manor house. She was ready to be more than the Fieldings' ward and Sir Peter's rescued waif.

Genevieve thought she was mostly ready to be his wife. She even knew what it meant. Abigail and Gloria had sat her down during a visit to the Meridens' in Warwickshire earlier in the summer and explained the mechanics in great detail. While shocked, Genevieve had retired to her room with several illustrated books on the subject that Abigail had extracted from

Meriden's library. The art alone had fascinated Genevieve, but it had also sparked her imagination. Still, her sisters had emphasized, again and again, that marital relations were not just about procreation, but also about emotional intimacy. Women were vulnerable, Abigail had explained, because a man could so easily turn the experience into a terrifying ordeal instead of a pleasurable event. Genevieve would have no way of knowing if Sir Peter could be trusted to give her pleasure until she was vulnerable enough to find out.

That night, Genevieve had taken the book to her bed and by candlelight had touched her body in the same way the men in the illustrations had touched the women. She closed her eyes and from memory did the same now, brushing her nipples through her sleeveless nightgown, then lower to brush at the curls between her legs. It was pleasant, but not nearly enough, so she unbuttoned the top of her gown and slipped her fingers inside, rubbing the areola before she pinched the bud and pulled, hardening her nipple. It tingled deliciously, so Genevieve used her other hand to do the same to her second nipple, wondering whether it would feel better or worse were a man to do the same. If it were Sir Peter, she pondered, would she be terrified that she'd disappoint him or eager to have him try it harder?

Her breath caught in her throat as a sudden horrible realization overcame her. He'd undoubtedly had a mistress before their marriage, and Genevieve hadn't been sharing his bed. What if he had someone else that he preferred to her? They had never discussed such things. Her heart thudded heavily as she considered the idea. The chances were high that Peter had had a mistress in the two years since their marriage. He had, after all, been well-known as a rake and a card sharp. Neither of the Fieldings had ever referred to his reputation directly, but her mother and her sisters had been blunt enough about it when she'd seen them.

Genevieve swallowed hard, fighting back a sudden urge to cry. If he did have someone, Genevieve would just have to show him that he could like her, too. She very much wanted to stomp her feet, throw things and yell at him, but she wouldn't. For a moment she thought it would be better if she never knew. A few seconds later she decided she had to know one way or the other or she would go mad from curiosity and suspicion.

But it was common, exceedingly common, for noblemen, married or not, to have mistresses. Whether they were opera singers, paramours or high-born matrons like her mother who were unsatisfied with their marriages, noblemen were not expected to stay faithful. The vast majority did not love the brides they were bound to through arranged marriages and, by far, most noblemen had been shamelessly indulged since infancy and were accustomed to having their way whenever they wanted, whether it was the purchase of a finely bred pair of high-steppers, a pretty parlor maid or the acquisition of a nobly born bride. Baronets were not usually considered high aristocrats — not being members of the House of Lords — but Sir Peter Devon was not just a baronet. He was a war hero, knighted for his service and filthy rich, both as a matter of inheritance and from fleecing every young pup who had wandered through the hell in St. James that he frequented. Thus, he was accorded much the same respect as many peers who were considerably higher than him on the social scales of rank and class.

Genevieve and Peter had an arranged marriage. He did not love her. Ergo, the probability was high that he had a mistress — or at least that he'd indulged in affairs during the time of their marriage of convenience.

Someday, though, Genevieve was certain she would share his bed. After all, he'd want a nursery and an heir to inherit his title and lands. Even though Sir Peter wasn't at the top of the aristocratic ranks, he was one of the wealthiest men in England, and he'd assured her that she would be well provided for her entire life. It wasn't as if he could marry anyone else.

Unless he annulled the marriage. It was another unbidden thought, but this one truly frightened Genevieve. If he wanted to end the marriage, she realized, he could. They had not consummated it, not even kissed properly.

Her heart beat faster, and her fingers dug into her thighs. The thought of losing Sir Peter, of being cast away and ending up back with her mother instead of Lady Fielding, made her nauseated. She left the window seat and paced the room, wondering what she might do. She wouldn't be of legal age to consent on her own standing for more than two years, which meant if Sir Peter decided to look elsewhere for a wife—

No, she wouldn't be returned to Winchester's guardianship. The earl had been committed to an asylum earlier in the summer, which meant that if Sir Peter sought an annulment or a divorce decree, she'd have to throw herself on the mercy of Lennox, Lord Alden, Abigail's husband or Gloria's husband. She couldn't contemplate it. She clenched her nightgown in her fingers and paced. She knew of Winchester's original plan to marry her to General Malone and how

Sir Peter had sacrificed and gone to great expense to prevent Malone from fulfilling the obligations of the marriage contract. Both Fiona and Lady Fielding had told her the story. Sir Peter was her hero. He'd protected her for so long already that it seemed nonsensical to imagine him walking away from that role now. Surely if he intended to end their marriage, he would wait until her twenty-first birthday.

But what if she hadn't truly become his wife by then?

Genevieve escaped the studio. In her bedchamber, she lit the candles on the bedside table and sank onto the chair nearby. Her fingers pressed anxiously against the curls between her legs and she rubbed there through the thin white silk of the nightgown. It was a fine garment, one purchased with the funds that Sir Peter had allotted for her wardrobe and accessories. He'd given her an exorbitant amount that she couldn't have imagined spending each quarter, but Lady Fielding had been ruthless. The older woman had said it was sufficient but not excessive, and she'd made certain that Genevieve's wardrobe was fashionable, stylish and expensive. While Genevieve had definite ideas about colors and styles that suited her, Lady Fielding had detailed lists upon lists of items that were necessary to complete it, in addition to the gowns. Silk nightgowns had been relatively inexpensive compared to the reticules, fashionable jewelry, perfumes, soaps, gloves, cosmetics, fans, shoes, hats, bonnets, hair ribbons, parasols, chemises, chemisettes, riding habits, walking dresses, evening gowns, morning gowns, tea dresses and mourning wear.

She pressed the curls again and rubbed her fingertips against them through the silk, trying to think of something other than Peter's generosity. But thinking beyond Peter was difficult. He was manly — beautiful, even — and she never tired of seeing him. Every time he had ever touched her, whether for a dance, to escort her in to dinner or to kiss her hand farewell, Genevieve had had to suppress a shiver. He had large hands that could be astonishingly gentle when he touched her. When he looked at her, she thought he was kind and considerate. When he spoke to her, he always complimented her in some way, so his deep voice made her insides purr with happiness.

Genevieve wondered what he would taste like when they finally kissed. From dancing with him regularly, she already knew he wouldn't taste of stale whiskey or smell of cheap cigars. But in the crowded ballrooms of London's Season, it was difficult to appreciate how he would naturally smell or taste when they were close.

Her palms pressed against the silk and moved in a circle, until the fabric beneath her hand was damp from her efforts. She whimpered, wondering if he would do the same to her someday or if he knew of some other way to bring her magic — some way she couldn't imagine. She prayed he would give her pleasure, but conversely, she couldn't imagine him acting as an insensitive clod who ignored her while seeking his own pleasures. Genevieve sucked in a breath, aching as her nipples tingled. She shifted on the chair and they rubbed painfully against the silk.

Genevieve glanced at the door, but Ellen — who was more duenna than maid, anyway — had retired for bed more than an hour earlier. Ellen was forever lecturing her about polite appearance and behavior, and Genevieve knew that what she was about to do was quite improper. She dragged up the long skirt of the nightgown and slipped her fingers up over her knees and across the fronts of her thighs. Except for bathing, she rarely touched herself in such places, but her skin was warm and both her fingers and the flesh between her knees and her hips responded to the light touches she brushed over her skin.

The moment had an odd energy to it, as if she was awakening something she might not be able to put back to sleep. She listened to her instincts and moved her fingers to the blonde curls between her hips. Even in the darkness, she could see the moisture leaking from between her legs, leaving a glistening beacon at the bottom of that golden triangle. Genevieve closed her eyes, remembering how it had felt to see the illustrations in Abigail's books, of how the men had put their fingers between the women's legs, intent on bringing them pleasure and release.

Genevieve knew what release was, at least in theory. But she'd never been able to bring herself to that point. Nevertheless, she moved her fingers more firmly between her legs until they slid between the moist folds of flesh. She rubbed there, letting the pressure in her spine build and the ephemeral sense of desire bloom in the back of her brain.

But it wasn't enough. She explored the folds, imagining Peter's manhood and how it would fit if they ever copulated. She slipped her fingertip inside and thrust gently up to her middle knuckle. With her thumb, Genevieve stroked the hard pearl at the front of her womanhood and wished desperately that she knew how to relieve the throbbing there.

The sound of the butler extinguishing the lamps in the corridor startled her, and she jerked her hand away and let the nightgown fall into place.

Her body shaking, Genevieve slipped into the dressing room and wiped the evidence of her exploration from her fingers, donned a clean nightdress of white linen and wiped the arousal from between her legs. Stiff and tired, she slipped back into her bedchamber and climbed into the bed, staring at the ceiling as she grappled with the frustration rising inside her.

She was fairly certain now that there was only one cure for the ache she experienced whenever she saw or thought about Sir Peter Devon. Even better, there was one way to prevent Sir Peter from annulling their marriage, whether before or after she was twenty-one.

She was going to have to seduce him.

The sooner, the better.

* * * *

Ellen clucked her tongue in disapproval, but Genevieve resolutely ignored her. She directed the groom, Jem, to set up her drawing easel and spread out a picnic blanket for Ellen to sit on. At least the attentive woman had thought to bring a book. Genevieve had spent many hours painting, so Ellen knew what to expect.

At the time of her engagement, Genevieve had had a governess. The stiff, severe Miss Colchester had been outraged and quit on the spot when she'd learned of Genevieve's imminent marriage.

A few days after their wedding, Peter had hired Ellen as Genevieve's companion. He hadn't embarrassed Genevieve by calling her a governess. Even so, Peter had given very clear instructions to Ellen and his own mother regarding his expectations of Genevieve's decorum. She wasn't to be alone without a chaperone — especially not with him, he'd said.

Of course, that had been almost two years earlier, but Ellen hadn't seemed to notice that Genevieve was no longer sixteen. Lady Fielding, thankfully, hadn't stuck quite so close to Genevieve, at least not when they were out in society, but in those places, Sir Peter shadowed her anyway.

She wondered what Peter would think when he arrived at Fielding Manor this morning, as he was expected to, and found his dutiful wife-in-name-only absent, instead of waiting to submit to the polite relationship he'd instituted between them for far too long now.

"Thank you, Jem. If you'll return at about two o'clock, I should be ready to return then."

Ellen grimaced, but Genevieve simply sat on the rug she'd spread at the base of the easel, set a fresh page of paper from her case to the frame, hunted up her pencils and began to draw. Jem would return with the gig to take the two women and Genevieve's supplies back to Fielding Manor, unless Peter was concerned enough at her absence to seek her out himself.

But she couldn't spend all morning worrying about Peter, if he would come hunting for her or about Ellen's grumbling. Suffolk was full of wonderful scenes to sketch and paint, and she'd already completed a number of canvases that had been well-received. Alden had insisted on keeping one of the Ipswich marina, and Peter had one of Framlingham Castle hanging in his library. She'd painted cottages and hayfields, pastures and tree stands. This particular view of the River Alde was a colorful curve at a narrow point, where both sides of the river were dominated by reed beds. A wood dotted the landscape in the distance, and hayfields opened up on the opposite bank, with a lovely stretch of green pasture running down from her feet to the water.

Perhaps it wasn't the most dramatic of landscapes, but it would certainly be a challenge for her to paint.

The sun rose and Ellen forced a floppy hat onto Genevieve. She hated to admit it when Ellen was right about such things, so Genevieve sighed, set aside her pencils and sat on Ellen's blanket with the picnic basket.

"There's no reason to work yourself to exhaustion, my lady," Ellen chided gently.

Genevieve shrugged. She knew it was foolish to let her skin be flushed too red by the sun, but she'd set out deliberately to spend all morning away from Fielding Manor. In that exercise she'd already been successful. The true difficulty would be in working out a way to meet with Sir Peter without Ellen or Lady Fielding present. She pondered that as she nibbled on the cucumber sandwiches and plum tarts, and she picked at a cabbage salad with pears and beetroot.

Eventually, though, the hours of quiet were enough, and Ellen was there, after all. "Ellen, do you think Sir Peter will ever see me as something more than a little girl?"

Ellen's eyebrows lifted. "Is that what this morning is about? Are you tired of him courting you?"

Genevieve shook her head. "Oh, I know you think he's courting me, but he's not. He's always very kind and attentive, but he barely touches my hand, has no interest in discussing anything more serious than my latest painting or his mother's next dinner party— which he won't attend anyway—and won't even contemplate the notion of walking in the garden, riding together or any of the other outings that couples who aren't even married might engage in. I'm an obligation, nothing more, and none of that is because you're sitting at the other end of the room just out of hearing range."

Pursing her lips, Ellen thought, considered. "He's thought of you as too young for a long time now, my lady—perhaps too long. You've been trained to run his residences, manage your own financial affairs and have a successful future with those paints of yours, I'm sure. But Sir Peter hired me, not your mother, so I'm the first to tell you this. He didn't hire me only because he was afraid of other men taking advantage of you, of other men being alone with you or even only because he feared you would be hurt or your reputation somehow compromised. His first and primary order of business when he discussed the position with me was that *he* shouldn't be left alone with you. Now that you're a young woman, if you want him to rethink that stance, you'll have to convince him of it—and without managing to get me dismissed from my post, please."

Genevieve pondered that for a long while and wondered what she was to do about it. But she really only had one battle plan, so she made the conscious decision to be stubborn and see where it led.

The next morning, Genevieve asked the boy, Jem, to bring an awning to the site she'd selected. On the third day, he ferried out an armchair.

There was no reason Ellen ought to be uncomfortable.

Even so, as the days turned into a week, Genevieve grew despondent. She knew that Peter continued to call every morning and visit with his mother. But he made no effort to seek her out, and his reticence bothered her.

For someone so intent on protecting her, how could he have so little interest in interacting with her?

And what would either of them say when they did meet, as was inevitable?

Maybe her admiration of him really was only one-sided.

Chapter Five

Peter's hands clenched so hard that his knuckles were swelling. He'd managed to survive her absence, almost certainly deliberate, for six full days. Only his mother's calm assurance that she was painting and in Ellen's company—not off on her own or in a crowd of young ladies almost certainly under the observation of gentlemen—had gotten him through the fifth day. On the sixth day he'd hunted down the groom, discovered their destination and made a secret detour to be sure they were doing exactly what Jem and his mother had said.

She hadn't seen him. He'd kept far back and used his spyglass to identify Genevieve, with Ellen comfortably ensconced in a chair under a picnic awning.

August was waning into September and he was so close—only two months—to her nineteenth birthday, when he would be free from the vows he'd given to Genevieve's sire and her sisters. They'd put their faith in him, that he would respect her youth, and he *did* respect it. He wanted to prove to the world—but especially to her family—that he was a good enough man for her, that he could keep his promises.

Of course he wasn't good enough for her. He never had been.

At first she'd been just what he'd thought. She'd been a child, not suitable to be anyone's wife, let alone the wife of a thirty-three-year-old man who spent his nights half-drunk and his days working out ways to avoid sleeping at night. But Genevieve had grown out of that shell and blossomed into something so much more than a well-mannered young lady with a fabulous figure. He'd given her a refuge and a place to call home and provided for her, and all he'd asked for was her safety and the right to watch over her.

What he had was a young woman who looked at him as if he were her angel.

He wished he could be an angel—at least her angel.

Thankfully, today was Sunday. She couldn't avoid him, not completely. She would sit between his mother and Ellen in church, but he'd be at the end of the aisle and his stepfather would be at the opposite end, with the women between them. Even if she didn't speak, he would see her, see her reaction to him.

Was she angry? Had she learned something about his past that disappointed her?

He was no saint, but he'd given up women when he'd married, knowing full well such exploits would reach her ears. He still gambled while in town, but what else was he to do all night in smoky London? In any event, he lost only rarely, and his winnings far exceeded any losses. The sound of horse hooves on cobblestone and the rank stink of firewood smoke still gave him nightmares.

In the country, which she miraculously appeared to prefer, he could sleep at night. He credited her with giving him that — the ability to sleep — and prayed she would always prefer the country. He danced attendance on her, as much as was allowed given their age difference. He ached for a time when he was free to observe her from nearby instead of from across the ballroom or under the eye of a chaperone. He still drank whiskey — and occasionally too much of it — but what man wouldn't in his place, with his past and present? And, more importantly, she'd never seen him drunk, so she didn't know.

He tied his horses and phaeton beside the church and looked around for the Fielding carriage, breathing a sigh of relief when he found it several lengths away.

Perhaps it was better if she cut him now. It would hurt, but at least he would bear it, and no one would think it out of character if he disappeared to Scotland for the nonce. Doubtless he would do something asinine eventually anyway and drive her away.

Peter grimaced. He knew it was wrong, but he liked that she looked at him with all her heart and hopes on her face. He dreaded the day that expression disappeared, knowing that day would come all too soon. His failure was inevitable. The only question was how long it would be before he disillusioned her.

She was there, in the family pew. To his surprise Ellen was missing, but Genevieve's blonde curls bounced on her bare shoulders, catching his attention. The sunlight through the stained glass windows fell on her hair and that tempting flesh, highlighting her perfect form. She was the angel.

Peter froze. Bare shoulders? She was supposed to dress modestly. He'd made it clear to both Ellen and his mother that she couldn't try to attract—

He swallowed heavily as she twitched a fine silk shawl over her shoulders and across her back.

Someone behind Peter cleared her throat and he hastily stepped forward and slipped into the seat beside Genevieve, praying that he did not sit too close and scare her. She didn't smile, only looked at him steadily until he bent to the side, grabbing onto and clenching the hymnal, unable to fathom how to touch her. He hadn't touched her since the last time they'd waltzed in London, back in June, and he'd carefully kept as much space as possible between them then.

"How have you been, my dear?" he finally managed.

Her lips, her gorgeous, moist pink lips, curved slightly. "I'm working on a painting of the river and the light is best in the morning hours," she murmured. Even as the confession spilled out from her, her hazel eyes darkened. It was a curious reaction. Her eyes usually only darkened when she was frustrated. Had she thought he would be satisfied today merely by a polite greeting?

"I know." He frowned, not intending to sound disapproving. But it was clear to him that she took his words to be a criticism by the way her shoulders slumped and her head turned stiffly to the side. "No doubt it will be fantastic," he whispered, hearing the people around him quiet in expectation and unable to say more without drawing the attention of others in the sanctuary.

He offered to share a hymnal with her at the first music, but she had her own. Still, nothing could prevent him from, inch by inch, closing the space between them. He stood close, much closer than he would have with Ellen between them, and breathed in the fresh aroma of soap and lavender that clung to her. Once Peter looked down at her and afterward had difficulty looking back up to the rector's stern visage. Her breasts swelled out of the bodice of the low-cut summer gown, reminding him vividly of exactly how much she had grown, and where, in the twenty-two months of their marriage.

He barely stopped himself in time from groaning. His mother looked over at him and frowned, and Peter stilled abruptly, as if he was eight and fidgeting again.

Only when the service ended and the congregants around him were shuffling toward the door, did he look down at Genevieve. She, too, had stood. Because of his machinations in moving closer to her, she was almost touching his hip. She bent forward a few inches, tucking her hymnal into her reticule, and Peter drew a harsh breath as her gown gaped away and gave him a stunning display of sweet breasts barely covered by her chemise.

Stiff, he held out his arm for Genevieve, lacking the polite words to invite her to take it but commanding she do so by blocking her exit from the pew instead. He couldn't look down at her again, but he desperately needed her skirts to hide behind. Church was no place for a man in his condition, and she wouldn't understand if he tried to explain, anyway.

She exhaled softly as she acquiesced and slipped her arm in his, but he made no mistake about her true opinion. Her chin was high and her cheeks were flushed, and as soon as they were out of the crowd and could halt in the small courtyard at the foot of the steps, she slipped her arm out of his and turned aside, hiding her face as she settled her bonnet and tied the ribbons firmly over her cheeks.

"Peter, good morning," his mother interrupted. Of course, she and John had come up behind him. Peter was forced to turn and acknowledge her, knowing even as he did that Genevieve was escaping. He gritted his back teeth to prevent any other change in his expression.

"Mama, John," he returned, nodding his head to his stepfather and bending to kiss his mother's cheek.

"So polite of you to greet us when you arrived," his mother chided. Peter winced, but then again, he knew she was aware how disturbed he was by Genevieve's recent behavior. Hopefully she'd forgive him the lapse before the Little Season. Otherwise, he was likely to receive short shrift in her drawing room and wind up at dinners seated as far from Genevieve as practical.

"Where's Ellen?" he asked first.

"Taken to her bed," his mother sighed. "She felt well yesterday morning, but by last night she was pale and shaking. I think all those mornings outdoors last week have caught up with her. I've never known the woman to be ill, but there's always a first time."

Peter raised an eyebrow. Ellen was a hardy soul. He'd never have hired someone delicate and defenseless as Genevieve's companion. He laughed at himself then. He'd hired her as a damned guard, but he supposed everyone was susceptible to illness at times. "So you are headed back to Fielding Manor from here?"

"Yes, and you are invited to lunch. I already told Cook to expect you," Lady Fielding nodded at Genevieve, now across the grass and chatting animatedly with Lady Framlingham. "I'll make certain she comes to the table."

Peter's jaw tightened. "I'll take her in my phaeton and drive her back."

Beside his mother, Sir John cleared his throat. "Peter, is that a good idea?"

"Probably not, but she and I have something to work out, and you can follow us down the lanes in the carriage, it's not as though we'll be private—just out of hearing range."

Peter's parents dared not argue, not in such a public place, but he could see Sir John's jaw tic a bit. Turning from them, knowing they'd head immediately to the carriage so as to be prepared to follow him closely, Peter strolled over the lawn, coming up behind Genevieve without her even knowing he approached. By the time he stepped into the space beside her, it was too late for her to bid the lady adieu and escape, not without drawing the older woman's notice.

He slipped her hand onto his arm and covered it after bowing to the matron before him and exchanging the customary greetings with her ladyship. Lady Framlingham eyed the small maneuver speculatively as she bade him welcome. Peter smiled and looked down at his charming wife, who had suddenly become very quiet. "Genevieve, my dear, I did not mean to end your conversation. Pray continue. You were saying?"

"Ah, we were just confirming plans. Lady Framlingham, if you'll excuse me?" Genevieve murmured, curtsying slightly. Lady Framlingham, a baron's wife, did precede her in rank and age, but Peter still felt irritated by the small measure of respect she'd given the woman. Genevieve ought to be treated as the woman's equal, at least. She was still thought of as an earl's daughter, even if the earl was a madman and it was well-known she was not his progeny.

"I will hear from you next week then," Lady Framlingham nodded graciously, staring at Peter until he inwardly growled and proffered a short bow.

Peter steered the young beauty beside him away, leading her toward the carriages.

Genevieve, too well-bred to look frantically about, hissed at him in a quiet set-down instead. "Where are you taking me? Lady Fielding will be looking for me."

"She and Sir John are ready to depart. They will follow us to Fielding Manor."

"What are you saying?" She chanced a look at him that was more a wifely glare than the polite inquiry of an acquaintance.

Peter refrained from laughing and gestured to his phaeton. "My horses needed exercising, so I drove this morning instead of riding. Now I can escort you to Fielding Manor, and on the way you can tell me why you're avoiding me. We'll be in plain sight of the Fielding coachman the entire drive."

Genevieve paused and stared up at the high seat, one she could not reach without assistance. "I'm not avoiding you," she denied.

"No?" Peter asked, openly disbelieving.

"No," Genevieve said firmly. "I've been painting."

"Up you go, then." Peter reached for her hips, swinging her up onto the bench.

Genevieve struggled to hold back a surprised screech, sliding over immediately as Peter climbed up after her.

"I accept that you've been painting," Peter acknowledged, as he released the brake on the phaeton and carefully moved the horses onto the lane, tossing a coin at the Fielding Manor groom who'd held them through the service. The lad trotted off to climb up onto the Fielding carriage. "And I accept that the morning light is best for this particular piece. However, I do not accept that you blithely went off for six mornings in a row, never once having a bit of conscience. You knew I would be calling but didn't leave a note or a message to relay through my mother, and that is quite unlike you."

He glanced over quickly, wishing her bonnet was not quite so wide. The shade of her eyes was concealed by the shadow, but she was biting down on her bottom lip quite adorably.

"She knew where I was," Genevieve said faintly.

"She did, and Ellen was with you," Peter agreed reasonably. He let the silence stretch between them.

Genevieve, as he'd expected, broke the impasse. "I apologize for my bad manners," she allowed, but Peter heard the reluctance in the words.

Sighing, knowing full well she didn't grasp his fascination with her, he asked, "Have I done something to upset you, to have you avoid me, Genevieve?"

Her head turned sharply at that, staring up at him wide-eyed. "Of course not!" she denied.

"So when I call tomorrow morning, you'll be there?" he asked, thinking of Ellen's unexpected illness.

"No. I mean, not in the morning," Genevieve stumbled. "I still need to work on the painting. I wanted to go this morning, but Lady Fielding insisted I come to church."

Peter's eyebrows shot up. "So you were planning to avoid me today, too."

"That's not what I meant!" Genevieve exclaimed. She drew a deep breath and tried again, while Peter kept his gaze on the horses. "Lady Framlingham asked me to paint this particular view, and she needs it by mid-September as a gift for her daughter. That's what we were discussing before you joined us—how soon I could finish it. I know it doesn't seem like anything significant, and she's not giving me an advance commission. But she's excited about the sketch and agreed to a fee, and if I want to paint for anyone outside of the families, she's the perfect patroness to advocate for my work in London."

Peter frowned. Genevieve did not need to paint for a fee, because he would happily and easily support her. Neither did he want to sound as if she wasn't talented enough to sell her work, because she was. "Yes, but Ellen is ill. And you aren't going down to that spot alone."

"I'll take Jem—"

"Jem is a twelve-year-old boy, not a proper chaperone." Peter gritted his back teeth and prayed this wasn't going to go where he thought it was headed.

Her posture stiffened and her chin went up, then Peter's gut tightened.

"I need to work on the painting. I'm going to need to go to the river nearly every day, at least for another week at the site, and several hours each of those days," she stated.

Ellen was sick and his mother—while doting on Genevieve—could not be expected to sit outdoors some four to five hours every morning. She wasn't ill, but she was aging. She slept later than Genevieve, rested more and ran Fielding Manor, in addition to having a daughter she'd never expected under her roof. He wouldn't ask it of her.

He turned the horses into the short drive between the lane and the house, his thoughts grim. How would he keep from touching her, from holding her, if he spent so much time in her company, virtually alone? Rural Suffolk wasn't exactly a back London alley or a dangerous stand of trees in central Spain, but Genevieve wasn't going to wander the countryside unguarded.

"I'll do it," he grunted.

Genevieve turned her head fully to him at that, her eyes wide with surprise. "I'm certain I'll be perfectly safe. There's no way you want to spend... It's—"

"You want me to believe you're not avoiding me for some mysterious reason. You want to paint every morning, and you're not going to be out there without a proper companion," he said sharply, pulling the reins short as one of the grooms came running to catch his pair's heads. "I think you know how this is going to turn out. You refuse to let me escort you, Genevieve, and I'll be waiting for you at the river tomorrow morning. It's not as if I don't know where you will be."

Without waiting for a response, Peter jumped down from the phaeton. Genevieve grasped the back of the seat, glaring down at him, but he simply waited.

She couldn't climb down from the contraption on her own. Obviously reluctant to accept his assistance, and at the same time, unbalanced on the high seat, Genevieve ended up glaring at him. He watched as she slid over gingerly and turned, then he reached up and swung her down beside him, determinedly ignoring the *frisson* of awareness that rushed him when her supple body was in his hands. It had happened so rarely, usually when they'd waltzed, but he understood the sensual reaction, even if she didn't. His reaction was aggravated by her natural response, something she was too innocent to conceal from him.

Taking her arm, he led her in, stopping in the front hall for them to divest themselves of their outerwear. The Fielding carriage was proceeding down the drive, so Peter knew that his mother would be in directly. Genevieve removed her bonnet and handed it to the young maid who'd appeared, then her gloves, while Peter doffed his hat and driving gloves. He turned, and his heart slammed hard against his chest.

Genevieve shrugged off the silk shawl from her shoulders, her breasts rising and bouncing with the motion. A lump caught in his throat.

Peter took her by the arm. He did not touch her bare skin often, and he knew immediately she hadn't expected it this day. She stilled, her breath hitching, but she walked calmly beside him into the drawing room.

"Very well. If you insist, I cannot stop you from being my companion on the morrow."

The cool, distant tone of her voice ripped into him, as powerful as any bayonet jab would have done. "Have you finally grown up enough to challenge me now, lass?" His quiet question did startle her, but behind them in the hall, Sir John and Lady Fielding were removing their carriage jackets. He didn't give her time to speak, only bent his head, set his lips to her ear and whispered words he knew would raise her heart rate and force her to seriously think about the challenge she was presenting him. "Think very carefully about what you're doing, Genevieve, trying those wiles on me. You may think I'm an overprotective man now, but you have no idea how obsessed I will be once you end in my bed."

His mother swept into the room before she could formulate a reply. He'd already taken two steps back, knowing full well that his mother would focus in on them immediately. "Now, my dear Peter, lovely Genevieve, Cook has lunch fully in hand. We just have time to refresh ourselves before it's served. The maid is waiting, Genevieve. Peter, come along, son."

Peter sighed, but took his mother's arm. He knew full well what she was going to say, but he honestly wasn't certain anymore that he could wait until Genevieve's nineteenth birthday to start the slow process of wooing this treasure who was his bride.

It turned out that he'd had no idea what she was going to say.

What she said changed everything.

"Sir John wants to take me to Italy this winter," she said. "Genevieve is welcome to come. I'm sure she'd love to visit Rome. The museums and architecture would be educational, and you know her artistic senses would welcome the experience. We'd like to leave from London near the beginning of December, and we'll stay until March or April. If you'd prefer she remain in London, I'm sure she'd be welcome at Lennox House."

Peter barely followed the conversation at lunch, except to note that Genevieve was nearly as quiet as he was.

Before he left, he did remember to ask about Ellen. "How long do you think it will before Ellen is well?" he asked.

Lady Fielding raised an eyebrow. "She's sniffling and stiff. It's a summer cold. She's not accustomed to those morning hours outdoors that Genevieve's been keeping. I'd expect at least a week."

Peter nodded, knowing there was no way he'd hold out a week without touching her. Along with his mother's travel plans, the time frame for Genevieve's transition to Devon Place was rapidly shifting forward. "I'll call for Genevieve in the morning and take her out myself. She's already agreed. We discussed the matter on the way back from church."

His mother patted him on the cheek, and he bent down obediently for her kiss that spot. "Genevieve is perfectly safe with you, you know," she whispered.

Peter hoped so, because there was no way on God's green earth that she was spending the winter at Lennox House or any of the Lennox's palatial country residences, especially not in Wales. He was also certain she would not be spending her winter admiring statues of ancient nude Romans. He hadn't been lying when he'd warned her about his tendencies. Unfortunately for her, Genevieve had stoked his greedy instincts. With her maturation from young female to lady, that protectiveness was already evolving.

Genevieve was going to discover, eventually, just what a possessive bastard he truly was. Maybe someday she'd forgive him for the temerity, too.

Chapter Six

Genevieve was fidgeting. Without complaint, Peter had loaded her easel and canvas, paints, picnic basket and blankets into the boot of the estate gig, the basket in the back and also on the seat behind. He'd helped her in very politely, climbed up beside her and whipped his pair of bays, directing them down the drive.

She sat close beside him, close enough that her body heat warmed his side a bit. The morning was cool enough that she had a pelisse on over her summer walking dress. It was not a heavy fabric, but at least her delectable shoulders were covered. Maybe he would make it through the morning hours without tasting them after all.

Beyond a brief greeting, Peter was conscientiously silent. She seemed to be relaxing now that they'd departed. Perhaps her twitchy limbs would still if he could speak to her reasonably, without scaring her off. Then again, where was she going to run off to?

Genevieve had consented to be alone with him, even if it was to paint.

Still, before he could think of any reasonable remark, Genevieve broke the silence. "It's very kind of you to chaperone me today, Sir Peter."

He threw her an incredulous look. "Did you just call me *Sir* Peter?" he asked.

"Yes," Genevieve sniffed. "That is your name."

"That's my title, and you are not one of the villagers or a stranger." He frowned. "Come to think of it, you must have called me that at times in the past. Don't do it again, though."

Openly bewildered, Genevieve looked away. She'd only spoken one sentence, and he'd been critical of it. Peter reminded himself he was an ass, then compounded the opinion by speaking again without thinking of how his words would sound coming out of his mouth.

"And it's not *kind* of me," he objected. "I'm not your chaperone."

He turned the horses off the lane and into the pasture. There had been enough traffic through the area in the last week that the wheels and horses had begun to wear a path through the grasses. Ahead of him, he could see the awning Jem had erected the week before. It was easy to identify where to park the gig. Jem had pounded two hefty stakes into the ground to tether the horses, so Peter braked and jumped down. He tied off the bays and returned to the carriage to help Genevieve down.

"If you're not here to be kind, then why are you here?" Genevieve challenged.

Peter, who'd spent hours of the previous night with the mantra *four more months* running repeatedly through his head, was tired. Genevieve was there, her straw hat pushed back and her gaze firmly on his. If any unidentified observer who might want a view of her happened to be nearby, they would find no joy, as she was shielded by the carriage.

He had no defenses left…at all.

"I'm here because I'm a possessive, selfish specimen of mankind," he returned. "I'm here because it's high time you knew it."

Genevieve's face scrunched up for just a second.

Peter bent his head. This time, he kissed her.

Genevieve stared at him, her lips burning from the seconds of unmistakable caresses. Peter didn't look away, didn't apologize. What was she supposed to say? Thank you? More, please?

Peter's lips tightened. She remembered how strange they'd felt pressed against hers, before the leather of his glove cupped her cheek and she'd tipped her chin up to better accept his kiss. What would he do if she kissed him, now that he'd begun it? Was it too forward of her?

Instead, she watched those tightening lips curl and twist into a half-smile.

He took the same two steps back that he'd done the day before, to separate them. "Jem isn't far behind," he said, reaching out for her hand. He lifted it and unbuttoned her glove, pressing his lips to her inner wrist. "Why don't you show me where you want everything in the meantime?"

Genevieve reached out with her other hand to steady herself on the black wood of the gig. His lips had felt remarkable against hers, the warmth of them scraping over her sensitive skin, a sensation she'd never experienced before. But the caress of his mouth against her wrist sent heat spiraling up her arm and neck then into her brain. She wasn't thinking clearly now.

Peter was watching her, though, and from his small smile, she knew he had deduced his effect on her. That would not do at all, she told herself belligerently, stiffening her spine and pulling her hand out of his. She tilted her nose and began to speak, but she had to clear her throat to deliver the words.

He worked without further comment, rolling out the rug where her easel would sit and the larger rug under Jem's awning. Genevieve carried the easel from the gig and, despite his frown, constructed it herself.

"I could have done that," he scolded, striding over to where she reclined on the rug, sharpening her pencils.

Genevieve looked up, and up, until she found his face scowling down at her. Without thought, she laughed. "I wouldn't be much of a painter if I could not carry and put together an easel," she pointed out. "I've done it hundreds of times, all without your help."

Even as the words left her lips, she realized why Peter continued to stare. She'd already slipped off her pelisse, leaving it in the gig, and wore only the low-cut summer walking dress. She had a painting smock to slip on soon enough, but for the moment, Peter was looking straight down her bodice.

He'd looked yesterday too. She looked down at her lap, so that he would not see her smile. He grunted from somewhere above her, an uncharacteristic noise given their previous formal relationship. She peeked, but he was moving away.

Not that the view was bad. From her position on the ground, it was easy to see the power with which he moved. His hacking jacket was well cut and his leather breeches fit even better. Genevieve admired the form and flow of his muscles, her fingers itching to draw him.

Of course, she couldn't — at least not today. Today she needed to take the blank canvas and begin to sketch out the painting. She had a week's worth of sketches in her notebook and knew now how she wanted to paint the rays of the sun as they hit the golden hay and the quiet river. Tomorrow she would begin painting, a bit every day, but once she had finished daily, the canvas would need to dry before they could take it back to Fielding Manor. She could sketch him then, when he wasn't aware.

She'd tried to draw him before, from memory, but she'd never been successful. This time she was determined to have every detail of his form and face. When would she have another chance like this? Ellen's *illness* wouldn't last forever.

He'd already kissed her. When Ellen was again in her company, would he try to withdraw and treat her as a distant acquaintance again? Genevieve knew she would fight that tooth and nail, even if it did end with Ellen's dismissal. The kiss may have been her first, but she wanted more of them — soon.

Jem arrived as she was settling the canvas into place. She turned it slightly to the side, so she could look at both her sketches and the view she was painting. The adjustment put the awning to her right, so only a slight twist of her head would bring him into view. However, once Jem departed, Peter did not behave as she'd expected. He didn't sit in the chair and read or watch the river. He didn't sit in the chair at all. Instead, he paced. He marked out a perimeter around her and walked it once, then again and a third time, until

Genevieve was spending more time watching him than working.

His face had changed, too. When he had been setting up the site, he'd smiled at her. As the hour had passed, his expression had gotten grimmer, as if he might be rethinking the kiss.

Genevieve didn't want him to rethink the kiss.

Finally, when the morning sun was high enough to warrant a break, she unbuttoned her smock and let the breeze whip her walking dress around her. It took only a moment for Peter, whose eyes seemed to constantly roam the countryside, to see Genevieve. She raised her arm and waved to him.

A moment later he was standing in front of her. "I don't like this," he said abruptly, sweeping his hand out in a wide circle. "You're too exposed. There's no protection, no concealment, not for hundreds of yards. Anyone could see you. Anyone could have spotted you and Ellen here last week and taken advantage. What defense would you have had, the two of you?"

Genevieve raised both of her eyebrows. "It's a good thing you're here, then," she replied, patting his arm. "I need to rest. Come. Let's open the basket and see what Cook has sent."

He frowned, looked up at the sun and reached to tilt her wide-brimmed hat down, shielding her face even more. "You should have something more comfortable than that awning and a single chair." Peter took her hand and turned her. In the sunlight, it was difficult to study his eyes, Genevieve thought, but the grim determination of his face was like nothing she'd ever seen from him.

"It's not as if we need to construct a summer house for this one canvas," Genevieve objected, stepping into the shade and sinking onto the rug. Peter looked at the chair, frowned and moved the hamper basket in front of them, joining her.

"Perhaps," he allowed, but Genevieve could see he was not convinced.

"We are on Framlingham land, anyway," she added, opening the basket. "You are welcome to concern yourself with the matter when I paint Devon Place."

"I will do that," he answered, his voice rather lower than she expected.

Genevieve turned quickly, but Peter was already there, his hand sliding into the hair at the back of her head to hold it in place. With his other hand, he untied the ribbons that held her hat on and plucked it from her head.

He lowered his head, and meeting Genevieve's eyes, pressed his lips to hers. She shuddered, her hands clasped his shoulders, and she forgot the world around her.

It happened that way every time Peter kissed her. A third time that day, then several times each day that passed. Friday, after they'd demolished the picnic luncheon, Genevieve leaned against him, her head on his shoulder, her mouth to his neck, and whispered reluctantly, "Ellen says she is well enough to return to her duties tomorrow."

Genevieve did not want to give up these moments alone with Peter, did not want Ellen's impromptu vacation-illness to interfere. But in the drawing room after dinner the previous evening, both Lady Fielding and Ellen had advised that Peter needed to be denied her company for a few days, or at least required to make an effort to see her. They both believed he needed to find a way to be alone with her when she wasn't painting, when she could focus on him.

Beneath her cheek, a low noise rumbled through him. She kept her eyes closed and pictured him frowning, his eyebrows drawn down toward his nose, the elegant shape of his hairline smooth across his forehead. Genevieve had studied him intently, both as he'd paced in the sunshine and as he'd sat nearby, and she had taken to sketching him. It was hard to capture his eyes with a simple pencil, but she'd cataloged his facial features thoroughly, hastily recording as many of his expressions as possible. Someday, she thought idly, she'd sketch his hands as well. At the moment, they were wrapped around her frame, hugging her close. Before this week, she hadn't thought much about his hands or about how stimulated she would feel when his hands burned her body through layers of cotton, linen and silk.

"How many days do you have left to paint out here?" he asked instead.

"At least tomorrow, possibly Monday," Genevieve estimated. "After that I will be spending many hours in the studio, adding shadow and subtle shades of paint that I just can't make up and bring out here in a jar."

"I'll see out your painting expeditions," he said, surprising her. "We wouldn't want her to relapse."

"Yes." Genevieve agreed, not willing to say more. She wasn't going to disagree with him and wanted his escort, though she wasn't certain how Ellen and her mother-in-law would react to his pronouncement. Before eating, she'd slipped off her smock. The temperatures had been rising and earlier she'd also discarded her slippers. Her bare feet were on the rug, between Peter's boots. On Wednesday, she'd done the same, and caught him staring at them. He hadn't touched, but he had tried to resist looking, and couldn't, so she'd done the same yesterday and today, happy with the attention. "After I'm done with this one, I want to paint Devon Place. Summer is almost over, and I won't have another chance until spring, but I'll be in London for the Season then, so truly, it would be next summer."

Peter was quiet, but his hands shifted, rubbing up Genevieve's bare arm. She shivered against him, wanting to turn and rub her body against his marvelous chest. Her fingers itched to explore him, to study him, but she knew better than to hurry him along physically. It shocked her that he'd accepted this much intimacy between them without arguing.

"We don't have to go to London in the spring, if you wish to stay in Suffolk."

Genevieve blinked, even squirmed a bit, unintentionally. Peter's arms actually tightened, pressing her body up to his, a deliberate provocation. Her nipples, through her gown and chemise, hardened and scraped the lapels of his jacket.

"Your mother will insist. I've only been out for two years."

He snorted. "To be perfectly candid, you're not a young miss on the marriage mart. Not even the most outrageous gossip in London would expect a nineteen-year-old miss who had married this last spring or earlier this summer to be in town next spring, and many young ladies your age did precisely that. Indeed, the gossips will only talk if you were there, instead of on your husband's estates." His fingers traced her cheekbone — an intimacy Genevieve craved already — then her lips, her jaw, her collarbone. When he spoke again, his voice was much quieter, deeper. "From now on, your participation in the Season won't be my mother's decision," he murmured, turning her face to meet her eyes. Genevieve flattened her palms on his back, holding herself close to him, but his fingers feathered downward, between them.

She drew in a shocked breath when he brushed the edge of her bodice with the pads of his fingers, abrading her skin with the roughness.

"By springtime, one way or another, your presence or absence from town will widely been seen as my decision," he added, his eyes intent on hers. The sunlight was shadowed by the awning and the gig drawn up on one side, to shield them from anyone driving up the path they'd beaten into the grass. Genevieve didn't know what Peter thought he would see in her eyes, but she heard his words clearly, understood their meaning. "If you wish to remain in Suffolk or go up for only a few weeks, that is what we will do."

Genevieve tried to think about that announcement, but her body was much more interested in the delightful sensation of his fingers against her skin. She arched back against the arm he'd wrapped around her waist and her breasts rose.

His finger slipped down inside the fabric, between the mounds and settled there, twitching.

Both Genevieve and Peter froze.

In the stillness, they both heard the pounding of hooves coming closer.

Peter jumped to his feet, straightened his coat and stepped to the side. To her astonishment, he retrieved a pistol from a narrow door built into the space beneath the gig and dropped to the ground, looking outward.

"It's Jem," he announced, after a moment of fraught silence.

Genevieve already knew that. She'd glanced around the side of the gig and was tying her hat back on as he spoke. Without comment, she watched him stand and brush off his jacket and breeches as if nothing unusual had occurred. He replaced the pistol as she put her feet into her slippers. "He's early," she finally said.

"He's on horseback, and riding at breakneck speed," Peter said, striding out to meet him. "He's not come early. He's come on an emergency. Pack up the basket. Something's wrong."

Genevieve hurried to obey, knowing that Peter was right. Jem was expected at two o'clock with the dray to take the armchair and rugs, not on horseback at half-past eleven. Hurriedly she re-packed the remainder of their meal.

"I know you don't want to return," Peter said after a few minutes. He'd gone to meet Jem, but they'd been too far away for Genevieve to hear their conversation. "But I need to take you back. One of the outbuildings has caught afire. It's out now, but John was hurt. The doctor has been sent for, but Mother wants us both to come to the house."

"Can Jem stay?" she asked, clutching the side of the gig for support. "The canvas needs to dry or it will be ruined. At least an hour—and even then it can't be covered."

"Yes, I'll take you back and send someone else with a dray to help Jem transport everything. Go give Jem his instructions."

In a very few minutes, Peter had her in the gig and headed the horses out to Fielding Manor.

"How is he? What did Jem say?" she asked Peter anxiously. They moved quickly enough that Genevieve was bouncing on the seat, so she grabbed hold of the rail in front of them for balance, not daring to complain.

"Only that he was burned helping put down the blaze in the old dovecote. I didn't see any signs of smoke, but with the wind burning to the northwest, it's possible that we wouldn't have seen anything. Thank God it wasn't the granary or the barns."

"The dovecote is only used by the gardeners now for their tools and supplies," Genevieve stated. "Why would it catch fire? And in the middle of the day?"

"A very good question." Peter urged the horses to a faster gait. It wasn't a dangerous speed, but certainly Peter was driving the horses more aggressively than he normally did. She stayed silent thereafter, wanting Peter to focus on his driving.

As they approached, Genevieve scented the acrid smoke as it drifted through the breezes. Determined to remain calm — to not panic or assume the worst — she watched the skies and the large country manor as it came into sight. From the drive, they could hear the shouts of the estate's men as they worked behind the house. Genevieve presumed they would have to rake out the coals and pull down the stones. She swallowed heavily. Sir John had been a good man to her these last years, certainly more a father than Winchester had ever been. Not only had he been generous with his home and his wife, but he was also kindly paternal, easily outshining Lennox's careful cordiality and stiff reserve.

They rolled to a stop directly before the front doors, which were standing open. The doctor's carriage was also standing in the drive and two of the younger lads ran up to take Peter's pair. Though she knew Peter normally wouldn't have left them without an older, stronger groom present, they were breathing hard, and Peter was clearly rushing. He swung her down to the drive without comment, but, for once, Genevieve hesitated. She didn't want to trap Peter through social machinations. She wanted him to choose to make their marriage a real one.

"Wait!" She tugged on his sleeve when he turned to escort her up the steps. When Peter looked down, she whispered frantically. "Dr. Mabry will see us arrive together."

Peter only gripped her arm and drew her along. "We are married, you know."

"But you've always said that we should never be unchaperoned—"

Peter paused on the front step and turned her to face him, his hands on each of her arms. "Genevieve, after these last few days, do have any intention of suing me for an annulment?" he demanded.

The bluntness of the question was shocking. Genevieve stared at him, her mouth gaping open for a second. "Of course not!" Peter was her hero. She wouldn't leave him. She loved—

He wasn't ready to hear that. She wasn't even ready to think it, let alone say it.

"Come along then. You are of reasonable age, even in the *haut ton*, to be courted and wed, and after all, we are already married, whether your family likes it or not."

She wanted to ask him about that, demand what he meant, but it would have to wait. Instead, he marched her into the house, up the stairs and into chaos.

Chapter Seven

The household was as upside down as Peter had ever seen it. Neither the butler nor the footmen were about to greet them. A maid scurried out from behind the green baize door, dropping a rushed curtsy, so he sent her running for washing water to be delivered to wherever they ended up. He and Genevieve both needed to wash their hands and faces. Upstairs, they ran into the housekeeper bustling toward the main stairs, which she rarely used.

"Sir." She bobbed. "Pardon me, the doctor needs —"

"I only want to know if they are in the master chambers," Peter asked abruptly, watching the woman's eyes drop to where he was clutching Genevieve's hand in his.

She answered affirmatively, so Peter sent her on, gripping Genevieve's hand even tighter. The last days, days where he'd drawn closer to her, had been both miraculous and heart-wrenching. He'd gone to sleep with an ache in his groin, had woken on the verge of spewing in his own hand and had spent those agonizing hours at Genevieve's side wound tighter than a clock spring.

And now this, just as he'd thought he might be able to set aside his past, as soon as she might be ready for more. Without question, his mother would need her here, need her time and attention. He couldn't think of it, wouldn't think of it. His mind produced old visions of men burned, explosions that had taken limbs off, left the men dying—

"Peter," Genevieve gasped and he halted, then resumed at a more reasonable pace. Even so, he didn't loosen his grip. He was going to need her to keep him sane when he saw Sir John.

The doors to the sitting room were open and he went through them. Beyond that, he could hear his mother crying. He paused again as dread sent streaks of pain into his chest. Then he heard a low moan from his stepfather. The dread turned to panic.

"I can't do this again," he whispered, not even intending to say it aloud.

Once again Genevieve came to his rescue.

"Peter, they need you," she said softly, tugging on his arm.

Sir John let out a loud cry, and Peter jerked, but Genevieve was dragging him along now.

"Genevieve, angel, you don't have to see this. It will be ugly."

Her jaw firmed. "Your mother will need me. She asked for us, correct?"

Even so, she stopped in the doorway and he bumped into her from behind. Both of them stared. Dr. Mabry was a young medical man new to Suffolk and his practice, by which Peter knew that Mabry had finished his training only two years earlier and had never seen a battlefield. As a result, Mabry had little practical experience with treating large burns. Such skills had been widely practiced in surgeons' tents and field hospitals during the Napoleonic wars, so Dr. Mabry's inexperience was immediately apparent to Peter.

John's shirt had been cut away. Both of his arms were blistering, but the doctor — or perhaps someone from the household before his arrival — had dredged flour over the wounds. Thankfully, his chest looked to be burn-free, so John must have been wearing his waistcoat, but not his jacket or gloves, when he'd fought the flames. The leech jar sat nearby, and already the doctor had been bleeding him, attaching the leeches to John's biceps above the burns.

"What the devil are you doing?" Peter roared, barely remembering not to push Genevieve out of the way. She scurried from his path anyway, making a beeline for his mother, who was clinging in horrified fascination to Ellen on the opposite side of the chamber.

Dr. Mabry glanced up, started to explain, but Peter cut him off. "Leeches won't help him, man. The vesicles need to be pricked to drain before they burst, and the wounds need to be dressed to try to stave off infection."

The man looked up at Peter and sniffed. "And what would you know of it?" he dismissed. "Bleeding him will remove the bad humors."

"Bleeding him will kill him, you bloody fool," Peter growled, pushing Mabry back. He frowned at the leeches but knew there was no way to remove those few until they had fed. His stomach turned, but even as the memory began to play in his mind, Genevieve's voice behind him speaking to his mother reached him. He clenched the bed then finally looked at John's face.

It was twisted in agony, but John was conscious. "Peter," he whispered. "Son, do what needs done. I trust you."

Peter tugged off his coat, thrusting it out. Ellen took it from him. He frowned at her, the picture of good health, with a shawl around her shoulders, but he remembered that Genevieve had said she was ready to accompany her out the next day.

"I can assist you," she said. Her stalwart voice was determined. "You know my history."

Peter did know. She was a long-time widow of genteel birth, forced to seek out domestic service to support herself. But once upon a time, her husband had been an officer. Ellen had followed the lieutenant to Spain by becoming part of the supply machine that kept them fed, armed and serviced. She'd buried her man near Toulouse.

"You know what will have to be done to save his arms, possibly his hands," Peter murmured to Ellen, looking at the evidence spread out on the bed. "It will be painful, devastating."

"We sent for hot water," she agreed. "And I can hold his arm down if I have to."

"And a long needle, scalded in a fire. Light a lantern. It will be a sufficient flame." In a field hospital or surgeons' tents, there was always a fire burning, heating water. At the end of August in Suffolk, the only fire would be in the kitchens. "We're also going to need cotton, lots of it. Wadding is best, but clean cloth if it's all that's here. Eventually we will need bandages too, enough to wrap him multiple times. The maids will need to find the cloth to make them—and quickly. Whatever we need the first time will need to be replaced at least twice a day."

"I'll go now for the needle. Your mother's sewing box is in the sitting room."

Ellen hurried away, and Peter glanced down at his stepfather then back to Genevieve. "He's going to need whiskey. Bring the decanter from the library and a glass. Mother, come and sit on the opposite side. You may need to keep his head in place."

Mabry finally spoke up as the others scurried to do Peter's bidding. Peter rolled up his sleeves as the man asked sourly, "What makes you suitable for this?"

Peter glared at him, then ripped off his simple necktie and jerked open the ties that held his shirt in place, revealing the long edge of a burn scar down his pectoral muscle. "I've already survived it," he snapped. He left the shirt gaping open as he turned away and rinsed his hands in the water basin by the window. Ellen returned from her search and lit the lamp. Peter watched her for a moment, holding the needle steadily in the lantern flame, fighting back the urge to remember, to experience.

Eventually he looked up at Mabry, accepting that he'd need the doctor, if the man was not pompous enough to storm out of the chamber. "The flour trick only works where the burn does not produce blisters. The blisters need to be carefully lanced and drained, and the skin pressed down with cotton to provide a protective layer. After, we'll need to stretch his arms and hands out as much as possible and bind them tightly with bandages. His arms and hands will need to be cleaned and re-dressed at least twice a day, possibly three times, since this isn't a battlefield, and any new blisters will need to be treated the same."

Mabry swallowed, looking every inch the boy instead of a man. Peter suddenly felt positively ancient, realizing precisely how much of a lecher he appeared to be from society's perspective. The doctor was older than Genevieve.

The next two hours seemed interminable. His mother poured Scotch down John's throat until the man sniffled into her skirts. Peter prayed John didn't remember these hours, because Peter knew they would join his own nightmares. Ellen and, surprisingly, Mabry, held John in place when he would have fought them, and Genevieve became his impromptu assistant, handing him cotton and taking away the detritus from the procedure.

When it was over, when John lay still in a drunken stupor and all the lanced blisters were tightly bound inside bandages, Mabry drew the leeches from John's upper arm. Peter looked at him approvingly.

"Not for burns," he said bluntly. "And definitely not on him."

"I'll come back in a few hours." The doctor nodded. "He may need sedating once the whiskey wears off. The pain must be terrible. And I can do the lancing, if you insist that's what must be done, although it seems more of a surgeon's duty."

"It is what needs to be done," Peter's mother insisted, looking up with eyes still full of tears, but her chin was set with stubborn determination. "And he'll need laudanum. As you know, there's no surgeon in our part of the county, so if you can't do it, say so now. Peter is strong enough for today, and I can send for someone from Ipswich." She looked as exhausted as Peter felt from the tedious and careful procedure, as if she should take to the bed herself.

"When you unwrap the dressings," Peter said severely, "try not to tear the old skin away. Just leave the cotton if it sticks. All of that damaged outer layer of skin will come off in time. He must heal from the inside out."

Genevieve drifted to him, her eyes lacking their usual vivacious brightness. "Come, Peter. You need to rest."

She led him to her studio. He supposed that made sense. Her rooms had been his in childhood, and no maid could be bothered with airing out a guest room, not today. Without comment, she helped him onto a wide daybed. He frowned at his boots, pondering what to do, but she'd disappeared, so he simply sat and stared at them. But just as he decided to collapse and worry about it later, John's valet appeared.

The valet, thankfully, had a boot horn. He removed the offending apparel and took them away. Peter wanted to ask where his jacket had gone, but he simply stripped out of his shirt, spotted and stained with his stepfather's blood and skin, and surrendered that as well. It was unsalvageable, but better the valet dispose of it than he sleep in it on the pristine fabric of Genevieve's daybed.

Now that the immediate crisis was over, he couldn't function. He ought to be checking on the men working outdoors, caring for Genevieve, organizing the household so that his mother could nap. But he didn't do any of that. Instead, he just sat.

At least he sat until Genevieve returned. She had yet another pitcher of water, one that had followed pitcher upon pitcher of it that the women had used to clean John and the bed beneath him. Genevieve dipped a rag in it before taking it to his face. It was an intimate thing, to have her wiping that cloth over his eyebrows, his cheeks, his jaw, even down to his neck, while he sat bare-chested and woodenly silent. She wrapped his hands in the cleansing rag, and cleaned them, rubbing the skin. He stared at her shaped fingernails, the elegant fingers, watched the tender way she was ministering to him.

Peter simply absorbed it. He didn't have the energy to even convey his gratitude, but she urged him back onto the daybed and kissed his cheek as if he was boy instead of a man. "Rest. I'll look after them for now."

He nodded, letting his eyes fall shut. He didn't want to rest here, didn't want her to know that he couldn't sleep, but what else could he do?

She hummed for a moment as she moved around him, cleaning up, and he forgot to stay awake.

* * * *

The head gardener had reported to the butler, who had passed the word to Genevieve and Lady Fielding that the fire had been caused by one of the lads spilling a lantern. It had broken, and the lad had dropped his shovel to the slate floor, setting a spark to the oil. Sir John apparently had already known. The boy had set up the alarm himself but hadn't been able to extinguish it before the flames had caught the hay stacked inside — and the tools and the roof.

Lady Fielding had naturally refused to leave Sir John. The maids had made up a cot beside the bed, because Sir John needed the entire bed the couple usually shared. His arms had to remain stretched out, his fingers stretched open and apart by the cotton bindings.

With Lady Fielding at her husband's bedside, Ellen had taken charge of the household staff, preparing them for the challenge ahead, leaving Genevieve to settle her mother-in-law. She'd organized for the dear woman to have tea and a cold collation. Lady Fielding had tried to refuse, but Genevieve had pointed out that she'd need her strength, and she'd likely have to feed her husband, as Sir John was likely not going to be able to feed himself.

Genevieve sighed tiredly as she slipped into her studio. Jem had transported the canvas and her other supplies back to the house in the mid-afternoon. The unfinished painting sat on the traveling easel in her bedchamber, waiting until she could return it to her studio, but Genevieve wasn't even tempted to check it, beyond ensuring it had not been damaged. Peter remained asleep in her space, his arm flung over his face and one leg hanging off the side of the daybed. He was mumbling, twitching in his sleep, and Genevieve desperately wanted to comfort him, but she knew not to try to wake him. Instead, she sat and studied him, wincing as his language deteriorated into mumbling mixed with curses.

Peter was going to be hungry when he woke. He'd slept already for a good two hours, while she'd done what was necessary to settle Lady Fielding. Genevieve already had scones and sandwiches waiting, as well as ale, and there was always tea. Like Peter had been, Genevieve was exhausted.

Tea sounded like an excellent idea. She hadn't had more than a pastry when they'd opened the hamper earlier for the late breakfast.

She was brewing the pot when Peter sat up with a shout, swinging out his arm in a wild punch. The violent motion startled her, but she bit her lip and tried very hard to be still. Peter had already come to his senses, and the dawning horror on his face did not bode well.

"It was only a bad dream, and hardly a surprise after this horrific day," she finally offered, gesturing at the waiting tray of food. "Come. You must be starving."

If she didn't know better, she'd think Peter was panicking. He looked first at the tall clock over the mantel, then paced back and forth impatiently, glancing at her in open consternation.

"Peter, do sit down. There's ale," she invited again, pouring herself a cup of the steaming tea, trying not to stare at the heavy muscles in his chest and abdomen that flexed as he moved.

"No, I-I-I-I'll be back," he finally stammered, practically slamming the door behind him as he ran out. She could hear his bare feet running down the back stairs outside her corridor, then brightened as she came to an obvious conclusion and laughed.

At least it was funny to her until fifteen minutes later, when he still hadn't returned.

After thirty minutes, she wiped the tears from the corners of her eyes and went to check on Peter's parents. She'd caught Sir John's endearment earlier, calling him 'son'. Sir John had no children of his own, having married Lady Fielding some ten years after Peter's birth, when she was nearly thirty-five. He had taken Peter under his wing, and while they weren't father and son, they were certainly closer than neighbors—or many step-fathers and step-children.

Peter wasn't there, either. Sir John was mumbling, Lady Fielding asleep beside him, but she would wake soon. Nearby in the sitting room, Ellen and two maids were quietly making bandage strips from old sheets.

Instead of returning to the studio, she entered her bedchamber. It, too, had been Peter's as a child, though no one would know it from the current décor. The walls were covered in Chinese papers of gold-and-red stripes, the floors with similarly colored rugs. The ceiling was plastered with a gold leaf pattern, and the furniture was a beautiful black wood with red-and-gold upholstery, highlighted with the barest hints of ivy green. It was a wild color scheme, certainly not suitable for many, and the exact opposite of the light, airy *white* feeling of the studio next door. But two summers ago it had suited her mood. Lady Fielding had grimaced and expressed her opinion that it was entirely too dramatic, but that had been expected, and Lady Fielding had not refused her plans. At least Peter had not tried to parent her by refusing to pay for the outrageous design. He hadn't even seen it, but had taken the bill of sale from the decorator and paid it without a single comment to her.

She flung herself into a chair and stared out of the window. In the distance, she could see over the wide front lawn, the lane and into the fields across the far hedgerow, dark green with alternating rows of beans, sugar beets and cabbages that were nearly ready for harvest.

Sighing, defeated, at least for the day, Genevieve wandered into her dressing room and stripped her gown. It was limp from her morning excursion and the ensuing crisis. "No wonder he didn't want to touch me," she muttered, looking at her flattened hairstyle and drooping eyes. Quickly she washed her face and settled her hair, then washed herself with soap and cool water left from the morning. While it was almost tea time and she had no expectation that she would be dressing for dinner, she also didn't want to appear in any dowdy or countrified morning gown, such as she might wear in the studio covered by her smock. No matter what, Peter might still be about.

Genevieve ended up choosing a pale green gown. She couldn't remove the corset or tighten it by herself, but she did change her shoes for sensible indoor slippers that did not click on the floors. Without Ellen or ringing for a maid, she could not don any of her newest gowns with gigot sleeves or anything that fastened in the back. Under such limiting circumstances, the low-scooped green neckline with ribbon highlights at her waist and elegant buttons up the bodice was her most sensible choice.

And, as the last few days had demonstrated, filling the front of her bodice with an unnecessary fichu or chemisette was counterproductive. She held the gown to her front and studied herself in the mirror.

When she heard the gasp, her gaze jerked around and she found Peter standing in the dressing room doorway, which she'd failed to close.

Peter was fully dressed again, his hair still wet from where he must have washed it. He wore a different outfit, but his own boots were in place.

He looked fresh and lovely and she wanted to stare at him.

He was staring at her.

That was when Genevieve realized she wore nothing but her chemise, corset, stockings, and a gown pressed to her bosom. And she was standing in front of a mirror.

Her pulse pounded heavily in her throat. Peter was not moving, but she did not mistake his stillness for a lack of interest. He was intensely focused, on her. Her hands shook, and the gown shook, but she held on for a moment.

She held on until he stepped into the room, reached out and took it away, leaving her facing him in her underclothes.

A bright blush covered her cheeks. She started to turn away — to run away — but he dropped the gown to the floor and held her arms to her sides, examining her from the tips of her toes inside the velvet slippers, up her stockings to the hem of her chemise, and higher to her waist and hips, where the corset smoothed out her curves and slimmed her waist. His gaze lingered admiringly on her breasts, barely concealed by the whalebone frame covered in white silk. But he didn't stop there. He went higher, examining her shoulders and neck, and higher until their eyes met.

Genevieve shuddered at the blatant hunger on his face.

Chapter Eight

Peter was too dazed by the sight before him to even pick one of the curse words swirling through his mind. So he stayed silent and stared at her—first at her spectacular form then at her expressive eyes, wide with shock. She flushed, the faint pink tinge of her skin rosier with every second.

He hadn't meant to walk in on her changing, but the door between her studio and her chamber was open, so he'd peeked in, looking for her. She hadn't been visible, but he'd seen a door open beyond and wondered if they'd converted that chamber to a sitting room. So he'd strolled through the empty bedchamber, wanting her to join him for tea and sandwiches.

Except the room wasn't a sitting room, it was a dressing room, and Genevieve was barely covered.

Her pretty underthings did as much to feature her form as hide it.

"You left the bloody door open," he accused hoarsely. Immediately he wanted to kick himself. He hadn't meant to accuse her. He'd meant to excuse himself. "You were gone when I returned." Even worse. Her eyes dulled. She was obviously hurt by his rudeness, so he cleared his throat and tried again. "You are so damn pretty without your gown."

Christ, he was an idiot. He stepped forward, reaching out for her jaw and tracing it softly.

She blinked.

"I'm going to kiss you now," he whispered. "I can't stop myself."

She nodded, so he let his hands drift down the back of her corset and pressed his lips onto hers. A curious relaxation washed over him, as though an out-of-sync joint had finally slid neatly into place. She was with him in the kiss, not fighting him. She parted her lips and he experienced her taste and her scent and nearly wept for joy. He wanted to spend hours staring at her half-dressed loveliness and even more hours with her beautiful lips against his. He couldn't think further than that — not now, not on a practical level.

Insidious lust whispered that they were close to her bed, and he could sink inside her, so deeply that she'd not be able to refuse him, that she'd have to stay with him if they consummated their marriage. Yes, she'd admitted earlier that she had no intention of asking for an annulment, even if Lennox wanted to offer the choice when she turned nineteen.

Damn it, he wasn't giving her the choice. She'd refused already. By the time her birthday came around, he would have been unable to resist her.

But not here. Not now. Peter's mind quickly balanced all the positives of bedding her against the negatives — the returning doctor, his mother and Ellen in the house, his stepfather in pain, Genevieve as she'd looked before she saw him, trying to refresh herself without bathwater after a strenuous day. He'd have to hurry.

He didn't want to hurry—not with Genevieve, and definitely not her first time.

Reluctantly he pulled away. Without speaking, he kissed her forehead, helped her dress and led her back to the studio, staying silent until he had finished two sandwiches, a glass of ale and three biscuits.

"Thank you for thinking of feeding me," he finally managed, having struggled with what to say for the entire time he'd been eating. "And I want to offer my apologies for my behavior earlier."

"It was my fault. I left the door open." Genevieve shook her head as she spoke.

"Not that," he corrected. "For running out when I woke. I'm not used to waking up in strange places, and I was dreaming. I didn't mean to swing at you, I wouldn't hurt you for the world, but I didn't know what I was doing."

"Peter, I was halfway across the room, and I don't think you were swinging at me. You were swinging at someone French and swearing in Portuguese."

Peter felt his ears pop as a sudden change in pressure in the room surprised him. She'd understood what he'd been saying?

"Fiona knows all the curse words in all the languages. My governess insisted on teaching me how to greet most Europeans in their native languages, which includes both French and Portuguese, so Fiona secretly taught me how to curse in those languages too."

"I thought your sisters were a good influence," Peter muttered.

She tipped her head to the side and considered him, then smiled tauntingly. "They also told me about what will happen when we consummate our marriage, what it's like the first time when I'm still a virgin and how to know if you've enjoyed it." She paused and added, "That was Abigail and Gloria."

"Christ." Peter said the expletive without thinking, then sighed.

"You should probably send them a letter and say thank you," she said seriously. "Or were you planning on telling me all those things yourself?"

"I was planning on... Hell, no, I didn't have a single plan. Don't women just know these things?"

"No, Peter, not until we experience them. It's a good thing they told me, you know, otherwise I'd be really confused about what just happened...in my dressing room." Genevieve was calm and collected, and Peter felt as if he was going to perspire out the collar of his shirt. He stared at her, willing her to continue. "What happened is that you kissed me and thought about taking me to the bed. You wanted to, but you didn't. I could feel y-your —"

"Cock," Peter supplied, perversely happy that she was finally struggling with saying something, since she seemed utterly confident about everything else.

"Yes, that. I could feel it against my stomach. So I know you wanted to, but you didn't. I'm guessing you were weighing what you wanted against everything else."

"The doctor is going to come back, my stepfather is gravely injured and so on," Peter affirmed.

Genevieve leaned forward. "So that means, later, when the timing is better, you're going to want to take me to your bed."

"Yes." Peter was relieved to hear the word come out of his mouth without embellishment. He knew better than to curse in mixed company and Genevieve was definitely a lady. His lady, in fact.

She nodded briskly, seemingly pleased by his agreement. "Well then, we should go check on the household, don't you think?"

"Yes," he said again, and was relieved when she took his arm and let him escort her into the corridor.

* * * *

Privately amazed and happy with how far Peter had come, Genevieve let him escape that night without comment. He needed to rest, and the day had been mind-numbingly difficult. Besides, before the crisis had begun, both Peter's mother and Ellen had advised her to not seek out his company for at least a few days. Saturday was the same, with Sir John in excruciating pain, so much so that he was grateful for the laudanum. By Sunday, Genevieve withdrew from the master chamber, leaving Lady Fielding in charge and Ellen as a capable nurse. By late afternoon, she sat down in the morning room and took up the wearying task of informing her family and Lady Fielding's closest contacts of the news. Lady Fielding had copied out Sir John's instructions to send for his solicitor, crying the entire time, and Peter had sent it flying by courier to London.

Genevieve did note that Sir John neither requested nor sent for his heir, his sister's son. Bartholomew John Queshire's presence would, to Genevieve's mind, require more work than his absence. Though he was in his late twenties, Genevieve thought of him as a spoiled brat. Luckily, he only called in London. He'd only come to stay in Suffolk one time, the previous summer. Peter had unhelpfully been gone, visiting some property he owned in Scotland, but Ellen had stayed staunchly at Genevieve's side and eventually Genevieve herself had simply retreated to her studio and painted. It had taken days, but eventually Sir John had routed the houseguest and sent him fleeing to his mother's household in Ipswich.

This morning Sir John had said to Lady Fielding that he had no intention of dying. Genevieve hoped that whoever did work the pearly gates felt the same on the matter.

As she sealed the note she'd written to Abigail, the door behind her opened. Genevieve looked up, surprised, when Peter came in, shutting the door behind him.

"Dr. Mabry has the skill to tend to him. He just didn't have the knowledge. And now he does," Peter claimed, coming up behind her and leaning over the back of her chair.

Genevieve gave a short nod, fingering the penciled draft on the desktop. It wasn't a complete letter, only the part that she had to re-live in each edition. Peter rested his chin on the top of her head and perused it. "You know, this is likely to bring a houseful of guests," he surmised.

"Surely not!" Genevieve shook her head, horrified. "Your mother can't entertain. I don't think she could even cope with callers. I turned away the rector's wife a few hours ago." Genevieve pursed her lips. "She only went because the housekeeper and butler were both backing me up. I'd never have gotten her back in her carriage if she'd suspected you were here."

Peter snorted then drew Genevieve to her feet. "Speaking of me," he said, drawing her into his arms and shifting her hands to help settle them on his shoulders, "are you thinking to avoid me now?"

"Of course not," she declaimed immediately, though she silently rejoiced. He'd sought her out for this?

"Good." Peter leaned forward and kissed her, but this kiss was different. Hungrier. He was no longer leading her along a path toward intimacy but was dragging her along as he raced toward his goal. Genevieve experienced a hot rush of desire rip up her spine, and she moaned, instinctively rubbing against him. Her nipples hardened, and an ache formed in her stomach. "Have you finished with the letters?" he whispered.

Genevieve forced her eyelids open, meeting his dark eyes. She shook her head slightly but couldn't bring herself to speak. Instead, she pressed closer, moving her hand so that her palm pressed against his jaw, abrading the stiff hairs that were beginning to appear there.

He groaned, twisting his head and moving so that his lips pressed against the palm of her hand. One of his hands caught hers, holding it in place. His tongue came out and licked the center of her palm, then moved up to the inside of her wrist.

"Peter," she gasped. "I'm burning inside."

"Yes," he agreed, pulling her with him as he backed toward the small seating area behind them. This room did not have a convenient chaise or daybed. Lady Fielding used the morning room for running the household and her correspondence, so the sitting area in the corner consisted of two French-style settees arranged in the corner with a low table between them.

Peter sank onto the silk velvet upholstery, drawing Genevieve down onto his lap. She went eagerly, happy to have his hands roaming her back and sides, wishing she wore a low-cut evening gown instead of a cotton day gown in burgundy pinstripes that fastened in the back, had sleeves to just below her elbows and bustled up under her breasts. Though the dress was perfectly acceptable for turning away callers like the rector's wife, the apron she wore over it was decidedly inappropriate for dalliance. But if Peter wasn't complaining, she wouldn't either.

Unfortunately, Peter discovered he wanted to complain. Or fortunately. Genevieve couldn't remember at this point if she did or did not want him to have any success paying her intimate attentions. "Damn dress. What are you wearing?" he muttered, his palms trying to cup her through the apron, gown, chemise and corset.

"I dressed for letter-writing, not seduction," Genevieve said quietly, hiding her face in his shoulder.

"And again, I don't intend to seduce you in such awkward circumstances," Peter said grimly. "But I've barely seen you in two days, even though we've been in the same house."

"And we don't have time. The dinner gong's about to ring, and I need to change." She looked up at him and conceded one point. She wanted to see him, to spend time with him, despite the advice of the older women in her life. "You are staying for dinner, yes? I've already told Cook to expect you. It will just be the three of us. They are setting a table up in your mother's sitting room so we can be close to Sir John. Ellen is resting so she can sit up with him tonight."

Peter smiled at her, breathed in slowly and pressed a kiss to her forehead. "Yes, angel, I'm happy to stay."

* * * *

He hadn't wanted to leave, but Peter had done so after dinner, when Sir John was dosed with laudanum and sleeping heavily. With the butler hovering, he hadn't been able to kiss Genevieve again, despite her charming ivory silk gown embroidered with blue flowers and trailing green vines.

Oh, how he'd wanted to. Peter had spent all of dinner following the intricate embroidery on that gown, over shoulders and down the bodice, from her knees up over her abdomen, along the curve of her bottom to the high collar at the base of her neck.

He'd toed the line and been denied any private moment alone with her on Saturday. By Sunday evening he'd been ready to seize whatever chance fate handed him to simply hold her. How things had changed from only two weeks ago, when she'd avoided him like the plague.

Still, he couldn't seem too eager to flit to her side, and Devon Place didn't run on its own. He met with Mrs. Inglebright, Grady and Robin, as he customarily did on Monday mornings, dutifully listened to his steward as he walked from the house to the stables and rode past the river spot where Genevieve wanted one more day of painting, before he headed to Fielding Manor.

It didn't take long at all to see what had gone wrong.

Bartholomew Queshire had heard, seized his chance and was determined to make the most of it.

Peter strode into John and his mother's chamber and ordered him out.

The toad — there was no other description for the unpleasant, whiny creature in front of him — tried to stare him down, but Bartholomew was no match for

Peter. "As if I could leave my dearest uncle in his last days," Bartholomew objected.

"He's not dying," Peter pointed out.

"The poor man's just wasting away, with inadequate medical—"

"I *beg* your pardon," Mabry said from behind him. "Sir John will be as fit as a fiddle soon enough."

Peter smiled grimly. If Bartholomew had thought to sound officious, instead he'd brought out the doctor's pride with his foolish prick. "We have full confidence in Dr. Mabry's excellent training and skills. Sir John has already much improved. Now, Ellen will show you out."

Ellen rang for the butler and smiled at him blankly. "You'll want to wash up before luncheon," she said blithely.

Peter followed them all the way to the corridor, in case.

Sir John looked to be in agony, and his mother gripped the bed sheets so tightly that Peter thought she might leave a permanent mark. "Who sent for him?" Peter snapped.

Lady Fielding pursed her lips. "Neither of us, and Genevieve wouldn't invite him to the house. One of the locals must have told John's sister. She still has friends here."

Peter whipped his head around at that, frowning at his mother, struck by his mother's reference to Genevieve. "Why," he asked, keeping his voice admirably under control, "would Genevieve have reason to dislike Bartholomew, Mama?"

John answered, gritting his teeth against the pain as Mabry cleaned a section of the burned skin. "Couldn't help but notice when he was here last summer that the fool spent more time looking at her than at the estate."

"She was never alone with him, because Ellen was always with her," his mother pointed out reasonably.

Peter's fists tightened, his fingers digging into his palms, suddenly feeling extremely unreasonable. "And why," he asked, "was I not aware of this before?"

"You were up in Scotland, son," John managed.

His mother sighed. "There was nothing to fret about, Peter. He left after a few days."

Ellen reappeared and went back to gathering up the discarded bandages that Mabry was removing from his patient. "She noticed him watching her, sir, and after that, stayed in the studio and painted as much as possible. She wasn't seeking attention from him."

"Of course she wasn't," Peter acknowledged. Genevieve wouldn't have sought out another man's attention. He'd spent enough nights following her around ballrooms to know that she regularly received much more male admiration than she was aware of or desired. "Where is she now?"

"Painting, sir. She doesn't know he's arrived. I checked on her an hour ago and she was painting in her studio. She said she's going to try to finish that scene for Lady Framlingham without going down to the river again."

Peter nodded, then looked to Sir John. "He is your heir, like it or not."

Sir John's lips pinched together and his eyes narrowed. "Estate's not entailed. You're the executor," he managed. "He doesn't know, but he won't see a red penny more than a quarterly allowance—not even residency in the house—as long as your mother is alive. Those are my wishes, son. Understand?"

"Even if something did happen to you, and Bartholomew somehow did get his filthy hands on Fielding Manor or your funds, you never have to worry about Mama, John." Peter vowed it, raising his hand and lightly touching it to his breast. He stole a glance at her, but Lady Fielding was daintily pressing a handkerchief to her eyes. She was crying again.

"I know, son." John swore under his breath as Mabry repositioned his lower right arm and began to wrap it again. "Why I called for the solicitor. Want to make it clear to m'nephew. He has instructions. Not surprised he showed up here once he heard of it."

"Your man won't arrive for at least two days, John," Peter warned. "Can you tolerate him that long?"

"Will have to," John said grimly.

Peter agreed.

At least he agreed until he discovered a few hours later that Bartholomew Queshire had insisted on inhabiting the bedchamber directly across from Genevieve's rooms, in a part of the house where he shouldn't be wandering unless he wanted Bartholomew — and thus all of London — to know he and Genevieve were more intimate than ever before.

After a vitriolic litany of curses that the butler pretended not to hear, he had the poor man send for Jem, who arrived shortly in the morning room. Peter had been scratching out a note in pencil to Robin. "I need you to deliver this to Grady at Devon Place. He's my gentleman's gentleman. No one else, Jem, not even Mrs. Inglebright, no matter how good her biscuits. I want you to wait. He'll send a box back with you."

Jem bobbed his hand and left on his errand then Peter returned to his mother's chambers, finding her and Ellen in the sitting room. His mother was asleep on the chaise longue, but Peter wanted Ellen anyway. "I need you to warn Genevieve that he's here and he's expected at luncheon. Make sure she knows to keep her doors, including her studio door, locked."

Ellen nodded and obeyed, while Peter sat with his mother and fretted.

He didn't like Bartholomew — he never had — and the thought that Genevieve had felt it necessary to hide herself away in her own home because the toad was visiting had brought out every one of his protective hackles.

Chapter Nine

Grateful to Ellen for the advance warning, Genevieve was modestly dressed and had her guard up when she opened her door to descend to the first floor for luncheon. As well as anyone else in the household, she knew Sir John and Lady Fielding could hardly cope with an extended visit, and Sir John especially wouldn't want his nephew to see him weak or, worse, out of his mind or sedated.

His nephew, having excellent peeping skills, emerged from his chamber as Genevieve did, and preened, practically inviting her to admire him.

She turned and proceeded up the hall, leaving him to hurry after her. She knew it was rude, but she couldn't help herself, and she definitely did not want him to touch her.

"Lady Genevieve, you are as stunning as always."

Genevieve stopped. Her eyes went to his. "I believe you are well aware that I am married, Mr. Queshire, and I use the name Lady Devon now."

She turned and went on before he could offer his arm, turning the corridor.

The sight before her was a great relief. Peter and Ellen were both in the upper anteroom. Peter immediately held out his arm to her and she took it with a happy sigh, rather blatant in her intention to cling to her husband.

Bartholomew was forced to offer his arm to her companion, and he did not like that at all. He looked down at the older lady and sneered. "Surprised you're joining us at the table, Miss Ellen."

Peter stiffened beside Genevieve. She pressed her palm to his arm, descending the stairs sedately at his side. She wondered if he would make a possessive display of her. He didn't need to, but he didn't know about Bartholomew Queshire's frequent attempts to touch her. "Apparently you did not realize, Queshire, but Mrs. Wyman's late husband was one of my officers in Spain. He was commissioned as a lieutenant and died a hero's death, trying to rescue two infantrymen in the river."

Genevieve nearly turned around to see how that information — news to her that Lieutenant Wyman had been under Peter's command — affected their unwanted houseguest.

But instead Ellen spoke, and her quiet words nearly caused Genevieve to dance on the steps. "My late husband considered it his duty to serve England during the war, and he was proud to be under General Hill and Colonel Devon's command. If only all men were so honorable. The world would be a much better place."

The small set-down did not impinge on Bartholomew's awareness at all. At the bottom of the stairs, they turned into the dining room, and their guest sneered. "How informal this is, then. Not what I expected at all for a house of this standing, what with no suitable hostess present and Lady Fielding refusing to grace us with her presence."

He started to move, to sit at the head of the table, but Peter intercepted him, pointing out one of the chairs that graced the sides. Bartholomew started to challenge him, but Poindexter appeared and gestured him to the same seat.

They sat, Ellen and Bartholomew on one side of the table, and Peter with Genevieve opposite. "Mr. Queshire," Genevieve said brightly, "Lady Fielding says you have turned thirty. A remarkable age. I trust you are planning to pursue the matter of your marriage and nursery soon? You wouldn't want to find yourself without a proper heir, given the small size of the Fielding family."

Bartholomew paled and blinked, looking uncomfortable, but seized on the obvious gambit. "I hardly think there's any rush. Devon here doesn't appear particularly enamored of the condition and he's several years beyond me."

"Ah, I confess I'm finding much of marriage to recommend it," Peter chuckled.

"Yes." Genevieve nodded. "You might go up to town for the Little Season. I'm sure there's someone for you."

Ellen agreed, but Bartholomew seized the mention of the Little Season to ask Peter about what gambling haunts he most favored.

Peter gave a very long answer and actually offered to take Bartholomew out in London. Genevieve tried not to glare at the infuriating man, but Peter turned and asked her about her afternoon plans.

"I'm working on the canvas for Lady Framlingham. I've decided I don't need to go back to the river. My sketches were thorough enough, and if I decide there is a critical element missing, I'll take Jem and ride out with my sketchbook when that time arrives."

"Excellent."

Peter smiled at her, but when Genevieve blushed happily, trying not to fidget in her seat, she found Bartholomew Queshire staring at her. Again.

"Mr. Queshire, you are enjoying your fish, aren't you?" Genevieve asked anxiously. She smiled at Ellen. "Lady Fielding and Sir John do so enjoy it, so Cook was sending some upstairs, too. The lads who work for the gardener and gamekeeper all went fishing this morning."

"You've gone into *trade* with your art?" he asked, his lower lip curling in disgust.

Peter laid his fork down rather harder than necessary, catching everyone's attention. "Isn't it wonderful that she's already so recognized that she's being offered commissions?" he asked. The question was apparently rhetorical because he went right on. "Given that her work is now hanging in the public rooms of several notable hostesses in London, I suppose it was inevitable that my darling wife be recognized for the genius she is. I understand the Earl and Countess of Sefton had a very public disagreement as to where Genevieve's painting of Croxteth Hall should be. She sketched it last autumn, when she and Mother stayed there before going up for the Little Season, and presented the painting to them as a gift, on the occasion of the New Year. Sefton thought the proper place to hang the painting was in his library."

"Of course it hangs in the drawing room, where all of Lady Sefton's callers can see it," Ellen finished the tale.

Genevieve flushed. Lady Sefton had been her sponsor at Almack's when she was presented under Lady Fielding's aegis.

"It's becoming quite the cachet to have one of Genevieve's paintings hung in a *tonnish* drawing room," Peter said, pride and satisfaction practically beaming off him, as if he were the one who was being celebrated. "So a rush of commissions is hardly a surprise."

Genevieve could barely restrain herself from leaping from her chair and pelting him with kisses. It was that or cry, and she didn't want to cry, not in front of Bartholomew Queshire. Even if her paintings hung only in the drawing rooms of Lennox House, Fielding House, Sefton House, Arlington House, Lauderdale House and Canning House, everyone knew the artist.

Even Queshire's name sounded distasteful, and the way he wrinkled his nose and looked down at her aggravated her reaction. "You can't have known what a mistake you were making without the guidance of...of—"

"Of a husband?" Peter suggested mildly.

"Of a father," he sneered, ignoring Peter now. "Sir Peter might be an expert at caring for my uncle John's estate, but he can hardly claim to have your best interests in hand, after all."

The outrageous statement shocked the other three to silence for a moment.

"Winchester would have auctioned my art to the highest bidder in Trafalgar Square, if he'd known I had any sort of skill," Genevieve finally claimed. She smiled at Ellen. "And Sir John thinks it an honor to be known as my patron." Her eyes turned to Peter, whose small smile encouraged her to be as outrageous as she wished. With a glance at Queshire, Genevieve added, "As for my husband's approbation, I assure you, Mr. Queshire, I hold his opinion of the highest regard."

She looked to Ellen, who had stopped eating, and abruptly changed the subject. "I do believe it's time we excused ourselves. Mrs. Wyman?"

Ellen agreed.

Genevieve only threw one paintbrush against the wall before hugging herself and dancing around the studio. *Someday,* she thought, *Peter and I are going to be alone.*

Ending by the window, she stared down into the forecourt and grimaced. Bartholomew trailed after Peter, who was filling in for Sir John's regular schedule and going out to look at the crops, so that they might decide when the harvest would begin.

At least she'd have the afternoon to paint.

* * * *

Ellen came to extract her at teatime, and the two induced Lady Fielding to join them in her sitting room while Sir John napped. "That pest had the temerity to come in here and protest every decision poor Peter made today," she snapped. Lady Fielding's lips were clenched and her form stiff.

Genevieve poured her tea and added an extra lump of sugar.

"Peter was so frustrated by the end of his tirade that he went home to Devon Place," she went on. Glancing at Genevieve, she added carefully, "He said he'd see you later, but it may not be until tomorrow. He had business to attend to there, as well."

Genevieve groaned. "You're not going to make me sit down to dinner with Mr. Queshire in the dining room, are you? Alone?"

"Never alone with him," Ellen added. "Sir Peter was *very* clear about that."

"Pray that the solicitor arrives expeditiously," Lady Fielding sighed, sipping from her cup. "Otherwise John may leap from that bed and swing his entire injured arm at his nephew's head."

In the end, they abandoned Queshire to dine in solitude. Lady Fielding did not wish to leave Sir John. Ellen, as she pointed out, rarely joined the family for dinner anyway. Peter did not appear, and Genevieve simply didn't go down. Instead, she nibbled on a delicious cinnamon cake and drank watered wine that Jem delivered to her studio door at half-past eight.

At half-past nine, a quiet knock distracted her from the book she was reading. Expecting Jem returning for the tray, she was surprised to see Peter on the other side. He pushed through and shut the door almost silently, setting his boots on the floor and turning the key in the door so quietly that the tumblers engaged without a sound.

Genevieve stared at him in shock. "What are you doing?" she asked, then pointed to his hose. "And why have you taken off your boots?"

Peter turned, squinting at her in the dim light. He seemed tired, yet resigned. And he carried a saddlebag. "You didn't think I'd leave you alone in a house with him, did you?" he asked, picking up his boots and striding through the bedchamber door. Genevieve watched him find space for his things in her dressing room, and her heart beat hard in her chest. "Again, what are you doing Peter?"

"I'm staying here," he announced, advancing on her suddenly.

Shocked, she stared at him and waited. "I'm not alone in the house," she whispered.

"He's across the damn hall, and the locks on these doors are too easy to pick. My parents are too far down the fucking hallway to hear you scream. Ellen is tucked away upstairs." Peter's voice rose from a low explanation to a loud accusation at the last.

Genevieve was simply bewildered. She gestured to the doors. "It's not as if I'd let him come in here," she told him. "I don't even like the man, and he's entirely untrustworthy."

"Of course, angel. That's not it at all," Peter explained. She could see he was trying to explain, was struggling to explain, so she remained quiet and let him try again. "He intends to stay, you know, using John's injuries as his reason to move himself in and become a dependent. And he won't be able to resist taking a turn at you. Maybe not tonight, maybe not tomorrow, but he's going to. If I'm not here to stop him, to keep him from touching you, I'll go after him and kill him for the insult afterward."

"He hasn't even knocked on the door, not that I'd open it to him. But don't do that, Peter. I'd like to visit Rome and Amsterdam and Copenhagen and Paris — I'm sure they are beautiful — but I don't want to live any of those places. I like Suffolk. I'd like to live here," Genevieve objected.

Peter laughed. He was close enough to her now that the husky noise reverberated in her ears. Her body shivered in wicked anticipation. They were alone. It was late, and the doors to her suite were locked. Neither Ellen nor a chambermaid would come until Genevieve called for them and Peter had clearly snuck inside.

Her eyes flew open. "Does anyone know you're here?" she asked.

He paused. "Jem," he admitted. "He stabled my horse. He thinks I came to see John and Mother. I waited until Cook banked the kitchen fire and retired then came in through the garden door and up the back stairs."

"So in the morning, everyone will know."

"I'll slip out at dawn to go riding and arrive just in time for breakfast." Peter's lips tipped up a bit at the corners. "The household already knows we're spending time alone. It doesn't matter if it's outdoors, in my bedchamber at Devon Place or here."

She stepped closer to him, pressed her hands to his jacket and rose on the balls of her feet to press a kiss to his lips. "Are you staying for breakfast?" she asked.

"I can walk out of the room now and spend the night on the daybed in the studio, if you choose. Or I can stay here, in this chamber, with you. Do you want me to stay?" Peter asked, reaching for her hips and holding her an inch away from him.

"Yes. Oh yes, Peter," Genevieve answered, her fingers slipping into the hair at the nape of his neck. "Stay."

Peter held her slightly apart from him, looking down her dressing gown. It was in Genevieve's favorite color, a pale sage-green edged with white piping. Buttoned down the front to the floor with white buttons, she'd left several buttons at the top loose, and the embroidered round neckline of her white batiste nightdress showed through.

"You'll let me guide us through this?" he demanded. "I don't want to hurt you."

Genevieve tried to drift closer, to press against him, but Peter held her still. "You aren't going to hurt me," she whispered.

"Angel, I won't be able to help it." Peter frowned at her. "You're a virgin. It's going to hurt, though I'll prepare you as best I can."

Genevieve decided agreeing with him was the fastest way to get him to move forward, so she nodded and tried to wait for him to release her. She stared at his face, noting the short bits of hair that were beginning to create a stubble at his chin and jaw. His dark hair was smoothed back, but glimmers of its color were visible in the light of the lamp and the candles. His eyes were barely discernible in the shadows, but she wanted to smooth out the frown in his forehead and press her lips to the corner of his mouth.

She moved forward and looked down, surprised to find that his hands were no longer holding her away from him. Instead they were fiddling with the buttons on her dressing gown, slipping them open, silently parting the panels to reveal the white nightdress beneath.

Her breath caught. His fingers were wondrous, magical digits that were easily removing her clothes.

He reached her waist, looked up at her and reached out with one hand to remove the pins that held her hair in place. They fell, unremarked, to the floor, and her gold curls tumbled down around her face, tickling her ears.

Genevieve's hair was not short, but she'd cut it over the years, so it fell to the middle of her back. Peter played with it for a moment, laying two tresses over the front of her shoulders. He stared, then drew her across the room to stand in the lamplight near the table where she'd been reading. Without speaking, he pushed the bodice of the dressing gown apart and drew it down her arms, removing the sleeves and letting the entire garment fall to the floor. Beneath it, Genevieve's white summer-weight nightwear was hardly enough to feel decent. The garment wasn't cut any lower than her silk evening gowns, but it was sleeveless, lacking even a gauzy overlay. It was decorated with tiny white embroidery and white ribbon, but such detailed work was obviously not Peter's attention.

He only looked for the way to unfasten it.

Genevieve shrugged and smiled. She clutched the fabric of his waistcoat. "I wasn't expecting you tonight."

"Don't be shy, angel," Peter demanded, his hands already tugging at the fabric. She felt the fabric sliding over her legs, falling around her silk slippers. Those were tied up around her ankles with a wide satin ribbon. Peter stared down at the sight and smiled.

Then he stepped back and inspected her. It was the only word that she could think of, to describe the way he deliberately ran his gaze up her legs until she trembled. He seemed to stop at her knees, but when they shook, he moved his inspection higher, to her thighs. She couldn't hold back a gasp at his brazen response. His lips thinned, he breathed heavily, his cheeks hollowed out and the furrow in his brow deepened.

Suddenly nervous, Genevieve reached down.

Peter caught her wrist and held it out to the side, his blazing eyes now fastened onto the gold curls that hid her innocence. "Angel," he murmured and Genevieve blushed, but before she could respond, his eye was roving upward.

She sucked in a sharp breath but couldn't stop him from perusing her bosom, ever so slowly. In fact, his other hand reached out to capture hers. He held both wrists out to her sides and simply stared.

Forever. No, he stared until she gasped and swayed, overwhelmed by holding her breath.

"You are perfection, angel," he said, tugging so that she would step away from the nightdress. She obeyed, and he led her to the bed, kneeling in front of her after seating her on its side.

At her feet, Peter picked at the knotted ribbons. Despite her nudity, it was an intimate, loving gesture. The heat of his hands, his gentle stroking of her skin, was almost too much. She cried out, arching her back and nearly begging for more off his caresses.

Genevieve bent forward, wanting to kiss the top of his head but settling for stroking it instead. Her palm grazed over his ear. He slipped her footwear off, reached up and caught her hand, pressing a hot kiss to her palm.

Almost instinctively, she slid back across the gold brocade of the coverlet. With the summer warmth, the crimson-red curtains were tied tightly back, so she could watch Peter. He moved the lamp to the bedside table, then tugged another small table to the opposite side and moved the candelabra to it, throwing more light at the bed.

Genevieve moved to pull back the textured satin bedding, but Peter shook his head. "Be still and wait for me," he commanded.

The words made Genevieve's blood heat and liquid pool at her core. She stared, watching as he doffed his jacket and waistcoat. He'd already dispensed with his boots, so once he was in his shirtsleeves, Peter sat on a chair and tugged off his stockings, baring his feet.

Genevieve stared at them, remembering his fascination with hers on previous days and the sensitive reaction of them when he'd removed her shoes earlier. She wondered what Peter would do if she returned the gesture. She wanted to study the shape of his toes, the way his feet arched, the fine skin over the top of his feet.

His back to her, he dropped his breeches.

The long shirt hid his hips and buttocks. As he turned around and approached her, though, his manhood tented out the fabric near the hem. Genevieve noted the dark shadows beneath his white linen. She understood now why he'd moved the lamp and the candles.

She licked her lips, unconsciously, but recognized his hungry gaze as it fixed on her mouth.

At the side of the bed, he unpinned his sleeves. Her breath catching, she gripped the brocade in her palms, practically rubbing her bottom against it in hopeful anticipation.

His chest was as glorious as she'd imagined — wide, lightly dusted with hair with a dark line of a scar spread from below his navel up and around his right nipple. She knew he'd been injured, but this evidence made her heart ache.

Even so, Genevieve lusted. Her body actually ached with the need to touch him.

She wanted everything—to take him in her arms and smooth away the furrowed brow on his forehead, to stroke her palms down his hot skin and know the texture and colors, to shine light on him so that no intriguing mark could be hidden from her.

Instead, she dropped her eyes farther, to his groin. His manhood jutted out from his body proudly, so impressive that Genevieve almost cried out just from looking at it. She knew a brief moment of thanks to her sisters for explaining about copulation before this time came. She almost wished Peter had approached the matter more conventionally and undressed both of them under the blankets, in the dark.

But then she wouldn't know how absolutely magnificent he was.

Genevieve opened her mouth to speak, to offer some compliment, but Peter cut in, his voice harsh. "Is the scar too much for you? I can put my shirt back on."

Chapter Ten

"No!" she cried out.

Peter jerked at the word, his knee already coming off the bed. He wanted, desperately, to feel her breasts rubbing against his chest, but he'd seen her reaction to his scars. She'd paused for a bare second and her hands, fisted into the coverlet, had loosened.

Only after her gaze had dropped farther and distracted her did she demonstrate the same hunger she'd had before he disrobed.

"Peter." Genevieve moved from the sprawled position back against the pillows, coming up to face him on her knees. He wanted to reach out for her, to caress the golden-white skin before him, but instead he stayed motionless as she reached out and cupped his jaw. "Peter, you are the most beautiful thing I have ever seen. Someday I want to sketch you, like this, so glorious. You're like a god come to life."

Peter nearly snorted but twisted his head and caught her lips. She responded generously, as she always did, her mouth opening and her body tilting.

He hardly dared to believe she had welcomed him. It was all too easy. Something certainly was going to happen to crush this exhilarating experience of having her against him. He moved his hands down her back, rubbing his palms over her hips and lower, so that his fingertips pressed into her buttocks. Eager, he tightened them, taking in the heady flavor of her mouth and the scent of her soaps. Out in the countryside he hadn't been able to determine what fragrance teased his senses. So closed and confined, in the hours after and near where she bathed, he recognized the rich aroma of jasmine. It was sensual, evocative—definitely not something he remembered her wearing in any ballroom the last two Seasons. He wanted to lick it from her neck and apply it to her hips and sink himself in it until he smelled of her and only her.

Against his chest, Genevieve's nipples hardened and brushed him.

He released her delicious mouth and bent to taste one of the teats, lapping at it with his tongue. She cried out, arching backward. "Quieter, angel," he whispered. "You don't want Ellen to hear from upstairs." He certainly wouldn't consider it amiss if Queshire heard her cries of pleasure—at least then the man would know he had claimed her—but Ellen was another matter. If Ellen interrupted, it would interfere with Genevieve's first loving. The experience had to be perfect, so that she'd wish to indulge with him again— frequently, at least eventually.

She moaned at his words, a sound Peter definitely wanted to hear again. He sucked in the bud and areola, wishing he could watch it change color under his mouth but was satisfied by the eager shudder that ripped through her. He held her through the spasm, then tried the same intimacy on her other breast.

He couldn't hold back his smile at her passionate reaction. Using his body to push her down on the bed, still clenching her rump in his hands, he licked and blew on each nipple until she clutched and pulled at his hair, trying to drag him closer.

She could tug on his hair all she wanted, but she wouldn't change the course he was mapping out in his head. Peter wanted more from her than a quick tumble, and she seemed willing to give. Despite the temptation posed by her plump breasts, he moved his lips lower, tasting her concave belly, circling her navel with his tongue. Below that, golden curls met sensitive skin at the corner of her pubis. He nipped there, using his teeth.

Genevieve pulled at his hair again. "I like that, you know," he warned, scraping her hips with his lips. "You're encouraging me. I'm going to be so patient it will drive you to the edge of the sun."

Her voice was shaky and distant, especially when he moved his hands to push her farther back, so that her thighs met just below his lips. He almost licked them. Peter needed her to feel every sensation, every new experience. He wanted her to come back, anxious to experience more, to seek him to explore her sensuality. As much as any London rakehell, he well knew that young wives were exceedingly vulnerable to seduction, particularly those women who found that illicit eroticism was more compelling than their inattentive, easily distracted husbands. Once London knew that

Genevieve had shared his bed, every wolf of the *ton* who had circled her for two years would try to pounce.

And Peter had no intention of sharing. He didn't want Genevieve even considering the notion that another man could please her more than he.

When had his mindset changed from believing firmly that she should not be seduced, to not being able to resist touching her? He had resisted—he knew he had—but somehow he had found himself alone with her, and without any polite distance to maintain, he had touched her and known he would never be able to stop.

He slipped his hands down to her thighs and opened them, pressing his lips to the damp curls at her apex. Genevieve jerked again, but this time he was ready. She didn't move an inch, even when he traced a path downward over her outer labia with his lips. He breathed in the natural musk that she couldn't hide with jasmine, the deeply erotic scent that was uniquely Genevieve, and he nearly lost himself in the sheets.

Instead, he struggled to push his tongue past his lips and he licked her. She wrenched under his hands, but he held her velvet thighs more firmly and licked again, this time lapping at the nectar at her core.

"Open up, angel," he ordered, but enforced the directive by guiding her thighs apart with his hands.

The revelation of her inner female rocked him. Thankful he wasn't standing, he sucked in a deep breath. The additional aroma from her arousal and perfume came with the extra air, tightening his body.

The lantern and the candles weren't enough. He wanted sunlight streaming in, exposing her pink folds to him, not these shadows that danced in her curls. Thankfully, darkness didn't affect taste. He lowered his head, intending to indulge that illicit desire, when her hands caught at his hair and tugged.

He looked up, obedient to her, and growled when he realized she'd distracted him.

"Y-y-you're— Th-that's—" Genevieve's voice was weak, but she was trying.

"Delicious," he proclaimed, licking the taste of her from his lips, where they had scraped against her sensitive skin. "Just don't fight it. Let yourself feel it."

"It's s-so—" Genevieve hauled in a breath, trying to look at him. "So much."

"Trust me, angel," Peter commanded softly. "Now, loosen your fingers and let me show you heaven. If you need to hold onto something, grab the coverlet and don't let go."

Slowly, she uncurled her fingers. He could see that nerves, while absent for the disrobing, had struck her, but she was making a fine effort to be obedient and conquer her anxiety.

"Good girl," he murmured. Inwardly, he flinched, but managed to keep his reaction from his face. He didn't want her to think he saw her as a child and was usually careful not to address her as such, but it was hard to separate protectiveness from paternalism at times.

He hoped if he put her underneath him often enough, she'd accept that he didn't see her as a child, even if he occasionally erred and idiotic words slipped from his mouth.

But most of all, Peter didn't want to ruin her state of mind, the hot luscious lust that seeped from her pores and wrapped around him. She quivered with it, a force so powerful she could not keep it inside her. That open desire she emanated, focused entirely on him, was as

Elle Q. Sabine

intoxicating as the best Scotch he'd ever tasted, as addictive as any opium or snuff, and infinitely more aromatic.

Before she could think enough to react, he lowered his head and set his lips to the innermost bud around her sheath. He speared her with his tongue, pushing up as he sucked.

Whether the noise she made was a shriek, a screech or a scream, Peter didn't know. But he liked the way it sounded, so he pulled out his tongue and thrust it in once more.

She tightened her hands in his hair again. Peter dropped one of her thighs and found her hand, tugging her fingers and settling it on the bed beside her, holding it down. She needed to be wild, almost mindless with arousal and desire when he plunged his cock inside her. He knew it would hurt Genevieve and he didn't want it to, but the best chance for minimizing the pain was for her to be slick and hot and as open as she'd ever been.

Genevieve hadn't come yet. He wanted her to come the first time when he sank into her, when she was so tightly full of him that he could feel every last contraction. Maybe that part of his plan was a bit selfish, but surely that's what would be best for her too, to have a breathtaking climax to counteract the loss of her maidenhead?

Peter used the tip of his tongue to trace the sensitive edge of her opening, up one side to the top, where the opening narrowed and her clitoral hood had been pushed back. He could barely breathe at the dim vision he had. It was a lovely, swollen nub, begging for him to torment it. Peter realized suddenly that he would have all the time of their marriage — months on end alone at

Devon Place, even – to play with it and listen to her lovely reactions.

Instead of frightening him as it ought to, the realization only made him want to fuck her more. Hard.

Before he had quite thought through the consequences, Peter pressed his tongue hard against it. The pressure was enough to cause a reaction in Genevieve, which was really all that Peter wanted. She arched her back, swung her hand off the bed and anchored it in his hair again. When she uttered a loud noise that he wanted to describe as pure joy, Peter nearly jumped up to dance in exultation.

Surprised at the volume of her squeal, Peter loosened his tongue and flattened it again. He felt the shudders start in her womb, the indication that an orgasm was imminent, so he surged up on his knees, his hands under her buttocks now, angling her. He set his cock to her entrance, moved his left hand to the center of her bottom to hold her in place then pressed his palm to her mons, lowering his thumb to scrape her clitoris.

She did shriek for the first instant, but the sound died away to a sobbing noise as the contractions overwhelmed her.

He thrust, pushing in past the barrier, until his balls rested tightly against the curve of her ass. She might be shorter than he, but she was the perfect depth, tight and hot around him. The tip of his cock swelled more and touched the elusive spot some men never found, sending Genevieve back into a frenzy of shaking. His mind numb from the effort of restraining himself, Peter looked up at her, finding her eyes half-open as she watched him. He was holding off from covering her, not wanting to press her to the mattress or roughly fuck her, but the end was inevitable.

Peter wanted her, desperately, and not just as a passive recipient. He stretched, adjusting the angle and position. "Too much? Ready for more yet?" he gritted out, wishing he could think of something sensitive and encouraging to say. He didn't know how some men could be poets in bed. He could barely think with the woman he wanted above all others beneath him, let alone put together more than one thought at a time.

Right now, the only coherent thought he could manage was holding off until he was certain she could take him driving into her.

Genevieve shuddered, her eyes rolling back a bit. Peter couldn't help it. His hips jerked and he stabbed his cock back inside her hot tunnel.

She squealed. Her beautiful eyes flew open. "Yes," she managed, the word clear. "Do that. Do that again."

"Fuck." Peter made an unintelligible noise in the back of his throat, too, but it was the ironic curse between them that echoed in the quiet room. He thrust again—and again. Each time, she opened a bit more, arched more. He bent forward, holding himself off her a bit, but low enough that her nipples scraped his chest as he repeated his maneuver over and over, until she was on the verge of sobbing once more.

"Peter, help. I need something more, too," she begged. "I hurt. I want—"

"I know, angel," he groaned, nearly ready to let himself go. He couldn't hold himself off her and put a finger to her clitoris. He surged into her, surprised when her desperation drove her to lunge closer to him.

She groaned happily at the deeper contact and repeated her experiment in time with his pace.

Peter caught on quickly. He used his knees to anchor himself securely and powered into her over and over, letting himself have that moment he'd thought was selfish, but now knew was actually as important to her as to him. She exploded in his arms, not the slow build from her first orgasm, but a sudden dispersion of power that radiated from her body.

She was the most beautiful creature he'd ever seen.

Even as the thought formed in his head, the pressure in his loins became too much to contain. His seed shot from his cock, filling her. The pleasure of the release shot up his spine, tiny starbursts forming behind his eyes. Even so, he kept his eyes on hers, first to watch the orbs glaze over, then to see her stir, even as she fought through the aftershocks of fading bliss.

Peter sank down, resting his weight on hers for a spectacular moment and brushing her nose with his. He pressed a kiss to her lax mouth. She attempted to respond but had trouble with her lips. Her hands slipped over his hips and held him close.

That small gesture of acceptance touched Peter more than he wanted it to. It also reminded him. "Thank you, angel," he murmured, carefully pulling his cock from inside her. "I'm not leaving, but let me up for a moment. We can't go to sleep with the lamp burning."

She made a small sound of disappointment. "I want to touch you," she whispered. Peter moaned at the thought.

"Another time," he promised, finally lifting off her. That movement—stepping away from her body—was enough to finally kill what remained of his erection. The room wasn't cold, but her skin had been a delectable sensation against his and now that stimulation was gone.

He wanted it back. Quickly.

Even so, he couldn't tumble her back down immediately. That had been her first time, and he'd been somewhat vigorous at the end, if not a complete animal. He hoped she didn't think— No, she'd practically begged him to thrust harder. Mechanically, he used a rag and her washing water to wipe away the evidence from his cock, noting the streak of blood. He left it and wetted a clean rag, taking it back to the bed.

She resisted his attempt to wipe her clean, but Peter would have none of that. Genevieve had been delightfully responsive, and caring for her afterward was part of the prize. "Hush, angel. I've already seen and tasted you there. Open your thighs," he demanded, capturing her wrists with one hand and pressing them to her stomach.

Peter knew already that Genevieve wasn't a naturally obedient woman but she tried, despite her embarrassment. Her cheeks were already pinking and her legs opened barely enough for him to slip his hand between her thighs and wipe away the fluid leaking from her. "Good," he praised, lifting her up and away to wipe at the small dots of blood dotting the coverlet. "Although we may need to replace this."

She promptly covered her face with both hands. "So everyone will know, tomorrow. The entire household."

Peter's mouth quirked as he fought back a smile. "Yes. But at least they won't actively attempt to keep you apart from me any longer." He managed to pull the coverlet and sheets back, and she helped after a moment, slipping underneath them and tugging them up to her chin.

Disposing of the rag, Peter returned to the bed, walking around it to douse the candles and return the table to its original place. He knew Genevieve watched him, so he made sure she had plenty of opportunity to study his nude form. His cock, long denied any companionship beyond his own hand, was eager to feel her velvet skin again. "All that being said, however, Ellen will remain your companion, as soon as she is relieved from being John's nurse. You are far too beautiful and far too vulnerable to wander England on your own."

Genevieve glared at him as he stared down at the bed then wrenched the covers back to slide in beside her. She promptly scooted over, so far as to try to slide out the other side.

Peter stopped her escape by the simple expedient of clasping her wrist and tugging her up against him. "Where were you going?" he asked.

Genevieve gasped as her form came into contact with his naked hip and torso. "To don a nightgown, obviously," she sniffed.

"Not when I'm in your bed, angel," Peter objected. He tugged her against him, settling her head on his shoulder with his arm around her waist, where he stroked her hip. After a moment, she began to relax and he sighed, content, organizing the sheet and coverlet over their bodies. With his free hand he reached out to douse the lamp, leaving them in the darkness. "Bartholomew is still here in the house, so this is where I'm staying, for now."

She sighed but didn't argue. He was grateful for that. Arguing would have only led to kissing, and kissing would have led to more worshiping of Genevieve. Genevieve had been a virgin and she was already going to be stiff and sore when she woke. Having his cock inside her again would necessarily be delayed until she'd recovered, which meant not tonight.

Peter repeated that reasoning several times, just to be certain both his body and his brain had the matter well decided, even if his cock seemed to have a mind of its own. She was luscious up against him, both her arousal and jasmine scents filling his nose, reminding him of her taste. "Go to sleep now, angel. I'll guard you tonight."

He didn't think he could sleep, not with the temptation she presented at his side. He didn't want to sleep, either. If there was one thing he didn't want to share with Genevieve, it was the nightly terrors. He didn't always remember them, but too often he woke as he had that morning during the Battle of Almaraz, his tent on fire. He'd escaped with little more than his life and his commission and had spent too much time in the damn surgeon's tent and field hospital. That morning hadn't haunted him in Portugal or Spain but had come later, when he'd returned to London. In the beginning he'd not been able to sleep at all—not in London, where Almaraz or Toulouse inevitably reminded him of the past. Since Genevieve had come into his life and returned him to Suffolk, he had been able to sleep better, but the nightmares occasionally returned, almost always as morning approached. With John's experience, the last few days had brought Almaraz back full force. Unfortunately, there was no gambling den in which to spend the night in his step-father's house, and Genevieve needed his protection.

"The doors are locked," she mumbled, clearly worn and already on the verge of sleep. "But good night."

* * * *

Genevieve woke in the night. Her window was open to let a breeze roll through the room, and one of them had pushed back the covers, so she lay bare in the bed. Peter was talking in his sleep, a low mumble she couldn't fully understand.

She tested her muscles carefully, noting that her thighs, buttocks and lower back were stiff, presumably from Peter's lovemaking. It had been delightful—no, awe-inspiring—and she couldn't wait to do it again, at least once her muscles worked properly. She thanked her guardian angel and all the godmothers in Britain that she'd gotten through it without letting any nervous hitch get in the way, at least not until it had been over. Then it had all caught up with her and she'd not been able to put up a brave, self-confident front any longer.

She did want a nightdress, she decided.

Peter faced away from her, on his side, so Genevieve slid out of the bed and moved through the dim room. Moonlight gave a bit of light, so she was able to find the garment and dressing gown from the floor. She collected Peter's clothes, too, and set them aside, clothing herself in the nightdress and draping her dressing gown at the end of the bed.

From the studio, she heard the clock mark the third hour.

In his sleep, Peter froze, then came up in the bed, punching wildly at the air. Genevieve drew back, watching him, remembering how he had woken from his nap a few days previously and how upset he'd been. Did he live with this agony every night?

Her heart ached, even as she realized that this was how the war still haunted him. He'd never spoken of it, but she knew he'd spent years with General Hill in

Portugal and Spain. His mother was inordinately proud of him, had spoken of his service. When she'd been introduced to the general in London, he had taken a moment to speak highly of Sir Peter's bravery and strategic skills. But now Genevieve's heart ached. If this nightmare was the legacy of his time in the Peninsular War, she wondered why he allowed his family to continue to remind him of it.

Peter's voice echoed through the room. She didn't want to interfere, knew she shouldn't approach him, but she had to try something to break the cycle.

She said his name, firmly, hoping it broke through.

Instead, she must have joined him in his nightmare. "Genevieve! Get out of here before you're burned to death too," he shouted. His voice muffled a bit as he rolled over and over on the mattress, back and forth, his feet thrashing at the blankets as he covered his face and smacked himself across his chest. "Run, Genevieve!"

"Peter, wake up!" Genevieve stared at him, remembered the burn mark on his chest and realized the cause of his agony.

Peter didn't wake. Unable to think of anything except to make him believe the fire was out, she ran to the dressing room and retrieved the pitcher from the basin. It only had a few cups of water remaining, but it was enough.

She threw it on Peter.

That woke him up. He stared at her, pain still evident on his face, then looked down at himself and the bed.

He paused long enough to grab his breeches and shirt from where she'd laid them on a chair, and he was out of the door.

She left the door unlocked — his boots and saddlebag were still in her dressing room — but he didn't return that night — or the next day. Or the next night.

That was when she cried.

Chapter Eleven

On Wednesday morning, Ellen sat her down in Lady Fielding's sitting room after breakfast. Genevieve had not slept well. The solicitor had arrived and had been closeted with Sir John throughout the breakfast hours, but Sir John was resting now.

"What happened, child?" Lady Fielding asked kindly, settling beside Genevieve on the conversation couch. "I thought he was coming to his senses, and I've been told he was in your room two nights ago. But clearly you were unhappy yesterday, and this morning you look as if you've not slept at all."

"And not for any good reason," Ellen added dryly.

Genevieve sniffled, fighting back the tears, but she did need to tell someone. Still, it felt disloyal to Peter to bring whatever problem he had to his mother, of all people.

"I thought... Well, we *were* together two nights ago. It was the first time," she admitted. She'd taken the coverlet off the bed and put a clean one on, making some inadequate excuse to the maid, but it had purely been for form. She couldn't hide Peter's belongings from the servant, though they were now tucked into her wardrobe. "I-I-I thought we were both happy about it. I wouldn't have changed anything at all. He was absolutely good to me in every way that Abigail and Gloria said could be between a man and a woman who care for each other."

Hesitating, Genevieve glanced at the two older women. But truly, what choice did she have? At least she had them to ask for advice. "In the middle of the night, he started dreaming…about the war, I think." At the very least, she wouldn't say she thought he was dreaming about being burned alive. She did not want to put that burden on Lady Fielding or Sir John. "I got out of bed, so he didn't ever hurt me, but I couldn't wake him, not even by shouting at him, so I dumped the remains of the washing water on him. That woke him and he was… Well, he was horrified. I don't know if he was afraid he would hurt me while he was dreaming or if he was mortified that I saw him like that. He didn't say a word to me about it. He just grabbed enough clothes to make himself decent and ran out. And he hasn't come back. Jem said his horse is gone from the stable, but he didn't even have his boots."

"I wouldn't worry about him riding barefoot." Lady Fielding patted her hand, looking thoughtful.

"Now I don't know what to do." Genevieve bit her lip. It might be unladylike, but she did it when she was painting — and when she was thinking.

"If I could, I'd ride over to Devon Place and knock that boy on his ass," Sir John suggested from the doorway.

Lady Fielding looked up at him and gasped, rushing to his side. "John, you ought to be in bed," she scolded. She couldn't take him by the arms, but slipped behind him, wrapping her arms around his waist.

Genevieve stared at him. She hadn't wanted to seek his advice, but Sir John was as much her father-in-law as anyone ever would be. She thought he understood Peter much better than Lady Fielding, especially now that Peter was an adult. "I was wondering if maybe he's been having them all along, since the war," she ventured.

"Surely not!" Lady Fielding promptly objected.

Sir John moved carefully through the room. How he'd risen, Genevieve couldn't imagine. He couldn't have put any weight on his arms or hands. That would have been too painful. "Don't you remember how much he drank and how erratic he was after he returned, Theresa? I wouldn't be surprised if the girl is right. Since we've been spending so much time in Suffolk, his temperament has improved dramatically. But do you remember before he and Genevieve married? After a few months in London, he would have that wild look in his eyes, and the next thing we'd know, he'd be off to Scotland or some other lark."

Lady Fielding pressed her lips together but didn't object when Sir John lowered himself carefully onto the edge of a chair, his arms stiffly held out at his sides. Genevieve couldn't imagine the amount of discomfort he was in, but it was a relief to see him out of bed, even pale and stiff.

"Many soldiers had nightmares, even while the war was still being fought. Mr. Wyman didn't, but he had me to think about and talk to after a battle. The others, particularly the infantrymen, rarely had anyone except each other and their ration of ale. Most couldn't write and wouldn't have confided such things to anyone in England, anyway. But everyone, even the colonel, saw — and sometimes did — terrible things." Ellen spoke quietly but firmly, and Genevieve listened. Ellen hadn't known Peter well then, but she had known of him, and they had been in the same place. "It's definitely possible he's been having night terrors, at least sporadically, since he returned."

"What am I to do then? Wait for him to come to his senses?"

The room was silent for a moment, but Genevieve heard the authority in Sir John's eventual answer. "Have Jem drive you and Ellen over, and you confront him. I would send Lady Fielding with you, too, but my solicitor is giving Bartholomew notice that he must quit the house tomorrow, before he's a legal hoghenhine. I would have preferred Peter be here when that nephew of mine receives the news. Feel free to use that to your own ends."

Genevieve rose, waving back his urge to stand. "No, stay, unless you're headed to bed. I'll do just as you say." She bade farewell to Lady Fielding and kissed Sir John's cheek with the affection of a daughter, something she knew he appreciated. "Thank you," she said sincerely and stepped away.

* * * *

The outing only muddled her mind more. Together, she and Ellen stood in the elegant marble-floored foyer of Devon Place and stared at both Mr. Grady and Mrs. Inglebright. Mr. Grady seemed apologetic, but it was Mrs. Inglebright who revealed most. "The master never tells us when he's going to knock off and go hunting. He does as he pleases, up and leaves without warning, my lady. Hasn't done it much since you've been in Suffolk, but m' youngest sister is the housekeeper in Clarges Street and says to me once that 'twas a regular occurrence in London, even after the wedding."

Genevieve supposed that was possible. Early in their marriage, they had gone as much as two weeks at a time in London without seeing Peter, especially before she'd been presented. She looked at Ellen, who seemed positively flabbergasted. Nevertheless, the duenna straightened up and spoke authoritatively. "With Sir John's heir unfortunately in residence, Sir John needs Sir Peter to return as soon as possible." A frown etched Ellen's forehead. "Beyond that, it's neither appropriate nor safe for Lady Devon to remain in the house except under constant guard. Since Sir Peter is gone, I'm going to suggest to Sir John that Lady Devon and I remove here, where she'll be safe. If he agrees, we'll return after dinner."

While Mrs. Inglebright beamed at that announcement, Mr. Grady gaped. "Lady D-D-Devon," he stammered, "I don't want to interfere, but is that such a good idea, what with..."

He paused, clearly not knowing how to continue and Genevieve blushed. Clearly the news of her change in standing from a wife-in-name-only to a wife-in-fact had not reached the Devon Place household. But how to—

"That's of no matter." Mrs. Inglebright waved aside the concern of the man beside her. "You know that the mistress's rooms are ready, Mr. Grady. We can air them out quickly and have the apartment ready in no time. She can lock the door to the master's chambers."

Mr. Grady, Sir Peter's gentleman's gentleman and sometimes his secretary, looked relieved. "Ah, yes, that's right. I do recall him saying only a few days before he departed as how the rooms were ready." His head bobbed in agreement, but Genevieve filed away that bit of reluctance for further examination. What did Mr. Grady know about Sir Peter that would cause him to worry about the lady of the house taking up residence?

In any event, Genevieve suddenly realized that Ellen was right. She did not belong at Fielding Manor any longer. Devon Place was her rightful residence, and it was proper for her to be there, even once Peter returned.

The women were silent as the carriage returned to Fielding Manor. It wasn't a long trip but quite long enough for Genevieve to inform Ellen that she believed Ellen had the right of it. "Indeed, I think all of our things should be brought over tomorrow, if only to make it more difficult for Peter to displace me."

Ellen agreed. "In any event, we all know my role is no longer to keep you from him, so I'm going to give you the best advice I know about marriage. My mother told it to me, and I lived it every day, following the army to Spain, even. She told me that the key to a successful marriage is simple. Commit to stay together through whatever life throws at you."

Genevieve was thinking about that advice and resisting the urge to think of whether Peter was practicing the maxim when she separated from Ellen in front of her bedchamber door. They'd discussed the matter with Sir John and Lady Fielding. Visibly weary after what had apparently been a loud and emotionally fraught interview with Bartholomew, the couple had reluctantly agreed, although Genevieve thought their reluctance was mostly occasioned by their affection for her. Devon Place, after all, was truly Genevieve's destiny.

Sir John had sent for his secretary, intending to write out a blunt message to Peter at his Lowlands hunting box and send it north by special courier. Genevieve had asked for a maid to come up and assist her with packing and for Jem to help her with her painting supplies. She opened the door as Ellen slipped up the stairs, going in and shutting the panel behind her. Still absorbed with thoughts of what might constitute a suitable space to paint in Devon Place, she began to turn the key—

A massive hand slammed down on her shoulder.

She screamed just in time, before a second hand reached around and clamped over her mouth. The fingers dug into her face, and Genevieve felt her attacker drag her backward. Instinctively, she slammed her foot down on his shoe, already glad she was wearing her half-boots with the little wooden heels. They didn't make nearly enough of an impact on the top of his feet, so she jabbed her elbow backward into his stomach.

The man grunted, and Genevieve tried to breathe, taking in the smell of his cologne and recognizing him immediately. Bartholomew Queshire released her shoulder to grip her around the waist, and Genevieve immediately lunged in an effort to escape. The hand over her mouth slid, so she bit down hard until he wrenched his hand away again, though he did manage to slam his palm down on her hip as she twisted. She screamed then, leaping for the door, but he pitched too, hard enough that she was thrown into the doorframe and, a second later, impacted the wall beside the door.

The panel obligingly flew open as Genevieve cried out again. Ellen screamed, and Genevieve heard the pounding of feet in the corridor.

By the time two footmen wrestled Bartholomew and pinned him against the wall, the solicitor, Lady Fielding and Poindexter were all in the corridor, and Ellen was hurriedly straightening Genevieve's gown. Genevieve knew instinctively what Ellen wanted to know and to keep her words very quiet. "He didn't have time to do more than bruise me."

"Yes, and that's exactly what everyone needs to believe," Ellen said firmly, quickly retying Genevieve's driving bonnet.

She swallowed, straightening, biting her lip for a second before raising her chin. It was time to rid Fielding Manor of Bartholomew for the foreseeable future, comfort Sir John and Lady Fielding and move into Devon Place.

If Peter wasn't here to see to the needs of his parents and his wife, then Genevieve would have to do it herself.

Genevieve felt a wrenching in her chest as she faced the doorway and set foot in the corridor, where the others waited, every face shocked or shaken. Even Sir John was carefully creeping toward them, one small step at a time, his face ashen. "He was waiting for me when I stepped into my bedchamber," she stated evenly. "Thank the good Lord that Ellen was still in the hall to hear and get help."

* * * *

Peter tossed the reins of his phaeton to the grooms, who came running. The afternoon was waning and with early September, the evening was cooler than had been expected even a fortnight earlier. At the door, he rang the bell, surprised when Poindexter admitted him without any of his usual enthusiasm.

"Sir John?" he asked, handing over his hat.

"Expecting you. They are upstairs, sir," the man acknowledged, taking Peter's dusty greatcoat. Peter went up the stairs, wishing as he did that he could peek into Genevieve's studio, just for the pleasure of seeing her. But Sir John's message, written in his mother's unusually shaky script and not delivered until three days after it was written, was now more than four days old.

The sitting room door was open, so Peter walked directly in, his ears catching Sir John's voice in the bedchamber. "Shameful," the elder man was saying. Peter took another step and caught another snippet. "Spend as much as you can before I die. Every penny. Give it to the poorhouse if need be."

The scene he walked into was not entirely comforting. Sir John was flat on his back, but mostly dressed in trousers, shirt and waistcoat. The sleeves had been removed, but he wore a necktie and slippers. Peter's mother saw him first and rose from the armchair that had been positioned beside the bed, the embroidery in her lap falling to the floor. At her action, Sir John grunted and adjusted himself into a sitting position.

Both stared balefully at him. Peter's stomach churned, but having no idea why he'd been called back, he said the only thing that came into his mind. "What's happened? Where's Genevieve?"

At that, his mother came forward, and, to his surprise, smacked him fully across the ear, as if he were a naughty lad instead of a man full grown. Tears formed in her eyes. She turned away and hurried to Sir John's side, carefully helping him put his feet to the floor.

Peter met his stepfather's gaze in shock. Sir John was angry too. "If I could, I'd whip you myself, son," he muttered. "Whatever possessed you to go running off when I — when we — needed you here? You knew how much I couldn't do for myself, and that rogue of a nephew of mine was in the house!"

The churning in Peter's stomach nearly made him heave. He knew precisely what had possessed him. The demons that haunted his dreams had driven him out of Suffolk and to the only place where he'd ever felt capable of banishing them. He hadn't fully done so when Robin had tracked him down in the forest, Sir John's missive in hand.

Peter's mother ripped into him. "What *happened?* Exactly what you feared would happen. The irresponsible cur attacked her, in her own bedchamber, in the house where she is supposed to be safe, where *you* were supposed to be guarding her!" His mother's voice was so full of betrayal and anger and sadness that Peter could barely parse out the words. The emotion in her struck him first, strong enough that Peter was momentarily caught up in remorse before he even understood. Then her words hit him, too, and panic shot through him, followed by a black icy rage that would only be satisfied by blood.

"Where is he?" Peter gritted the words out from between clenched teeth, feeling the pressure in his brain rise.

"Gone." Sir John snorted. "Though it was Poindexter who had the honor of *accidentally* shoving him into the wall on his way to the front door and the footman Willis who *unintentionally* kicked him in the back of the knee as they struggled to force him down the stairs. David may have shoved him a bit too hard toward the carriage, causing the horses to startle, and it may have taken Jem a few minutes longer than normal to subdue them, allowing the rear hoof of one of the pair to end up on Bartholomew's foot."

Peter made certain the fury on his face was self-evident. "I want him," he seethed.

"No doubt you will make an example of him," Sir John said grimly. "But it won't be because you've touched a hair on his head. You forfeited that privilege by fleeing at the first guns. Your damned nightmare was your problem, not Genevieve's, but she's the one who suffered for your foolishness."

Reminded of his precious wife, Peter swung his head toward his mother. "Where is she?" he asked, remembering that neither of them had answered his initial question.

"Gone," his mother bit out. "Do you think she would want to stay in this house after that? Even if we did send Bartholomew away, I couldn't have kept her here forcibly. Safety is the one thing we promised her when she came to us after the wedding, and now that trust is broken."

"*Gone?*" Peter couldn't contemplate it. Genevieve had been so full of tenderness and affection that last night he had seen her. She couldn't have left him. Incredulous, he repeated, "*Gone* where?"

His mother's eyes flashed. "You will have to discover that for yourself. I could hardly chase after her and leave Sir John in his condition. I will say, at least she took Ellen and Jem with her."

Lips pressed together, Peter stared at his mother, not quite believing that she didn't know Genevieve's direction. Where would she have fled? To her sister Abigail? To her sister Gloria? To her mother in London or to Wales? Peter knew Lennox had taken Lady Johna to Wales, but had Genevieve known? He couldn't remember telling her.

"I'm tired, Peter," John stated, drawing his attention. "And we aren't serving dinner downstairs. I suggest you return to Devon Place. I'm certain Mrs. Inglebright can serve you dinner and you can put your affairs in order, if you intend to hunt her down."

"I do so intend." Peter nodded, his mind still churning. Fury was still raging in his blood, but now he didn't know who made him angrier—Bartholomew, for daring to put hands on Genevieve, or himself.

* * * *

Halfway to Devon Place he had to pull his pair to a halt and jump down, where he retched in the bushes. He hadn't asked, and didn't know, precisely what they'd meant by *attacked*. The possibilities careening through his head caused his hands to sweat and his stomach to twist. His heart pounded and pulsed excessively, and what felt like panic had begun to stiffen his muscles. What had happened to his beautiful wife while he'd been off exorcising the demons in his head? He prayed that Ellen had had the opportunity to send a note, but nevertheless, he would head for London in the morning. It was her closest and most likely destination, and he had the townhouse there to take her to if she ever forgave him.

He'd damn well prostrate himself at her feet, though he couldn't imagine she'd appreciate the gesture.

Devon Place was better lit than Peter expected when he turned the phaeton into the drive. Lined with well-spaced conker trees, the gravel drive ended at the low ivy-covered wall that had surrounded the main house and garden for centuries. The gates had long since been removed, but the demarcation was clear. Past the gate, the drive was covered with gray macadam to complement the Palladian façade of the house.

Instead of dark, the front hall, drawing room and dining room were all lit, as well as the upper gallery.

Peter's eyes narrowed, but he knew better than to think Mrs. Inglebright and Mr. Grady would have allowed anything nefarious to happen under his roof. Behind him on the tiger's seat, his majordomo Robin—who often traveled with Peter—grunted. "Looks like they're expecting us!" Peter called back.

"Aye, or someone's visiting," the long-time retainer agreed. He'd been Peter's batman in Portugal and Spain and had simply stayed with Peter when they'd returned to England.

Peter nodded but his stomach clenched. There were very few people in his life that he would have invited to stay at Devon Place and most of those were related to his wife. Dear Lord, who else knew of this debacle? If someone had come expecting to visit, Grady may very well have invited them to stay overnight rather than sending them off to a country inn. But Peter wasn't going to entertain, not anyone.

A groom came running to take charge of the horses and phaeton, while Peter ran up the steps, already plotting how to remove the interloper from his house and get on with packing for an extended trip.

A footman took his greatcoat, cane and hat. "Who's here?" Peter asked bluntly. He vaguely recognized the servant, but didn't know his name. He only knew those of the three senior staff who he spoke to most frequently. This one was most frequently found removing his dinner trays from the library.

The footman's eyes widened, and he swallowed, turning away to set aside the garments. "Ah, sir," he began.

"Cut line, man," Peter demanded. "Who else is in the house?"

From behind him, a voice interrupted, firm and intensely feminine. "I am."

Chapter Twelve

Peter swung around, his mouth opening before he realized and slammed it closed. He stared at Genevieve in shock, gritting his back teeth. An initial rush of relief rocked him back on his heels, but it was immediately followed by a wave of anger so vicious that he actually stumbled as he stepped forward.

Without another word to him, Genevieve turned to the footman. "Please tell Mrs. Inglebright or Cook that Sir Peter has returned. He'll join me for dinner. Push it back a half hour so that he has time to wash the dust off first." She turned and retreated to the drawing room. Peter, helpless to do otherwise, followed her, shutting the door behind him, noting that she had dressed for dinner in an elegant gown of olive green. The sleeves were loose, almost medieval in style, and the front of the gown was similarly cut in a Renaissance fashion. Around her face, her golden curls shone brightly, a halo that glimmered in the lamplight.

She stood before the empty fireplace, staring up at the painting that hung there, one of the first she'd labored so carefully over. Her technique hadn't been perfect, but Peter had claimed it and had it hung in that place of prominence anyway, where any of his neighbors who came to call would see it. She didn't speak immediately but waited until he stepped close behind her. "I thought you would go up and change first."

"I'll go up in a minute," Peter managed. He took her by the shoulder and began to turn her, but her pained wince had him jerking his hand back sharply, as though she'd burned him. Both were silent for a moment, before he said quietly, "Please. Turn around."

Without further comment, she faced him. He silently said a prayer of thanks in his head that she didn't appear frightened of being so close to him. Moving slowly, using the tip of his finger, Peter traced the bruise around her eye and across her cheekbone. Several days old already, any swelling had faded, but the colors spoke of how hard she had been hit.

So full of emotion that Peter didn't know if he was crying or raging, he finally found the strength to speak, knowing the words would never be enough.

"I'm sorry."

Outwardly emotionless, she looked to him, waiting.

He almost wished she would have an outburst, to spare him this awkwardness, but in truth, Peter already knew that amends would be a major part of his penance. Genevieve liked pretty jewelry and other expensive tokens of affection as well as most women, but such a gesture was wholly insufficient to this abuse of her person.

"To be honest, I can't even think of anything that I could do that would be an adequate recompense or restore any sense of faith in me."

Genevieve nodded, still searching his eyes. "At least you understand that," she murmured. "I have some things to say, but I do not wish to discuss it until after dinner."

Peter couldn't help himself. He leaned forward and kissed Genevieve's forehead. "I am so damn glad you're here," he whispered. "Thank you for not running any farther than my own house. But know this... Even if you had run to the far edges of the known world, I would have come for you."

Dinner was a quiet affair, with Genevieve at the far end of the table from Peter. He despised the arrangement but could hardly argue with her. She was his wife, the lady of the house, and her seat was at the foot of the table. But he didn't like it and brooded over the thought that the two of them would sit here night after night for years, eight feet apart with the boards between them. He asked after her meal, and she complimented the kitchen staff. She asked about Devon Place's architect, and he relayed the history he knew of the house.

It was desultory conversation. She wasn't outwardly angry with him. Genevieve was detached. That was, Peter thought, worse than angry. It was frightening.

When Robin carried in Peter's decanter, he waved the man back and looked to his wife. "I believe we should adjourn to the library, my dear. Would you like a tea cart?"

Her eyebrows arched elegantly, but she agreed. "Yes, I do believe I should enjoy that," she agreed, rising as a footman pulled back her chair. Peter rose with her, moving around the table and carefully taking her arm to his. Peter didn't know where or how seriously she was injured, and even if his entire life hung in the balance of the upcoming conversation, he didn't want her to be in pain.

"Where is Ellen?" he asked as they left the dining room and traversed the wide front hall toward the library at the back of the house.

"She took a tray in her room. She was going to join me for dinner, but when she heard you had come home, she sent down that she'd prefer a tray. Ellen understands that we have much to discuss. I know you wish her to remain as my companion, but I think she might be of better use at Fielding Manor for now, Peter. Your mother needs help for the next few months, and Ellen excelled in that role."

Peter made a noncommittal noise. He would likely end up doing everything Genevieve suggested, out of pure thankfulness she was speaking to him, but he had no intention of showing his hand quite yet. He wanted to know, desperately, what she had to say and how much groveling would accompany the restitution she'd demand. Even more, he wanted to work out what would be required to bring back the happiness to her eyes, and the innocent, joyful glow to her face when she looked at him. He suddenly remembered, then prayed desperately, that she was not so damaged that joy had forever been taken from her.

He opened the door and escorted her through, leaving the library door open so that Robin could deliver the tea cart without delay. Genevieve took a seat in one of the high-backed club chairs upholstered in tufted leather. Unable to sit beside her, he took a matching one next to her, shifting it so that he could see her more clearly.

She sat quietly for a moment, looked up at him and half smiled. "After the tea cart comes."

Peter agreed.

Peter was watching her. He'd been watching her since he'd seen her in the front hall. Even when his eyes had been on his plate, she'd felt his attention. It was a steady regard, a focus she hadn't expected. He hadn't once glanced at his desk, at the stack of correspondence waiting for him, or been distracted by a book while they had waited for his butler Robin to deliver the tea cart. He'd simply sat and watched her.

She thought back to her parents. Winchester had spent as little time as possible with the family, often not even coming into the drawing room after dinner, many times not coming to dine with them at all. He spoke to his wife and the girls only as had been necessary for the family to function.

Lennox loved her mother a thousand times more than Winchester had ever felt a mild affection, but he was constantly absorbing the world around him. He read, wrote, studied, conversed. Occasionally Genevieve could recognize that part of Lennox's mind was on her mother. He would stand even as she did, assist her to her feet, hand her a glass of champagne from a servant's tray before taking his own or defer to her mother to speak when they were asked a question. But even so, Lennox's attention was often split between her mother and whatever else occupied his mind.

Sir John was more physically affectionate with Lady Fielding, and when they were together, he often touched her in some innocuous way, as if to affirm their connection. If her hand wasn't on his coat sleeve, he might lay an arm on the back of her chair so that his fingers rested on Lady Fielding's shoulder, or he might have a hand lightly at her back or hip to guide her. When in the same room, they could almost always be found at each other's side, and if Lady Fielding walked away, Genevieve knew that Sir John would soon follow her. But despite that closeness, Sir John still engaged with those around him or could sit in the drawing room after dinner and listen to Genevieve play the piano.

Of course, she and Peter were alone, which might account for his disinterest in any occupation other than her. Genevieve shivered slightly as she poured the hot tea, offering a cup to Peter before taking her own.

"Are you cold?" he asked immediately. "I can start a fire."

Genevieve shook her head and poured her own cup. She sipped at it for a moment, set it in the saucer to her side and said quietly, "I'm not specifically angry that you weren't there to stop Bartholomew from hurting me. In all likelihood, you wouldn't have been able to stop it any sooner than Ellen did, as he was lying in wait in my bedchamber, and it's unlikely we would have entered the room together, then, as I'd gone in to change for dinner. However, what I find hurtful, even reprehensible, is how you *abandoned me* without explanation or warning. I trusted that you would be there for me to lean on, at least figuratively, and you weren't. Instead, after the night we'd spent together, you had a nightmare, woke up and *ran away*. You didn't offer or send an apology or an explanation. You didn't ask me to be patient. You didn't even see to Sir John. You simply consummated our marriage then left me.

Bartholomew may have hurt my body, but you hurt my heart, Peter. How could you?"

The last three words were uttered with a bit more dramatic tension than Genevieve had intended. She'd wanted to be sensitive, to be kind and rational. She'd meant to ask what had been so upsetting to him that he'd forsaken all his promises to protect and care for her, but she didn't want to shut Peter down or push him away. She wanted him to confide in her, to trust her, but he was a man and on this topic he had been particularly silent, perhaps for years. He wouldn't turn to her for support if he thought he had to defend himself. She knew instinctively that he would not want her to think him a coward.

"What I mean is," she tried to explain, "I don't understand why you would behave in such a way. If I... If our situations were reversed, you would have tracked me down and read me a scold I wouldn't ever forget. Should I have chased you to Scotland? I need to understand what's happening, Peter, because I'm afraid it will happen again, and I won't know what to do then."

"It won't happen again," he said sharply, stiffening in his chair, the teacup clattering as he returned his to the tray. "I'll make certain."

"How can you be certain?" she asked, tilting her head. He looked tired and no wonder, given that he'd driven most of the day and come back to an emotionally difficult scene. But worse, he looked as if he'd gone without food or creature comforts. His features were drawn, the gray shadows in his eyes more than just a product of the lamplight. Her palms itched to smooth over his skin, to brush the rough hairs along his jaw and chin.

She saw his teeth clamp together and his jaw move, his fingers digging into the arm of the chair. "We can't sleep in the same bed, not all night," he said hoarsely. "I've thought about it — haven't thought about much else, to be honest. It's the only way I can keep you safe at night."

She raised an eyebrow but didn't want to concede any points yet. "I've been sleeping in the boudoir. It's a lovely apartment, and you clearly had it renovated with my more mature taste in mind. Thank you for decorating it so thoughtfully." The room was expertly executed in shades of white and a deep gold, with a few hints of polished walnut to offset the brightness. The dressing room matched and across the corridor was a long room that had been converted from a guest room into a studio for Genevieve. A large master bedchamber was on the other side of the boudoir, taking up the entire end of the wing, with Peter's own dressing room opposite Genevieve's boudoir.

Peter nodded seriously.

"But that doesn't address the issue. I need to know *why*, Peter."

He swallowed. She could see the lump in his throat pass beneath his cravat and out of sight. A good portion of her demanded she drop the subject, let it go in favor of rubbing her body against him, but the part of her that had somehow cracked open when she'd needed him still leeched pain and couldn't be ignored.

"Didn't realize the nightmare would come back," he said quietly. "Usually I only have them in London — not in Suffolk, not in Scotland either. Haven't had one here, not for years. But John's accident reminded me, triggered something in my subconscious. I've been dreaming every night since." He swallowed hard, so hard she could see the movement of his throat as he struggled to explain. "Even in Scotland. Never happened before there."

"You were burned." Genevieve remembered the mark on his chest. She hadn't been able to examine it closely then, but she remembered.

"Rocket exploded nearly on top of me that time," he admitted after an awkward pause. "But that was another time. Not what I dreamt about."

"It explains your scar," Genevieve nodded. "But it doesn't explain why you ran, Peter."

She watched the frustration flash over his face, fascinated by the play of emotions. His frustration was followed by shame, anger and a prickly reassertion of pride. "Yes, it does," he finally snapped.

At last, Genevieve thought. *At last he's letting me see an honest emotion, instead of a perfect construct.* It had taken her three days of dissecting their interactions and the manner to which he treated her to finally see a semblance of reality in their relationship. Peter had spent years constructing a façade through which he cared for her. He'd set himself up as her caretaker, her protector, even her provider, but he hadn't allowed her any reciprocal role. But now that they were closer, she could see the cracks in that façade, just as she could see the imperfections in the landscapes she painted. Even a beautiful garden had vines overgrown in places, trees that needed trimming or a deadhead on a rose bush. She hadn't seen those imperfections in Peter previously, but it made sense that they would be present. It was how she reacted to them that was important. In a painting it was possible to pretend they didn't exist, to portray the scene in utter perfection. But Peter was not a painting.

"So you left because you were embarrassed? You didn't want me to know that you were scarred—"

"No," he broke her off, his own voice shaking, his fingers gripped tightly on the arms of the chair. "Genevieve, I almost *hurt* you. I woke out of that nightmare with my fists swinging. If you had been closer, in the bed beside me—"

Genevieve jerked at the epiphany. Of course. Peter's main focus had always been to protect her—from Winchester and his machinations, from society's censure, from his own desires, from other rakes. He would be horrified at the possibility of hurting her. But he had left and she'd been hurt anyway.

She was going to have to concede the sleeping arrangements, and that thought made her want to scream. "I-I-I liked falling asleep in the same bed," she admitted, clenching her hands together. "I don't want to think I can never do that again."

The shock on his face surprised her, but it was quickly followed by an expression full of hunger and desire. His gaze deliberately slid down over her form, and she felt her body tense and tighten in response. "If you...that's what you need—what will make you happy—then I'm happy to make sure that you do. I can remove myself from your bed after you are soundly sleeping."

To her astonishment, he came out of the chair and to his knees at her feet, grasping her. He raised her palms to his lips and caressed them, one at a time, nuzzling the lines in her fingers. She trembled, wanting very much to release that tense place in her chest that had almost deadened her since his flight from her room. "Why Scotland?" she managed, needing to know but not wanting him to back away. To show him, she grasped his wrists and held them fast against her thighs.

He looked up, met her gaze. "The silence," he replied. She wanted to be suspicious, but he hurried along, as if he knew his words were insufficient. "The first time, it was as far from London as I could manage, not just in distance but also in landscape and daily life. The property had been my father's hunting lodge. He was a profligate, even worse than the rumors paint me, and he used the site as a place to indulge in excess. My mother would never set a dainty foot on the land, and I agreed with her completely. But I was running *away* from London that first time, many years ago." He paused, leaned forward and boldly pressed a kiss to Genevieve's stomach. Even through her gown, chemise and corset, Genevieve felt the force of that caress. "Now, whatever I'm escaping is not as important as where I'm going. Scotland, at least my two hundred fifty acres of its wilds, is where I can put away everything that haunts me."

To her own surprise, she nodded.

A fierce look passed over his face, but he didn't advance any additional intimacy. Instead, he gripped her hands more tightly. "What can I do for you to forgive me, angel?"

"Peter?" His name passed her lips almost unconsciously, surprised by his question. She released his wrists and traced his lips with her index finger. "Oh, Peter, I've already forgiven you. Didn't you know?" She bent forward, her heart pounding in her chest as she kissed the pale skin of his lips, tasting the tea still staining them.

He widened his as he cupped the sides of her face, cradling it gently, smoothing back the hair at her temples so that he didn't touch her bruised eye and damaged cheek. "Angel," he whispered hoarsely. "Angel, I can't even express how sorry I am that I haven't been here for you these last three days. And I promise, I won't leave again without telling you. Sometimes, I-I-I have to get away from whatever is wrong to keep from going mad, but next time I will tell you."

Genevieve shivered. His hands on her skin always left heat in their wake, and his lips were electrifying.

As if he knew the direction of her thoughts, Peter bent his head and kissed the upper mound of her right breast, where her bodice hinted at the flesh her garments concealed. It was a modest evening gown with its high collar dipping in front to a rounded neckline and sleeves to her elbows, chosen not for the weather but to conceal the bruising on her shoulders and upper arms. She uttered a soft gasp at the contact.

He said nothing but hooked a finger past the white silk piping that decorated the edge. When it didn't stretch, he frowned, but stood and drew her to her feet. "Will anyone be waiting for you upstairs?" he murmured.

"No," she whispered. "Ellen is at the far end of the opposite wing. Mrs. Inglebright introduced me to Annabelle, but I've given instructions that she's only to come at night if I ring for her." Annabelle was another of Peter's rescues, a young girl that Mrs. Inglebright had found on the steps of the Ipswich Cathedral, half-starved and desperate. She'd fled her home upon the death of her mother, knowing her male relatives were dangerous, and had been sleeping in the cathedral's narthex for a long two weeks. She'd been given a bath, clean clothing, a haircut and been presented to Peter as a new upstairs maid. He'd taken one look at the frightened child and told Mrs. Inglebright to train her as Genevieve's future lady's maid. That had been six months ago, and Annabelle still swore Sir Peter and the upper servants at Devon Place were angels in disguise.

"Excellent." He bent down and trailed his lips over her temple to her eyebrow, until Genevieve's body seized and she leaned into him. "You won't be needing her tonight. Come along, angel. It's time you retired."

The proprietary air with which he held out his hand nearly melted her. Genevieve could sense the shadows still in him, but she wanted him healed, not broken. She knew how strong he could be, if he believed.

She took his hand and let him draw her up the main stairs at his side.

Chapter Thirteen

Peter led her inside the door to her boudoir and closed it behind him, turning the lock. He knew none of the servants would enter without permission, but there was a primal instinct inside him to conceal Genevieve's vulnerabilities from the world. Only he would see her like this, nude in the lamplight, injured.

The thought of her hurting sent another spear of pain through his middle, but there was no help for it now. He would simply have to do his best to help her heal, to distract her. And his first order of business would be to find every inch of damage to her skin. Grady had given him the details of the incident while he'd washed before dinner, a tale he'd had trouble setting aside. He'd stared at her during the meal, trying to divine how much she was hurt, how tender she would be.

He let her go long enough to turn the lamps up. One on each side of the bed, not because he'd thought of them being used to light her skin while he loved her, but because he didn't know which side of the bed she'd sleep in. A third lamp was on the table between the two chairs by the fireplace. And a fourth lamp on the writing desk on the far wall, where it reflected in the cheval mirror that stood nearby. When he turned, he saw that she'd untied the ribbons around her ankles and removed her soft black leather slippers.

"Let me," he said, pulling her back to her feet and turning her around. He unhooked the buttons from their tight loops, and he stopped breathing as he pulled the panels apart to reveal her back and her shoulders. A great whoosh left him when he lowered the gown farther.

"I'm going to murder that sniveling weasel," he muttered. Peter sucked in his cheeks and bit his back teeth, letting the bodice fall to the floor before he remembered his stepfather's judgment that he'd forfeited the right of revenge. At her waist, he untied the tapes of her overskirt, pushing it down, then repeated the motion with the two petticoats below it. The knot in her corset took a minute longer to unravel before he unlaced it. When he pulled it away, leaving her in only her stockings and chemise, she stepped out of the pile of clothing and knelt to gather them. Even though he was distracted by the vision of his angel in a chemise of what must be the thinnest ivory silk in existence, he began removing his clothes. He felt the heat rush to his face as she bent forward and he actually popped the button off his jacket in his haste.

Good thing he didn't give a damn about explaining to Grady.

By the time he was down to his trousers, she had disposed of the clothing and was crossing the room. Catching her fingers in his hands, he drew her closer, bent his head and kissed her.

Her mouth was a lush haven, a succulent fruit. He delved inside with his tongue, even as he began untying that last ribbon that shielded her beautiful form from his sight. "I'm going to touch every part of you, angel. I'm going to find every mark he left and kiss it. And you are going to lie still and let me explore."

Her acquiescent moan was music to his ears, especially when the chemise fell and she was left standing before him in white silk stockings tied with charming bows above her knees. *His* knees almost buckled from the conflicting emotions. An angry bruise marred one thigh and he could see discoloration on her side above her hip. Higher, above her plump breasts, purple marks extended over her shoulders, where the bastard had gripped her so hard that the he'd left impressions of his hands. But Peter couldn't focus on the ugliness, not when so much beauty was waiting. The curls on her mons were trimmed, and she was already so aroused that he saw her juices were leaking. Her plump thighs framed her pubis perfectly. Higher, her raspberry-tipped breasts were heavy with promise. He'd basically ignored them their first night together, so caught up in tasting her honeyed juices that he'd neglected to explore how sensitive they were and how far he could take her by loving them.

He'd remedy that oversight tonight.

On that thought, he walked around her, patting her hip to keep her in place while he had his first view of her backside. She shivered, and he was reminded of the innocence that still clung to her, of how young and awkward she might feel, left to stand nude in the light while he inspected her body.

His cock hardened at the wicked thought, though he'd never subject her to a humiliating examination, at least not at this stage in her erotic education. Peter just wanted to see her behind. In the frenzy of their lovemaking, he'd never seen it, only held it in his hands and pressed his mouth against the alluring curve. But now he could see that it was well-rounded, curved just so to tempt his hands. When he slid his arms around her, he could cradle her sweet bottom perfectly.

Peter stepped close behind her, letting his trousers brush against her pink skin. Leaning down, he whispered in her ear, "Why were you wearing a corset over this?" Gently, he stroked the contusion on her side.

She swallowed and he looked over her shoulder to watch her thighs shake and her nipples, already pink and aroused, wave a bit in the air. She reached back and clutched him at the hips as she answered, her voice strained. "Have to. It's the fashion with these gowns."

"Then don't wear these gowns. That corset should stay off for a few days. You'll heal more quickly and be more comfortable." He shifted, moving his body to her side and bending. Peter swung her into his arms, delighting in her startled squeak, then laid her carefully in the center of the bed.

She reached out to draw him back when he stepped away, then blushed brightly when his hands landed on her knees and began to open her legs. "Peter!"

Unwilling to compromise, he pushed his knee down and parted her legs, quickly angling himself between them on his own knees.

She reached out and stroked his chest, hitting him flat with her palms and sliding sensuously down to his abdomen, slowly. Adoringly.

Peter felt the caress to his marrow, as though his soul had just been fondled.

The room vibrated with the silence, marked only by her breathing. He'd forgotten to breathe, and when he opened his eyes, she was waiting. Her eyes glittered, and she repeated the gesture.

He rumbled with delight and heady sexuality. Peter's ears rang with desire. He wanted to be so deep inside her that she would never forget him and wrapped so tightly in her arms that her skin would forever be marked by his imprint.

But Peter wanted to learn her, too, every inch, and if she touched him much more, it would be hours before he could begin discovering all the secrets her body hid.

"Put your hands over your head, angel," he told her, the words deep and almost unintelligible. Genevieve hesitated, looked down between them at his chest, directing one of her elegant hands toward his nipple, and stopped abruptly when he captured the wrist and moved it to where he wanted it. "Now the other one," he directed, waiting as she slowly dragged that arm into position. "Keep them there, angel, or I'll tie them down, understand?"

Her soft gasp was a clear acknowledgment. She might not have agreed, but she'd heard him. Peter smiled, and bracing his hands on each side of her head, bent forward and kissed her forehead. It was an innocent gesture, something he might have done a week earlier to gentle her to his touch, but now his lips traced her hairline, her eyebrows and the line of her nose, until her eyes rolled back in her head and she arched, seeking the caress of his hard body against her needy one. He ignored the tactic while he rejoiced in it, adjusting a bit so that his fingers could trace the bruise around her eye and on her cheek, learning its shape and size so that he could observe it over the coming days. He moved down to her jaw, feathering kisses along the bone and nuzzling the sensitive place beneath her ear.

If she'd been a cat, she'd have been purring. She stretched her body until she arched away from the bed, aroused little noises falling from her lips until he kissed them.

Peter delved deeply into her mouth, tasting her, until she responded just as fiercely as he kissed her. Her fragrance wrapped around him, the jasmine drugging him until he lowered his body to hers and pressed her into the bed.

Only his trousers kept him from plunging deep inside her. She wrapped her legs around his hips and thrust up against him, clearly inviting him. He had to draw back to unfasten them —

Genevieve tangled her hands in his hair. She tried to tug him back down but he growled a bit and managed to pull away, staring down at her.

She swallowed at his stare and licked her lips. Peter gripped his own thighs and dug his fingernails into his skin as Genevieve wriggled, pushing her lovely, pretty breasts forward in supplication.

"Oh, I'm going to taste them, angel," he promised. "But where are your hands supposed to be?"

She froze, then jerked them back over her head and Peter couldn't help himself. She looked so anxious. So expectant. So *curious.*

He slid off the bed and found his long ivory cravat, then sauntered back to sit beside her. "I warned you," he whispered, unable to pretend he was anything but pleased by her disobedience. "And now I have the pleasure of making certain you can't distract me."

Genevieve squirmed, but her breathing quickened and she rocked back and forth a bit. Still, her hands were unresisting as he clasped her fingers together and wound the cravat around them, knotting it securely. The other end he threaded through the rail that ran along the top of the headboard, congratulating himself on the unforeseen benefits of his furniture selection. He looked down at her, drinking in the glazed gleam in her eyes, and murmured, "Tug on it, angel. Can you escape?"

Obediently she squirmed, pulling on the bonds. Peter might have been celibate for almost three years, but he hadn't exactly been an innocent before, and he'd had some experience with tying knots. Although he certainly couldn't compare those adventures with the treasure in his bed tonight, she was in no danger of running from him.

Not my bed, he thought, despair gripping him for an instant. She couldn't sleep in his bed.

No. He pushed back the emotion. She was in his house, living in his house under his roof in a room and a bed he'd provided, looked after by servants that he paid, on land he owned. Indeed, he'd even selected the bedding that would comfort and cradle her through each and every night. She'd come here of her own accord, sought the refuge of his house, even though he'd been in the wrong.

Now that she was here, he had no intention of letting her retreat to any safe distance. She wouldn't be leaving him to visit family, to paint some rare scene or to prance through the London ballrooms, not without him watching over her. By the time the night was over, she would at least understand his perpetual fascination with her. She would also know how dedicated he was to seeing to her pleasure, how grateful he was she had forgiven his cowardice.

A wicked vision leaped into his head. "You are beautiful," Peter told her, knowing she would hear the arousal in his words. His erection was pressed against the placket of his trousers, but he would willingly suffer to see this particular fantasy come to life. Pulling his eyes from her wriggling, pink-tinged form was difficult, but he looked around the room quickly, hunting for something appropriate.

Peter glanced over at her, now watching him curiously. He could sense that her arousal still rode her. Approaching the bed, he bent and kissed her navel fondly, then reached down and untied the garters above her knees. "I'll be back in just a few seconds. We need something from my dressing room. While I'm gone, angel, see if you can wriggle those stockings off on your own."

She stared at him, her eyes wide.

"God's teeth, I don't like leaving you, not even for a moment," he grunted.

"Then come inside me instead," she begged, lifting her hips in a wanton move that had him stepping back to the bed. "Please, Peter, I can't wait all night. Please."

The desperation in her voice was more than Peter could stand. Her widened eyes, the tension strumming through her body, even the panic and angst over her injuries and his own absence all slammed into his gut simultaneously. He had his doubts about the safety of leaving her, too, for even a moment.

"On one condition, angel. You let me do this to you again, when I say it's time." Peter rubbed his palm over her nipple, scraping the sensitive bud until she cried out. He attacked the buttons at his trousers with his other hand, hurrying to free his erection.

She managed a soft noise of assent, twisting against his palm to scrape her own nipple against his hard hands. He pinched the bud firmly, holding onto it even as she whimpered and shook. At the same time, he jerked the trousers over his hips, stepped out of them and put his knee up on the bed.

This time her thighs opened for him without the need for instruction. She was past ripe, but before he shoved his cock so far up inside her that she saw stars, he had a promise to extract from her. Peter bent his head and latched on to the other nipple, the one he wasn't holding firmly. She shrieked, writhing underneath him.

He continued the torture, counted to ten and let her nipple free. "Promise me," he said, the words low and guttural against her harsh breathing.

Genevieve's form strained and stretched, pressing the pad of her mons against his staff. The golden curls abraded his sensitive tissue, up his staff and on his thighs as he moved above her. She grunted.

"Say you'll let me bind you, another time. Tell me how arousing it is to know that I can touch anywhere, taste anywhere, and you can't prevent it, can only accept it." Peter followed up those words by releasing his grip on the nipple he'd kept hard by simply squeezing it, then lashed it with his tongue until she sobbed.

"Yes," he heard her say around the frantic breathing. He smiled, leaned down to caress her lips with his, pushed his fingers beneath her bottom and opened her, made a silent promise to teach her how erogenous that particular forbidden delight could be, and angled his hips down so that his staff just barely impaled her rose-shaped opening. He stopped long enough to watch her eyelids flutter down, the lashes lush against her face. She stopped breathing, expectant.

Beautiful Genevieve shrieked in delight when his cock plunged inside her. Her head tipped back, her eyes opened enough to gleam beneath the lids as pulsations ripped through her. Feeling the contractions in the walls of her vagina, he pulled back and thrust again, heavily. A second wave of contractions shook her.

He repeated the motion, settling into a thrusting rhythm that built in his gut, tightening with each successive movement. Around him, under him, she softened in the aftermath of her orgasm. Emotion rushed him as he took in her blissful expression, too complex to explain but all of it urging him to finish what they had started. His fingers tightened on her bottom, holding her lower half in place so he could fuck harder without any dangerous tugging on her wrists and shoulders.

The release flooded him. Peter tensed on his forearms to keep his weight from crushing Genevieve as the after-effects made his body heavy. Deep satisfaction crept through him, from mind to groin, until he could no longer sustain his position. Despite the tremors still swamping him, he fell to Genevieve's side and curled her against him.

Her body was warm to the touch in the summer evening. Relieved he didn't have to stand to tend to a fire or move her beneath the blankets, Peter wrapped his arms around her and let oblivion capture him for a few precious moments.

Peter would have to leave her bed soon enough. He didn't need to do so yet.

* * * *

Genevieve stared at the ceiling, still shivering. Peter had stayed wrapped around her for a long time, but eventually he had kept his promise to find and kiss every mark on her body. He'd spent a long hour with his lips on her skin, loving her, before her soft sighs had become tinged by exhaustion. Then, Peter had stood up and doused the lamps. She'd tensed, awakened, expected him to leave, but he'd returned to the bed.

Instead of joining her in it, however, he'd lifted her, then jerked back the coverlet and slid her between the sheets.

She'd pretended to be asleep, true, and he'd said downstairs that he was determined not to injure her, also true.

It was a heartbreaking stand that he'd made, but at least he'd managed to discuss it with her, in any form. And it was only their first night together in the house. She and Peter had plenty of time to pay attention, consider each other and see how they fit together. Peter's sleeping issues might someday change for the better.

And if they didn't, she thought happily, she could always ask him to come and bed her. *That* benefit of marriage was truly extraordinary. If she had known how it would be between them, she'd have bullied her way into residence at Devon Place on the day of her eighteenth birthday and refused to leave forever after.

Genevieve understood not every woman was so blessed with a man who could cause fireworks inside her body. Since she had now discovered that she was so lucky, Genevieve had no qualms about demanding Peter indulge her, maybe every night.

She closed her eyes, letting the last remnants of the night wash through her memory and she slept.

Chapter Fourteen

As Genevieve had stalwartly demanded, they settled into living in the same house with little angst. She quietly took over running the house, first working with Mrs. Inglebright on the menus, then on the housekeeping schedules. When Peter was out supervising the harvest at Devon Place and Fielding Manor, she began working with the staff on standing orders for foodstuffs and other supplies.

With autumn quickly arriving and Sir John still recovering, Peter spent his days on his land and at Fielding Manor, organizing workers and crops and seeing to all the details of both estates. At first Genevieve focused on painting, but once her canvas for Lady Framlingham was finished, she made a point to have Jem drive her to Fielding Manor nearly every day after lunch. Calling on Lady Fielding and Sir John was not just a courtesy. She deeply valued their relationship and their kindness to her. They'd admitted to her that they'd been harsh to Peter when he had appeared at

Fielding Manor upon his return from Scotland, but Sir John had later taken him aside and they'd had a difficult discussion that in some ways mirrored the one that Peter and Genevieve had had.

Peter hadn't spoken to her of that reconciliation, but she could see that he was at ease in their company.

In the evenings, Peter joined her for dinner. After that first night, she had refused to sit at the end of the table, taking the chair next to Peter's carver at the head. As always seemed to be the case when they were together, she repeatedly felt as if she was his cynosure. It was exhilarating, unnerving and underscored by his behavior. He tended to stay away before they met in the drawing room prior to dining, but once they'd eaten, Peter rarely had his hands off her. Whether he guided her through the gallery with his hand at her back or she slumped naked on his chest with her legs wrapped about him, Peter touched her almost compulsively. After dinner, they rarely spent any time downstairs. Often, as soon as he knew the covers had been drawn, Peter would rise from his chair and guide her directly up the stairs.

Peter was a creative and focused lover. They'd been intimate in any number of locations, on every evening and sometimes in the early dawn. He'd taken her in his bed, her bed, on the floor in front of the fireplace, standing in front of the mirror, on her knees on the vanity bench, in the corridor against the wall, on the divan in her studio and in the window seat where she sat to sketch while she looked out on the gardens. Once when the evening air had been unusually warm, they'd walked through the gardens. She'd ended up straddling his lap in the gazebo, her skirts rucked up around her hips. He'd carried her most of the way back to the house.

Many nights after she had become exhausted by their play, he would curl her beside him on the wide-seated settee in the master chamber or on his lap in a leather club chair. During these hours, he would read her short stories from news-sheets or selections from the latest popular books. In this way, she'd learned he was an avid reader as well as a wickedly intelligent logician. One night he'd challenged her to a game of whist and when it had ended, she had been short her entire quarterly allowance and her diamond necklace, after which he'd forbade her from gambling without his prior permission, though he had returned her diamond necklace after she'd sank to her knees in front of his chair and pleasured him with her mouth until he'd begged for surcease.

She wasn't certain whether to take his order seriously or not, but she didn't find gambling entertaining anyway, though it was common enough in society.

But no matter how they spent those evening hours together, she always ended up alone in her bed. She frequently fell asleep in his arms, sometimes even in his bed, but he inevitably separated them. Sometime after she fell asleep, he would tuck her into her bed, douse the light, bank the boudoir fire and leave her.

Genevieve knew he wandered at night, too. She'd woken to see him in the doorway between their rooms, had noticed her sketchbook moved from where she'd left it, had found her clothes or other belongings carefully returned to their rightful places.

How often he dreamed was a question she couldn't answer. Genevieve tended to sleep heavily and though he left the door between their rooms open, she never woke. However, some mornings he came to her bed with a desperate determination that left her struggling to wake and respond. His eyes were sometimes darkened with exhaustion, but she would kiss him, run her hands through his hair and stroke his skin until he shuddered in her arms.

One evening at dinner two weeks into October, Genevieve asked Peter how he planned to spend the next day.

"I'll be in the library," he announced, sipping his wine. "John's crops are in. I've sold Devon Place's corn stock. John no longer needs me to oversee his workers, and I'd like to catch up on my correspondence before Parliament sits next month." He paused and eyed her carefully. "Did you want to go up to town for the Little Season next month?"

Genevieve stared. She didn't want to go to London then, but would go at the end of this month for her sister Fiona's wedding to Lord Oliver Morewell in Merton. But Peter knew that. He was asking something else, something she didn't quite understand. "Should I?" she finally asked. "Is your mother going up?"

Peter pursed his lips and looked her over. Finally, he said, "They've delayed their trip to Europe until mid-January and plan to return in early April, just in case. But I don't think John is prepared for London next month, and Mother won't leave him."

Genevieve considered. "Perhaps we should stay for a week or two after the wedding, make some appearances together, demonstrate how ridiculously happy I am to the nosy matrons who predicted such dire outcomes three years ago. But I have no desire to spend the entire Little Season there, unless you have legislative responsibilities?"

Peter chuckled but agreed. "No. Sir John is the MP, but I can't sit as his proxy in Parliament, even if I can act as his proxy as the local magistrate. I shouldn't mind a week in town but much past that and I'll get cranky. The Clarges Street townhouse is perfectly acceptable but not large enough to be suitable for entertaining. I doubt you'd be happy there for long."

Genevieve shrugged. "I can call on Mother and Fiona at Lennox House, assuming Fiona comes back to London instead of heading off on some exotic honeymoon."

"Hmm." Peter frowned. "I'll check with Mother and see if Sir John is well enough that Ellen can accompany us."

Genevieve inwardly frowned at that. She was happy to have Ellen in their households and wanted her to remain, but she didn't need a chaperone any longer, especially not to visit her mother or sisters. Still, it wouldn't do to outwardly oppose Peter's protectiveness, not when she wanted to encourage their closeness, and he wasn't using Ellen to separate them. "Aren't you planning to escort me in the evening?" she asked innocently.

"Of course," Peter replied immediately. Still, he remained quiet, watching her as he always did. She inwardly shrugged, not surprised at all when he took her hand and led her up the stairs as soon as she'd finished her pudding. "Will Annabelle be suitable as a maid in London, or will you need someone who knows all the latest styles and fashions?" he asked, surprising her halfway up the stairs.

"Annabelle will do perfectly," Genevieve assured him. The young girl was enthusiastic and detailed, learning quickly just how to suit Genevieve.

"Excellent," he murmured, tucking her into his side. "I did think she would suit you."

"You know me so well," Genevieve laughed.

Peter, however, took her seriously, and his voice was suggestively husky as he answered. "And I don't intend to halt my education, even temporarily."

To her surprise, he turned her into the studio, leaving her side to open the draperies, so that the moonlight spilled inside. Without comment or explanation, he lit the fire, then dragged the divan into the position he wanted it between the fireplace and the windows. After, he came up behind her, his hands sliding around her waist and clasping together over her abdomen. His warm breath flowed over her ear and he nipped the lobe. "Look there, angel. See where I've put it. Tomorrow, when the sun is shining directly on that divan, you're going to keep your promise from your first night in this house. I'm going to have you there, flat on your back, tied down, open to me and absolutely nothing your eager fingers, your seductive hips or your lovely lips can do will distract me."

Genevieve, who now had some idea of exactly how mindless Peter could make her, gasped. Peter slid his hands up over her breasts and kneaded there, then walked her backward to the window seat. In the moonlight, he caressed her temples with his lips, her hairline, the nape of her neck beneath the coiffure of double braids that held her hair on top of her head.

"Are you looking at it?" he murmured. "Wondering when I'll walk through that door tomorrow and strip you down?"

"Yes," she breathed, helpless not to fantasize.

"Will I disrupt your work, angel? Interfere in any way?" he asked. To her surprise, he'd been unfastening her hooks and buttons, and her gown slid down her arms, to her hips then to the floor. The bruises had healed, so he traced the lines of her bones over her skin until she rose on her toes and pressed back against him. He cupped her rear, massaging it and smacking it a bit so that she wanted to push it out and tease him. He slipped one hand between her thighs and stroked the soft hair. She reached back and slid her fingers inside the waistband of his pants to hold on tightly, then she turned to face him.

Immediately, he bent his head and captured her nipple.

As always, her mind swirled when he did that, but Genevieve had a plan and was determined to pursue it. She tugged at his waist, then pushed on his waistband to push down the trousers.

"In a hurry tonight, are you?" he moaned, after releasing her nipple to help. His trousers fell and his cock was free, already heavy and stiff.

Genevieve grasped it eagerly, having learned over the past weeks exactly how he responded to being handled. Some nights she stroked it with her palm with purpose and passion, pushing him rapidly toward an end they both desired. Other nights she traced the ridges and wrinkles with her fingertips in an erotic dance that drove him mad. He responded dramatically to the caresses of her mouth and tongue, unabashedly in her thrall when she worshiped him.

Tonight she tugged on his turgid staff almost roughly, until he stumbled backward against the window seat, bracing himself with both hands.

It was the opportunity for which she'd waited.

Before Peter knew what she was about, Genevieve dropped to her knees, her mouth already open. She tilted her head, then sucked him deep in her mouth.

Peter shouted hoarsely, his hands digging into her scalp. She grasped his hips and held tight.

This time, she wouldn't be moved, not when he tugged on her head, not when he moaned and thrust deeper, almost against his will. She only hummed deep in her throat and felt him shudder, until she tasted the sweet cream of his release.

When it was finished and Peter sat, sated, on the cushions, she looked up and smiled at him.

"Proud of yourself?" he murmured, his eyes fixed on her face for once, instead of on her body.

Genevieve nodded, happy. Peter chuckled, reached out and wiped a trail of moisture from her bottom lip. "You are a minx," he announced, then bent forward and picked her up from her knees to sit beside him on the bench. "And an angel." His lips found hers.

The next sound heard in the room was Genevieve's long, low groan. Peter carried her to the boudoir bed. Underneath his mouth and fingers, Genevieve couldn't help but scream. Peter never stopped until her world spun.

She fell asleep exhausted, content, excited, anxious and hopeful, with Peter curled at her side, his hand splayed over her stomach.

* * * *

She woke up alone.

When she went down for breakfast, Peter was out riding, so afterward she and Mrs. Inglebright adjourned to the stillroom. Without a lady in the house for many years, it was inevitable that some places in the house would be overlooked, and Mrs. Inglebright sheepishly admitted that the stillroom had never been a place she'd known how to manage properly, particularly with Sir Peter absent so frequently. Over the years, too much had gone to waste and had not been replaced. But Genevieve knew they would be in residence much more frequently now that she and Peter were living together, and this was one topic on which she'd been well-educated by Ellen.

The room should have been packed with fresh herbs, teas, coffee beans, preserves and other spices needed to support the manor, but over time many of the contents had lost their efficacy and usefulness. Living in town with dozens of apothecaries and markets conveniently located, Genevieve had not learned much about a proper stillroom, and Lady Fielding had not known more than the basics, but Ellen had religiously tended the herb garden and kept the Fielding Manor stillroom stocked, so Genevieve had learned from her what could be done when one was well-managed.

It took the pair two hours to clean out the old desiccated herbs, review the quantities of teas and coffees and make a list of what needed to be replaced. They cleared space for a stillroom maid to work over the autumn months, preparing jams and jellies from the fruit harvested in the orchards. Ellen would want to make lotions and creams as well, and the room needed to accommodate drying flowers and other plants required for such endeavors. Devon Place did not have an herb garden, but Genevieve knew that if Ellen remained in their household, it soon would. She advised Mrs. Inglebright to consult with Ellen on where to acquire the necessary contents and the possibility of adding herbs to the kitchen gardens, relieved that Mrs. Inglebright did not seem offended by Genevieve's overhaul of the room.

It was nearly lunchtime when Genevieve excused herself and went upstairs. Impulsively, she rang for Annabelle and bathed, then dressed in a simple day gown.

When she went down in response to the gong, Peter scowled at her in the hall. She blinked at him, but he grasped her arm and led her in, seating her at his side. "Did you forget I was in the house today?" he asked, once they were seated.

Genevieve, who rarely ate much lunch, was even less hungry than usual. She put a few spoonfuls of cucumber salad on her plate and asked Robin for a teapot and some toast. "No," she said absently. "But I spend the mornings with the household. I always have. I paint in the afternoons, when I'm not visiting your mother."

He gritted his teeth. "Are you planning to visit my mother *today*?" he asked.

She shook her head. "No. After lunch, I'm headed back upstairs, to my studio this time."

Peter glared at her, significantly, as if she still hadn't caught his meaning. "Good," he announced shortly. He ate for a few minutes, then set down his fork with a clatter. "I've just realized," he drawled. "You've taken over running the house. How did I not notice that no one was asking me to approve menus or linen expenditures?"

Genevieve raised her eyebrows. "I've usurped your authority over the gardeners too. They needed some direction on the back lawns and in the flower walks, and you were busy."

Peter sent Robin a look that had the servant exiting the room. "Have you had any difficulties?" he asked. "Any trouble at all?"

"Of course not," Genevieve denied. "Your mother taught me household management like it was an art form. Abigail, Gloria and Ellen have all tutored me on their experiences, and Mrs. Inglebright has been waiting for me to show up and give direction since the day we married."

Peter humphed under his breath. "If you need anything—and I mean anything at all, Genevieve—I expect you to come to me. I don't want to find out that there have been problems a year from now. And if there's anything you absolutely want to change—"

"Peter, you redecorated half the entire house after we married, in my taste, hung my paintings in the most prominent spaces. I'm certain that every single person on the staff understands what my role is here. But if it makes you feel better, I vow to seek you out the moment I am the least bit frustrated or uncomfortable with the responsibility, so that you can step in and protect me."

He sighed. "So, you're saying that I'm overbearing at times?"

Genevieve shook her head and sipped at the tea. "Hardly." She paused and added, "Not at times...all the time."

Peter stared at her for a moment before he laughed.

"Seriously, I appreciate your protectiveness, Peter. I do not seek to change you." She paused, thought for a moment about how to explain without drawing in the unlamented earl who claimed, then abandoned, the role of father or the benign and passive affection of her actual sire, the duke. "I appreciate your consideration, truly. And I will come to you if I need your intervention."

Peter agreed to that, and Genevieve smiled. She hadn't been oblivious to his frustration. He'd obviously expected her to be ready and waiting for him in the studio, but it would have been much too apparent to the entire household if she'd suddenly changed her day's activities. The night before she'd been far too distracted to relay her schedule, so she'd meant to share her plans with him at breakfast.

A little frustration would do him good, anyway. Her body was practically humming with anticipation. Now that her foray into the stillroom was over, she couldn't stop thinking about what the afternoon might hold for them both.

After lunch, she made her way up into the studio. Peter had created it from two smaller chambers that she guessed had been earmarked for children, once upon a time. He'd completed the work over the previous spring while they had been in London. She hadn't known until Mrs. Inglebright had imparted the information when Genevieve and Ellen had arrived with nothing more than Genevieve's bruises to lend them countenance. Their belongings, including Genevieve's painting supplies and canvases, had not come until the next day.

Under the old configuration, there had been two sets of French doors opening onto small balconettes to let in light, one in each room. The iron-railed exposures with stone floors were just large enough to set her easel up on them in warm weather, a feature Peter had thoughtfully insisted be maintained. Peter had added a third, a bay window complete with window seat, at the center. Aside from finishing the space, the cost of the glass alone would have been significant. But the view over the flower garden and gazebo to the orchard with its footpaths winding among the trees was stunning.

Genevieve had spent many hours sketching and planning a painting of that view. She was sketching when Peter opened the door and walked in. She glanced up and froze, staring at the stack of cravats he balanced in one hand.

Her mouth dried.

Peter found her immediately. He toed the door shut with his shoe and delivered the burden to the green velvet divan. Genevieve sat very still, waiting as he returned and locked the door, then he went into the attached dressing room to retrieve a pitcher and stack of washrags.

She set her sketchbook aside. When he had finished organizing and looked at her, she asked, "Why today? Why not a month ago or next week?"

"Next week we will be leaving for London. Ellen will be with us, so we will be less private."

His reasoning was straightforward enough, once he'd shared it. Genevieve nodded. She still disagreed, but she understood Peter did not want her wandering Bond Street or the Park without a female companion, and Annabelle wasn't enough of a duenna to deter those who would see her as a prize to claim. Her sisters would be occupied with children and husbands, and her mother could not be relied on to be available either.

"And last time, I made a vow to myself—that when we did this again, it would be daylight and nothing would interfere." He sat and undid his shoes, slipping them off and setting them nearby. Next off came his jacket and necktie. "However, as you know, I've been kept occupied by business, until today."

Genevieve caught her breath when he beckoned to her. She stood but remained still, tempted by his finger but also deepening her determination. "If I'm going to be denied the opportunity to touch you, at least give me the chance to look. Take off your shirt. Please, Peter."

His breathing hitched when the word please left her mouth. She heard him, felt her nipples tighten in response. He stripped off his shirt and beckoned again.

This time she obeyed.

He undressed her leisurely, as if he was in no hurry. Peter took each item he removed from her body, folded it neatly and set it aside, from the simple day gown to her final stocking.

Of course, she reminded herself, he had no reason to rush. He was going nowhere. She was going nowhere. Peter was the master of the house, and if he chose to spend his afternoon with his lawful wife behind a locked door, who would tell him nay?

Certainly not Genevieve. Not this day.

Chapter Fifteen

When she was nude, he took her hand and led her to the divan. It was wide and long, selected to accommodate Peter's height. Covered in crushed dark green velvet, rolled cushions at each end were covered with ivory silk and the edges were trimmed in ivory piping.

Genevieve imagined how she would look, spread out on that divan. Vulnerable and helpless, she wouldn't be able to resist or influence Peter, no matter how she struggled. She knew why he'd brought an entire stack of cravats. She was still unnerved by her own nudity in front of him, but there was no doubt he adored her bare skin. He'd worshiped her body over the past weeks, every inch of it, with his hands and mouth. But without his hands on her, all those maidenly fears reasserted themselves.

Despite her nerves, Genevieve didn't resist as Peter guided her down, sliding his hands beneath her and squeezing her behind as he settled her into the perfect spot. She was still breathing shallowly, her heart thumping, when he began talking.

She knew he spoke to help her relax. "These specific cravats are for the Mathematical." Peter stretched one hand above her and went to work. This time he didn't restrain her hands together but wrapped one wrist in the wide linen before securing it, out of sight. She tugged on it, but her arm didn't even budge. Still, he'd been gentle, and the fabric wasn't tight, just firmly knotted in place.

He grasped her other wrist and began wrapping it as well. "You've seen me wear one, but perhaps not here in Suffolk. It's an elegant knot, suited to dinner parties and balls. Have you ever watched me untie a Mathematical, perhaps that first night, the night I shamelessly extracted your promise to submit to this? These cravats are linen, over six feet long, but widest at the center, tapering to narrow width at both ends."

Genevieve shivered, but it wasn't because the temperature in the room had dropped. She remembered how he had loved her that night. Intimacy was always intense when he set his hands to her skin, but that night he had been driven, focused, almost ruthless. Perhaps it had been his reaction to her bruises or to finding her in his house, but Genevieve suspected that tying that cravat around her hands had affected his psyche, too. It had been a demonstration of trust on her part and one he would have valued.

Peter saw her shiver. "Are you chilly?"

She shook her head, trying desperately not to squirm.

"I like it when you wriggle." He tied off that wrist and tugged on it. "Go ahead. Find out how helpless you are."

Genevieve tried. His eyes didn't leave her for a moment. She twisted, tugged, pulled, pushed and finally got the idea to put a foot on the floor to try to tip over the entire divan.

Peter reacted to that, capturing her ankle. "Oh no, angel, you aren't allowed to hurt yourself." To her surprise, he trapped her foot between his knees and retrieved another cravat. She had to raise her head to see what he was engineering. He was wrapping her ankle as thoroughly as he'd trapped her wrists. She tried to lever against him, but Peter was strong. He pressed that wrapped ankle to the side of the divan and threaded the two free ends around that leg, securing it.

Genevieve whimpered when he rounded the end of the divan and reached out for her last free limb. Instinct had her pulling it away, wrapping it around her trapped shin, but Peter was hardly deterred. He slipped his hand against her backside, revealed where she'd shifted her hip. Peter ran his palm over the sensitive skin until he found the folds of her cleft and pressed his fingertips inside.

Already sopping from arousal, Genevieve flushed and squirmed, moaning when he shifted his fingers. Peter fixed his eyes on her as he stroked up and down the sensitive skin until Genevieve cried out and jerked, her ankle coming loose from where she'd locked it against her bound leg.

Peter immediately had it in hand. He held it firmly as he wrapped the widest part of the cravat around it and secured it in place. Genevieve, so aroused she could hardly function, struggled against the linen, but that only allowed the juices, freed by her spread thighs and open labia, to leak from her.

Peter chuckled when she realized it, her cheeks pink with mortification. "It can be reupholstered with a new fabric," he told her. "But I'll never have another wife, so I intend to enjoy this one."

She gasped his name, chiding, but that only caused him to chuckle again. He walked in a circle around her, staring, then stopped out of her sight, behind her head.

"I have to tell you, beautiful, that my original intent was to restrain you just like this so that I could caress you to my heart's content, and I have every intention of indulging myself in you. But now that I have you like this, I find there's something arousing just watching you, knowing how absolutely helpless you are, how dependent on me you are, right this moment."

His voice dropped as he spoke, as if the words became true as he uttered them. Genevieve did not know how to respond. She felt... She felt everything— wild arousal, a touch of fear, an inevitability she couldn't explain, a need she couldn't fight, even a measure of vulnerability. He could see all of her now, her imperfections as well as her features.

Almost before that thought was finished, he was beside her, sitting on the edge, bending down to press his mouth to hers in a kiss that blinded her to all sensations except his touch. As he promised, he took his time once the kiss ended, exploring her with his fingers and mouth, from the hollow beneath her ear to the contours of her knee.

But he avoided those places that ached for him. Her breasts were swollen and her nipples turgid with need. She still leaked arousal, and her hips thrashed up and down in desperation.

Peter hummed and sat up, licking his lips. Genevieve glared at him, almost ready to cry but staving it off with irritation. "One of these days you are going to wake up tied to the bed," she threatened.

"Will you torment me heartlessly?" he asked, raising an eyebrow.

"Try not to look so eager," she ground out, twisting her hips.

Peter's gaze fixed on them. "Why wouldn't I be eager? I'd be forced to wallow in your touch, slow to the pace you want, only lick and suck on the skin you offered me. Even better, you'd be completely focused on me, and there is nothing I can think of that is more arousing than the idea of having your complete attention for as long as I could stand it." He stuck out his tongue and blatantly licked his lips. "Fuck, you are the most alluring angel I have ever thought of, even better than my dreams," he said. He circled the bed again, watching Genevieve strain, before he returned to her side.

Another cravat dangled from his fingers.

Genevieve's breath caught. "Where are you planning to use that?"

He grinned at her. Grinned. Genevieve was tempted to be terrified but he calmly threaded it beneath her so the wide middle was below her upper back. He brought the ends up under her breasts, then twisted them together in her cleavage. The ends went separately around the back of her neck and back down around the outside of each globe, where he tied the ends under her breasts in a neat knot.

Then he gathered up a second cravat. When he was finished, her breasts, already oversized from Genevieve's perspective, bulged outward from the linen that confined them. Genevieve hardly dared to breathe. When she inhaled, her breasts swelled even further, the skin tightening and her nipples thrusting forward. She was exquisitely conscious of how the linen abraded her sensitive skin. Despite the temptation to be still, her hips and bottom wanted to move. In direct contradiction to her mind, her lower body was desperate to writhe, to develop some sort of friction that would stimulate her clitoris.

Every second that passed, Genevieve kept her eyes on Peter. He couldn't seem to look away, his eyes roving over her even as she desperately attempted to be still. "I wish I could burn this image of you into my brain," he rasped.

Genevieve wanted to offer to draw it, but she didn't know how she looked, and honestly didn't think she could accurately portray it if she did. She would be much more likely to draw Peter, standing straight, his legs shoulder-width, his erection pressing against the front of his trousers. She focused on that sight, on his hollowed-out cheeks and the flush in his face, committing it to memory.

Peter moved. She arched, inviting him and tormenting herself simultaneously. But instead of approaching her, he walked across the room, out of her sight.

Genevieve couldn't help it. She groaned, a pitiful sound, full of need.

Peter reappeared, the large mirror from the wall opposite in his hands. It took him a few minutes to arrange it, sitting against two straight-back chairs, but when Genevieve turned her head, she could see the profile of her body clearly.

Peter walked past her. "Touch me," Genevieve moaned.

"Not yet."

Genevieve heard the determination in his voice and held back an unladylike curse. She knew without being told that such a failing would only cause Peter to torture her even more. Instead, she bit her lip as he walked out of sight again.

"Once I touch you, I won't want to stop," he claimed.

Her clitoris throbbed. Genevieve moaned again, rubbing her backside against the velvet, imagining Peter pinching the hard nubbin between her legs that would beg if it could speak.

Instead, Peter reappeared with her sketchbook and a pencil in hand. She gasped.

It was too late to plead for privacy. Peter flipped through the pages, studying one sketch, then a later one. His breathing sped up, until watching him was more than Genevieve could internalize.

"Peter?" The word came out breathless, all her sudden nerves escaping in those two syllables.

Peter looked up and their eyes met. His gaze burned her, so fiery that her eyelids began to fall. "What a naughty angel you've been." He flipped a few more pages and stared. A strange noise—a growl—came from his chest.

Genevieve knew what he was looking at. Her first drawings of him, by the river, had been innocent. They'd captured his protectiveness as he stood guard, his gentleman's poise as he reclined under the canopy, his manliness as he brushed down a horse in the sun.

But her sketches had gradually gotten more salacious. He hadn't actually posed for her, so the renderings weren't as accurate as she might have liked, but the subject matter was clear enough. Since moving to Devon Place, she'd sketched his face in riveting detail, trying to capture the desire she saw there when he looked at her. She'd drawn him, bare-chested, as he knelt to light a fire, and again as he sat negligently in her window seat, book in hand and his bare foot on the floor boards.

Still, she knew he'd found the one she had spent too much time and too much energy perfecting. She'd actually done it several times, ripping out and burning the earlier attempts. In addition to pencil, Genevieve had added hints of pastels to bring life to the scene.

In her sketchbook, Peter was nude, his manhood fully erect. She had drawn him in profile, lit from behind by moonlight. The pale light reflected on his skin, highlighting the edges of his hips, half his chest and the line of his jaw. He faced Genevieve, who was just out of the scene, visible only by the length of her legs and her fingers draped over the end of the armrest of a chair in his chamber.

He was, to Genevieve, as handsome as a demigod, and if Peter couldn't see her devotion to him in that secret sketch, then he was truly oblivious.

Peter was still studying it. Genevieve twisted, finally bursting out, "I could do twice as well if you'd pose for me."

He actually chuckled. "If you drew any better, I'd be brought to life. This is spectacular, even if I find the thought of you sitting about thinking of me — drawing me like this — the most erotic concept to ever smack me across the face."

He turned more pages, then dragged a chair over to her at the foot of the divan and dropped onto it, just where she had to strain upward to see him, to watch him, watching her. "Lord knows I'm not the artist you are, but if I can represent even a quarter of what you did of me, I'll be satisfied."

He set the pencil to the page and Genevieve moaned. Her torment wasn't nearly over. Peter was just getting started.

Peter took his time. He had learned to draw as a youth, but his skills were elementary compared to Genevieve's. Still, the purpose of his sketching was to draw more of Genevieve's nerves to the surface and in that he succeeded admirably. She'd quieted, accepting both the restraints and her inability to push him to action.

Genevieve, waiting for him, aching for him, was a heady thought. She had been aroused by the act of binding her, but more inflamed by his fascination with her. He watched her carefully, looking for signs of discomfort in her limbs and discoloration in her breasts, but she'd responded beautifully to his games. Someday he would repeat this experiment on her bed, with golden ribbon instead of cravats, Peter decided.

In the meantime, he'd tormented his cock and his young wife quite enough. It was playtime. Setting aside the sketchbook, he knelt and lit the fire that was waiting.

Tense with expectation again, Genevieve was arching her back when Peter finally — finally! — returned to her side.

"What did you sketch?" she demanded.

Peter, surprised she had the focus to even ask, scowled and raised a supercilious eyebrow. He bent, lowering his lips to her temple and whispered, "You'll find out soon enough, angel. For now, just think about it. Imagine. What did I draw? Your breasts, all bound up and presented for me? Your pretty cunt, an unfurled blossom beckoning to me, full of your delicious nectar?

Those pretty ankles and feet bound so tightly against the velvet?"

A small moan escaped her. Peter lowered his mouth, tried to catch it and draw the sound into his chest but he was too late to capture it. Instead, he pushed his tongue onto hers and held it down while his lips rubbed hers. She didn't fight, her mind already captured, her body quivering with tension within the sturdy linen. Genevieve didn't strain against the fabric but neither was she pliant and lax. She was fully at attention, fully his. Inside his head, inside his heart, a kernel of glorious joy formed, tempting him to believe.

Maybe.

He was patient with her. He caressed, licked an inch of skin and waited for the shudders to recede, before he moved to the next square inch. The long minutes he spent on her nipples, then her areolas, then outward over the skin of her breasts, seemed interminable. Genevieve had tears running down her pinkened cheeks when he finally shifted. Lifting his head sharply at the sight, he heard her whisper faintly, "It's so much. I feel so much."

Peter smiled and lowered himself half-over the divan again, his mouth dipping to explore her belly and navel. "Just wait, angel. I'm saving the best part for last."

She whimpered.

He moved over her, settling on his knees at the end of the divan, between her calves. It was a tight fit, but he could bend forward, and he did.

Genevieve, covered now in a fine perspiration that spoke of her anticipation and the desire strumming her nerves, jerked hard against the linen bonds. He settled his hands on her hips, holding them firmly and bent, pressing his lips against her mons. Peter pushed his tongue down so that he could spear the weeping cleft between her thighs. A sob wrenched from her when he pushed the flat pad of his tongue against her swollen clitoris and rubbed.

Peter closed his eyes, almost faint with the erotic satisfaction coursing through him. The aroma of her arousal threaded through the jasmine scent that rose from her skin, a heady perfume. The sweet cream on his tongue was as seductive as any fine dessert he'd ever eaten, a rich mix of flavors he'd craved from their first night together. Under his hands, her skin was silk, a sensuous delight at every place they touched. He gripped her hips so that his thumbs were tucked into the neat triangle where her thighs met her pubes. He bent forward, his forehead brushing the slight curve of her stomach as she sobbed again.

And he stilled, suddenly and excruciatingly aware of the possibilities, his hope.

But she hadn't spoken, and he couldn't assume, despite the long weeks that they had spent together.

Peter drew a sharp breath and collected himself. He dropped his chin, so he shifted his hands and lifted her bottom slightly. The angle shifted enough for him to spear the pulsing walls of her cunny with his tongue. Around that muscle, those interior walls clenched and vibrated. From a distance, he heard her cry out again, and the vibrations became spasms.

He couldn't decide whether to hold his tongue in place or to look up and watch the expression on her face.

If he was looking at her face, he could be inside her.

The realization brought him to his knees. He considered a moment, but there was nothing to be done. He'd never be able to unknot the linen in time. Desperate, he climbed off, stood beside her head, and put one knee beside her shoulder.

Beneath him, she widened her eyes, her mouth and plump lips apart. She licked the bottom one, and a growl escaped him. Before he quite knew what he was doing, he opened her mouth with his thumb, and fed his cock past her lips, her teeth, over her tongue, until he bumped the back of her mouth. He grunted, uttering, "Breathe through your nose," and she tried to follow his instructions. She'd loved him with her mouth, but the angle and the depth of his penetration was difficult.

She was too dazed, though, to do anything but welcome him, and he was too desperate to do anything but come against the back of her throat after only a few thrusts. He let the ecstasy take him, cursing his lack of foresight in binding her legs so firmly that he couldn't quickly release her.

Next time, he promised himself, he'd find a simple way to confine her, or he'd leave her legs free and trap them with his own.

By the time Peter unpicked the lengths of linen and tossed them impatiently to the floor, Genevieve had gone past *sated* and progressed to *drowsy*. He drew her into his arms, against his chest, and suppressed the ridiculous urge to just carry her around with him and watch her. She'd be more comfortable, rest more deeply, in her bed.

He rolled her gently onto one side of the bed, then pulled back the coverlet on the other side and reached across the bed to settle her onto the sheet. Peter took his time tucking the blankets around her just right, cleaned up the studio then himself.

Genevieve slept on.

He stood in the doorway, debating, but she'd need to rise and eat. If he'd been a protective bastard before, he was going to be doubly attentive now.

Now that she was his… Now that the light in her eyes when she looked at him was full of trust, now that she belonged to him, body, heart and womb.

Now that she was carrying his child.

Chapter Sixteen

"Do you *truly* think they will hurt you?"

"Yes." Peter had no doubt the males of her family would at least try. He'd taken an oath to stay away from her until her next birthday, and he was easily six weeks ahead of schedule—and more, given they'd shared a bed nearly two months already.

Genevieve humphed but gripped his hand, clasping it tightly.

"But not likely in the coach," Peter clarified, covering her hand with his free one and squeezing slightly.

Genevieve gave a nervous laugh but held on, looking at the window. "We won't attract any attention from the family at all. We're old news, a long-established couple. Fiona is marrying *two men*, no matter how they disguise it as marrying Oliver only. That ought to have everyone's attention." She used her free hand to gesture. "And we're here, my lord."

They'd set out at first light in Peter's phaeton and arrived at the Clarges Street house in London at mid-afternoon, having sent their bags ahead with Robin and Ellen the day before. Their arrival had left them just enough time to dress and climb into the Fielding's town carriage. Peter didn't wish to be driving his phaeton over the dark roads into London at midnight, and the town carriage could accommodate a coachman and groom to assist them in an emergency. The late afternoon sun was just dipping in the western sky.

He sighed, slipped from the carriage, and turned to help her down. Easily, her gloved fingers slipped inside his, but they adjusted quickly and he properly took her arm and settled her hand inside his elbow.

Before they'd even reached the top of the steps, Lennox's butler, Carrington, was frowning at the pair of them from the open door. He must have been brought for the occasion, because Peter knew the only staff at this retreat was a Dutch couple Alden Swenson had brought from Amsterdam. The house was a Merton villa, set well back from the road behind iron gates and a tall, iron fence that ran along the frontage. Its back gardens ran down to the Thames, with high walls separating the villa's acreage from similar villas built to each side. The property was a luxurious venue in its own right, and the private residence of Lord Alden Swenson and Lord Oliver Morewell, and now also of Lady Fiona de Rothesay, Genevieve's eldest sister. The three lived primarily at Lennox House in London, where Lord Alden oversaw the affairs of his father, the Duke of Lennox — Genevieve's sire — and his very young nephew, Lord Eynon, the duke's heir and daughter of Genevieve's third sister, Gloria. Gloria had been married to Lennox's eldest son and heir, Lord March, but after March had died, Gloria had remarried as well, and was now Lady Clare.

The tangled affairs of Gloria and March, and March's death, had brought Alden and Oliver back to London from Amsterdam, where they had met Fiona. Now, Oliver and Fiona were marrying, with Alden symbolically giving away the bride.

Peter was frankly astonished that no one in the family seemed to find the entire triad repulsive. Indeed, while his mother had agreed to come, he suspected Lady Fielding was slightly relieved to have a reasonable excuse in the recovery of Sir John. But he had been silently fond of the females in Genevieve's family since Fiona had accosted him at that gaming hell and asked him what the devil he was about, engaging himself to her sixteen-year-old sister. Further acquaintance had only deepened his attachment. If it took two men to make Fiona happy, then he wished Alden and Oliver the best of luck.

Carrington was another matter. While he properly bowed to Genevieve and Peter, his expression was studiously blank.

Genevieve only laughed and smiled at the butler brilliantly, the vision beside him lighting up. Peter wondered how to make her don that expression all the time. She looked lovely in her dark-red gown and cape, embroidered and trimmed in gold, chosen for the evening autumn air. But the smile changed her, demonstrated the depth of character that she normally concealed behind her gentle, polite friendliness.

Carrington thawed somewhat and ushered them inside, taking Peter's hat and cane and leading them into the drawing room where so many others from her family had gathered.

Then the true test began. Genevieve's beaming smile was firmly in place at first, but it quickly dimmed. Her mother bluntly asked why Ellen had not accompanied them. Lennox tried to extract Peter for a consultation on the corn laws, but Genevieve clung to him tightly and informed the duke that it would be more prudent to discuss politics on another day. Abigail and Meriden made an attempt to separate them to discuss a commissioned painting, but Genevieve appealed to Peter, who informed the couple tersely that Genevieve was not available for a winter in Warwickshire. She already had plans for Christmas. Gloria, with her stepson Arwyn in tow, carried over young Eynon, who was dressed for the afternoon in a suit of white wool and formal little black boots. Even Peter recognized the young man's formal attire as stiff and uncomfortable, but the sisters admired him in a scene of mutual regard while the youth Arwyn, who seemed painfully aware of how he must behave, stood stiffly by and tried to engage Peter in conversation.

Peter responded, manfully putting Arwyn at ease, only to hear Gloria across from him say, "Oh, do let me take you in to see Fiona dress. She'll be so pleased!"

Genevieve had loosed her grip on Peter's arm to hold Eynon, but at Gloria's words, she hurriedly returned the child to his mother. Peter stepped closer and Genevieve reached out to him, brazenly gripping the sleeve of his jacket until they were aligned and she could settle beside him properly. "Perhaps in a bit, you know. We haven't spoken to everyone yet, and I know the ceremony will begin soon."

Peter listened to her words, heard the deeper meaning. *We haven't announced our change in status to everyone yet.* He excused them and moved them along.

Genevieve's aunts were less than enthusiastic, eyeing him disapprovingly. Her cousin Libby, married to Lord

Anthony Morewell—Oliver's younger brother, the third of four—was cool, and Anthony bluntly invited Genevieve to spend Christmas with the Morewells in Northumberland. He did not include Peter in the invitation. Genevieve declined, smiling politely as she turned away, Peter solicitously remaining at her side.

He could sense her growing discouragement, the dimming of her eyes.

Alden and Oliver strolled into the room side-by-side, and Alden looked directly at her.

Beside him, Genevieve again beamed. Sunlight was glinting in her golden hair from the front windows, and she must have simply glowed. Peter looked down on her sleek coiffure, mentally refashioned the glimmering sunlight into a halo, and murmured, "Come, angel. Let's congratulate them."

Genevieve agreed. It was quickly apparent that the others had already greeted the two men. Genevieve and Peter gained their company virtually uninterrupted, despite that the pair were the guests of honor, the hosts, and two-thirds of the wedding party.

Alden, a giant of a man, dwarfed Genevieve. That didn't stop her from stretching as high as she could and planting a kiss on his cheek. "You look lovely," she complimented him.

"He does, doesn't he?" Oliver shone with pride at Alden's attire. They were, for once, dressed nearly alike in white trousers and shoes, with dove gray jackets. Only their waistcoats were different. Alden's was a deep purple, striped with silver thread, and Oliver's was a soft silver with purple stripes.

"Congratulations, to both of you," Peter drawled, acknowledging what few in the *haut ton* had. Oliver was marrying Fiona in the church, but it was clear that she loved both men. He'd taken note of the few witnesses beyond the family who were present and wondered if that was circumstance or a statement on the *ton's* opinion of their wedding.

Oliver grinned. "No way to hold a giant gathering here. We didn't want to make a spectacle of it, you know, though now that the day is here, I want all of London to admire her."

"I suspect all of London is envious of her," Genevieve teased.

Alden raised his eyebrows. "Are you flirting with him?" he asked, slightly taken aback.

"Genevieve," Peter drawled, "is just being her mischievous self. If she's having fun with you, she likes you."

"Yes, well, I do like Peter, so he's one to know," Genevieve admitted bluntly.

Alden's eyebrows nearly shot into his hairline, they were so high, and Oliver laughed. Alden took a second to eye Peter narrowly.

"I returned from Scotland one day in September to find her firmly ensconced in the lady's apartments, running my household, and ready to order me about. What were my choices? To run away and hide, as a coward, or to stand and take orders like a man?" Peter asked dryly.

Alden laughed. "That much has become clear to us. No matter how much I insist, it is always Fiona who has her way."

"As it should be," Oliver agreed.

Just then, Carrington brought Oliver a note on his salver. Oliver read it briefly, then looked at the butler. "Give us five minutes, then everyone can be directed to move out to the terrace."

Alden stiffened, but Oliver smiled. "There's nothing to be nervous about," Oliver proclaimed. "I'm the one getting married."

At that Alden scowled, but Oliver only laughed. "Will you excuse us?" Oliver bowed.

They made their farewells, then greeted Genevieve's uncles, who were just arriving. Brothers to Genevieve's mother, Lady Johna, they were congenial men, and, Peter realized, they had not seen he and Genevieve arrive together unaccompanied.

They ambled outside with two of the few *ton* guests outside the family. Countess Lieven and Lady Jersey, both patronesses of Almack's and staunch supporters of Fiona through the years, sat one to each side of them. Before Peter quite knew what was happening, Lady Jersey, known as Silence in an ironic reference to her inveterate skill as a gossip, asked archly if he and Genevieve would be staying in town for the Little Season. On the other side of him, the countess asked pointedly if Lady Fielding had accompanied them to town.

He paused long enough to smile contentedly. The quality of the smile was as informative to Lady Jersey as his answer. Beside him, Genevieve calmly said that Sir John's health had kept Lady Fielding in Suffolk, and that she was unlikely to come up for any of the Little Season.

Telling enough, as it were. "Sadly no," he informed the lady beside him. "Genevieve and I have only come up for a few days, to see to dispositions at my house in Clarges Street, check on Fielding House for Sir John and attend this celebration. We only arrived this afternoon."

Lady Jersey's eyebrows arched and he steeled himself for another highly inquisitive question, when he was saved from further interrogation by the advent of piano music.

* * * *

The wedding breakfast, truly a dinner, was a continued exercise. Genevieve clung brazenly to his side, a delight Peter thoroughly enjoyed. The aroma of her delicious jasmine soap reminded him again and again of the delights that would accrue when they returned to his townhouse. Her light laughter titillated his senses, awakening his body. Her championing of him bolstered his heart.

She told Lennox of all the time he'd spent running the Fielding enterprises, as well as his own. He told Fiona of the beautiful studio he'd created at Devon Place, so she could paint to her heart's content. She told soft-hearted Abigail of how he'd rescued Ellen after her soldiering husband had passed, and provided other kind anecdotes to guests. Peter began to squirm under her praise, and had begun to intercede with his own tales of Genevieve's graciousness, generosity and talent.

When they escaped, together, it was only because Fiona, Oliver and Alden walked them into the front hall and bid them farewell there, a kindness that Peter wished to profusely acknowledge.

They both slumped, exhausted, in the carriage as it rattled back toward London. Peter drew Genevieve close to his side and kissed her hair, breathing in her essence, her tiredness. The exertions had been exhausting for her. He was humbled by the championing she had done of him, of her protectiveness. He knew well that if Genevieve's male relatives had separated the couple, Peter would have been subjected to an inquisition that would likely have resulted in fisticuffs. He could evade as much as possible, but the evidence of their relationship would be obvious within a few months.

Genevieve had been as silent as a monk on that topic, too.

"I suspect we should plan for a surprise visit from someone in my family, imminently — at Devon Place, as soon as they hear we've left London," Genevieve sighed. "Even though I didn't say precisely that I was living there, I remember you told Alden and Oliver."

"Yes. Meriden and Abigail will be first," Peter agreed. "They are leaving London next week, even though it's nowhere near the route to Warwickshire. Then I think Clare and Gloria, when they retreat to Norham Castle at the end of the month. You know Gloria won't wish to stay in London for the Little Season proper, and as Clare has not yet succeeded to the title, there's no reason for them to remain, except the social niceties."

"True. Lennox won't wish to miss the Session, and Mama wouldn't force the issue," Genevieve agreed.

Peter inwardly frowned. He was disgusted that Lennox didn't place a higher value on Genevieve's welfare, but, at the same time, relieved by the man's laissez-faire oversight of the daughter he'd never acknowledged. Alden seemed more of a sibling than Lennox a father.

"Yes. When do you think Fiona and her gentlemen might visit?"

Genevieve answered, and Peter let her quiet against his side. The ride into London was tedious but not extraordinarily long, and the two of them were in Clarges Street just as Genevieve began yawning.

The townhouse was a narrow dwelling built with identical homes on each side. They entered a narrow foyer on the first floor, with just enough room for a rectangular drawing room backed by a morning room over the gardens to the left. For the moment, the morning room made an adequate studio for Genevieve. They could just as easily breakfast in the dining parlor. To the right of the foyer, a dining room that could comfortably sit eight—nothing like the proper banqueting room at Fielding House or the large dining room at Devon Place, but absolutely appropriate for the house—was backed by a butler's pantry and stairs down to the kitchens and service rooms. At the back of the house, adjacent to the morning room, was a library-cum-study. In the center of the house, lit by skylights from the attics, a circular staircase led upward to the second floor, with its two large chambers. Each had a dressing room with bathing chamber attached, and here in the city, Sir Peter had paid a premium to have running water installed into both bathing chambers at the back of the house, where pails could be filled and set on the hearth to warm. Above the second floor was a third floor with a third chamber and the nurseries, with servants' quarters in the attics above that.

For a London house of a wealthy *ton* couple, it was small. It was too small for Genevieve to entertain. For all that Genevieve had smiled sunnily and said the morning room was a fine studio, Peter knew the room was barely adequate, with windows that needed to be lengthened. He wanted to add a set of French doors to open the room to the small back garden, and if it were at all possible to raise the ceilings, he'd do that, too.

Robin took Genevieve's wrap and Peter's greatcoat, and Peter impulsively carried Genevieve up the stairs. He detested saying good night to her and often avoided the problem by simply holding her until she fell asleep. He suspected that wouldn't take long tonight.

In her room, he helped strip her of her gown and underclothes, then set her on the bed and brought a wet washrag to clean her face. He went and stripped his jacket and waistcoat off, toed off his shoes then washed his own face, giving her a few minutes of solitude. When he returned, she was seated at her vanity, unpinning her hair, a burgundy velvet dressing gown hugging her.

Peter knelt and lit the waiting fire. She wouldn't need much of one, snugly tucked beneath the wool blankets of her bed. But it would warm the room for a few hours and in the early morning, Annabelle could rekindle it before Genevieve woke. Once he rose, Peter gladly took over the task of brushing Genevieve's hair, delighting in the silken tresses as he pulled the brush through them again and again, watching the gold glimmer in the lamplight.

Her tired sway was enough to call him to order. Peter lifted his wife in his arms and carried her to the bed, cradling her close to his chest. She was asleep almost before he dropped the dressing gown to the foot of the bed, but even so, he crawled beneath the blankets with her and tucked her into his shoulder, sighing contentedly when she nestled there.

Genevieve's room was at the front of the house. Peter, who'd rarely slept much in London anyway, had always occupied the back bedchamber that overlooked the rear garden. It kept the street noise to a minimum, which kept it from triggering the nightmares as badly, though nothing could dispel the smoke in the air, even at the height of summer. Tonight, still dressed in his trousers and shirt, he held Genevieve close and tried to ignore the sounds from outside. He didn't want to leave Genevieve, even though she slept. Both humbled by and inordinately proud of her, Peter wanted nothing more than to treasure the angel in his arms.

He fell asleep sometime after the low bongs of the eleventh hour chimed. By two, when the carriage wheels began rolling by with the horses clopping on the cobblestones on their way from the evening's entertainments, Peter was soundly asleep. He didn't even know when he fell into the nightmare.

With nothing more than the wagon wheel to protect him, Peter crouched low and shuffled along. The cannonballs couldn't quite reach them but sprayed rock and dirt at impact with the road beside them. The wagon drivers, those who were still on their seats, had left the road at the first indication of shots. The cannon must have been placed to land perfectly on the length of straight road that ran into town. Peter had quickly ordered his soldiers off the road too, though, in fact, most of them had already broken formation in their haste to obey. Their objective was to attack the entrenched French at St Cyprian, which was mostly to divert men and supplies from where the true battle was expected, at Beresford on the east side.

Even though Sir Rowland Hill's Second Division wasn't expected to succeed and had no intention of risking many of its twelve thousand-plus men, they knew it wouldn't be precisely easy. The trick was in letting the French think they were aggressing and regretting the few who were picked off one by one.

Despite all, Peter had no intention of being one of those who were picked off by French cannonballs. The wagon drew up, falling into position behind the one before it. They'd gotten the dry side of the operation away from the floods and mud on the east and south sides of the city. He gave a shouted order for the soldiers to reform their ranks behind the line of wagons, drawn up in front to hide their preparations.

Another cannonball hit, and this time it was accompanied by a scream.

Peter froze. The scream was eerily familiar.

He threw himself down on the wet ground and crawled under the wagon. Surely she wouldn't be –

Oh, but she was. His foolish angel, his wife – she who had vowed to obey him – was facing down the damned Frenchies in only her velvet dressing gown. Fully enraged, she was gliding forward instead of retreating like any sensible soldier, her scream occasioned more by her outraged temper than any injury. He shouted hoarsely but he didn't hesitate. He couldn't lose her, too. Peter reached her side, half-covered in mud, his uniform jacket torn away. Without even giving her a chance to excuse herself, he held her close, turning them to flee to the safety beyond the reach of those damned cannonballs.

The explosion at his left side was shocking, a searing pain that traversed his body and had him screaming. Still, he held Genevieve against his right side, both now on their knees as he dragged them forward.

Except that her hands were gently stroking his wound, healing him as only an angel could, a miracle in itself. Had he died then? Softly, her voice found its way through the roaring in his ears. "You've got me," she murmured against his throat, her drowsy voice almost sultry in its low tones.

He jerked awake.

The low light in the bedroom assured him everything was in place. The lamp was turned low, the fire in the hearth still smoldering. Outside the windows, the carriages and their horses were still rumbling by.

Genevieve was still asleep, had no idea that he'd been caught in that nightmare again.

Peter almost vomited but he couldn't do that to Genevieve. Instead, he struggled to control his breathing and his nausea, reminiscent of the weeks he'd spent in a military hospital after Toulouse and the war ended, until Sir John had arrived to escort him — just barely out of bed and unable to care for himself — back to England.

In his arms, Genevieve was wrapped around him, her head tucked under his chin and her arms around his waist. She lay partially atop him, though he couldn't understand why. He hugged her close to his heart. Peter knew exactly why he hadn't let her go, not even while he dreamed. He stared at the ceiling for a moment, closed his eyes and said a soft prayer of gratitude to a God to whom Peter rarely appealed. He hadn't had the nightmares in Suffolk in several weeks, but now on the first night in London, he'd succumbed to the weakness again.

What now? He hadn't panicked and run, hadn't vomited in her hair, hadn't struck out at her in his sleep. Indeed, he'd drawn her into his dream, where his imagination had placed her in the role of the champion she had played in the afternoon. There was some warped logic to the twist on his usual nightmare that Peter couldn't analyze. His heart was only beginning to slow, his perspiring forehead and palms beginning to cool. Concentrating on his fingers, he loosened his fingers one by one from where they'd gripped her hips and clung.

In her sleep, Genevieve murmured Peter's name. His heart nearly stopped.

Yet another incident, and he still hadn't hurt her. But he could. Peter knew well that it was not only possible, but inevitable, if he stayed here, where the nightmares would wrack him, particularly if he didn't collapse in bed in a drunken stupor. Whiskey and forcing himself to stay awake for thirty-six hours at a time had been the only way he'd ever slept in London.

How many times had he awoken thrashing in the sheets, his fists reacting as if he had a knife gripped in them and was in hand-to-hand combat with troops on the ground? Of course he'd never kept such weapons — any weapon — in his bedchamber. He was no numbskull. But he didn't need a weapon to damage his angel.

Why in the world had he agreed to spend two weeks in the City? Naturally, he wanted to make Genevieve happy. And she wanted to parade him through the *ton*, to demonstrate that he was a reformed gentleman and a loving husband.

He was, though she hadn't demanded the words and he hadn't offered them. But if he was forced to sleep in this smoke-filled, dank city, he wouldn't be able to live up to Genevieve's expectations.

Peter was strung up either way. "Damn it," he said aloud, though no one heard him. Reluctantly, he eased Genevieve off to his side and edged off the bed. If he hurt Genevieve's body, Scotland wouldn't be far enough to escape his nightmares. If he hurt her heart, the moon wouldn't be far enough.

Exactly what the devil was he to do?

Chapter Seventeen

Genevieve was smiling brightly as she breezed into the small dining room at the front of the house. She'd expected to find Peter still in his bed, preparatory to a late-night expedition to his clubs and gaming hells of choice tonight after dark. That he'd risen earlier than her was a surprise, but from the stairwell she had smelled the coffee and was happy to greet him there. They often shared breakfast, even when he was heading out to oversee work at Devon Place or Fielding Manor.

Her smile faltered a bit when Grady bowed and offered her a sealed note on his salver. She took it, noting Devon's seal, and slit it open with a table knife, too much in a hurry to wait for Grady to produce a more appropriate one. She sank into a chair as she read the brief, uninformative missive.

Dearest Genevieve, I need to return temporarily to Suffolk. I believe you planned to spend the day shopping and visiting.

If you go out this evening, pray ease my mind and claim an escort from your family. I intend to return tomorrow and be available for dinner and to escort you to your evening engagements. I love you. Yours, Peter.

She stared at the note, read it twice, blinked. Looking up, she asked Grady when her errant husband had left.

"Dawn, my lady. He requested I escort you today, in addition to your maid, if you went out."

Genevieve clenched her lower jaw for a moment, remembering the undisturbed coverings on his bed. In a sudden temper, she almost crumpled the letter, but she remembered the precious words and managed to refrain.

"Grady," she eventually asked, "I know you do not wish to violate your master's privacy but there are times when it is for his own good, and this is one of those times." She paused to draw a breath, thinking of how to phrase her question, then she finally uttered, "Does Sir Peter behave differently in London than in Suffolk?"

Grady blinked, hesitated, then drew himself up. "I'm not privy to all of his habits, my lady. But 'tis well-known that he drinks heavily and keeps odd hours in this house. I suppose you didn't notice before, because he would only see you at Fielding House, after he had slept."

"I see." Her voice was crisp. "Grady, we will not be staying in the capital. I'd like to return to Devon Place as quickly as possible. My husband took Robin with him, no? My maid can follow with the trunks—Sir Peter's as well—but I'd like to be in Suffolk before sunset."

Grady came to abrupt attention, his eyes blinking. "My lady, if you think it best?"

"I do, Grady. But you should not be anxious about your master. If all is as I expect, no doubt he will likely be asleep when we arrive and planning to drive back to London at dawn tomorrow. In his note, he stated that he intended to return in time to dress for dinner."

Grady nodded. "I'll make the arrangements at once, my lady, and send for the Fielding carriage to come around immediately. We can leave in an hour."

"That will do," Genevieve agreed. "I will have notes for my mother and siblings for a boy to deliver and will need to send regrets to those hostesses I agreed to meet today."

The servant withdrew, and Genevieve, suddenly so ravenous she could barely stand it, piled up a plate with the kippers she generally detested. Cook had made them for Peter, while Genevieve generally breakfasted on oatmeal and sweet cream, hot chocolate and boiled eggs. Sighing, she looked at her plate and carried it herself into the morning room to write her notes. Quite why she wanted kippers was a mystery. Doubtless it was the absence of Sir Peter that caused her to long for something familiar of his, like his breakfast.

With a disgusted humph, she sat down to write her missives, couching the unplanned return to Devon Place as a matter of Peter's business.

She didn't think about her breakfast again until she climbed into the Fielding town carriage and settled back. With only the coachman, Grady, Genevieve and her one small bag, they would make good time on the open road to Suffolk, stopping at each coaching station for fresh horses. A town carriage was sufficient for traveling quickly under such conditions, as long as the weather held. Luckily, the late October breezes had not turned into snow or rain yet.

Leaving London at nine o'clock and using the fastest carriage horses at each stop, Genevieve and Grady would not able to reach Devon Place until evening. At best, the light carriage could only travel about ten miles an hour. From her place inside the coach, Genevieve listened as Grady asked about Peter each time they stopped and they learned that he was several hours ahead of them. But as the hours passed and the jarring of the carriage wore on her, Genevieve began to lean wearily against the wooden frame. A chill came over her, and she was glad she'd remembered the great woolen cape she kept wrapped in, but there was nothing to be done about her feet, which grew progressively colder.

At mid-afternoon, Grady tried to press rolls with raspberry jam into her hands, but Genevieve dared not eat them. The rocking of the racing coach was simply too much for her to chance adding food to the mixture. She did descend and visit the necessary, however, and when she returned, she found that Grady had provided a hot brick for her feet. She barely had time to thank him before they were off again, rollicking along at a clipping pace.

When the conveyance finally pulled to a stop in front of Devon Place, the sun was setting and the evening air was chilled. It would be the morrow before her belongings arrived, but Genevieve inwardly shrugged. She remained slumped against the seat while the driver and Grady jumped from the top seat and Grady moved to put down the step, the vibrations still churning through her.

She shook her head to clear it and descended the steps, a bit shaky. Her knees wobbled in the foyer, but she gripped the staircase handrail and climbed, determined to find her recalcitrant knight. A brief word to Mrs. Inglebright had confirmed that he had arrived three hours earlier and gone immediately to his rooms, similarly sending Robin to rest, as they were returning to London at first light. He'd told Mrs. Inglebright not to bother with breakfast, so she informed Genevieve that she'd set Cook to baking apple turnovers.

"We'll be here for breakfast," Grady was telling the housekeeper. "Lady Devon does not intend to return to London. Annabelle is traveling with the trunks, all of them—Sir Peter's, too."

She sighed and reached out to push open her chamber door, then paused and proceeded farther down the gallery. This time when she reached out, she watched her hand shake. Even so, the door opened.

The room was dark, the drapes drawn over the long windows. There was no fire in the grate, so a chill permeated the room.

Peter slept heavily, the faint smell of whiskey on his lips as she leaned over him and kissed his cheek. She'd go to her rooms, bathe, dress, then return to sit and wait for him to wake. Quite where the desperate need to acknowledge his words had come from, Genevieve was not certain, but she knew with absolute certainty that she wanted to say them to Peter, to watch his eyes light as she uttered them. It was a gift she could give him, one not easily repeated.

Genevieve moved to stand. Swayed. The room tilted around her and she reached out blindly and tumbled against the side of the bed. Her right hand, beyond her control, came down on Peter's chest as she slumped to the floor. With a last gasp of consciousness, she bumped her bottom on the floor and her left hand and arm caught her enough to slow her fall. Her head hit the rug on the floor.

As the sounds around her faded, she heard Peter roar from a distance. Thank goodness she had gotten to him in time, she thought, and blessed blackness followed.

* * * *

She awoke to the sound of masculine disapprobation. Peter was not exactly yelling, but the clipped accents and volume of his voice were clear indicators of aggravation. She winced, turning her head toward him, but quickly shut her eyes again. The room was still spinning. Lamps had been lit, so she knew immediately she was in Peter's chamber, in Peter's bed.

Grady replied, his voice faint with shock. "My lord, Sir Peter, I did not know of her condition. I would not have agreed. I thought she had eaten but I found her luncheon in the carriage. If she had told me—"

Peter's grunt of annoyance was evident. "To be perfectly just, I am not convinced she knows yet, though after this episode, there's no doubt. From now on, the welfare of your mistress must take precedence over any other consideration, even her own desires."

Grady acquiesced instantly. "Of course, sir."

"Now, what the *devil* are you doing here? I said I was coming back!"

Silence met his reply, then Grady clearly tried to explain. "She insisted, sir, and that we come along as fast as you did, so that we would arrive today." When Peter didn't speak, Grady added, "The baggage is coming along tomorrow, along with her maid. But

Lady Devon was most insistent that she be home tonight."

"I see."

Genevieve shifted in the bed, still too weak to contemplate sitting up, but she tried to draw his attention, his fire, from Grady.

"If you know what's good for you, angel, you won't stir from that pillow."

The warning, clearly not directed to Grady, stilled Genevieve immediately. She opened her mouth to speak, licked her lips instead.

Openly anticipating her difficulty, Peter drawled, "Bring up the tea tray, Grady. And some food, for the love of God."

Grady escaped. Even with her eyes closed, the poor retainer forgot to slide silently and shut the door without a peep. She heard him scurry and the door click shut before Peter's presence was close enough for Genevieve to sense him.

"You can open your eyes now," he stated dryly.

She felt him sit on the bed beside her, began to shake her head. "No, I'd rather not." Genevieve touched her tongue to her upper lip. "What's wrong with me?"

Peter sighed. "You're half-starved from not eating all day, parched from not drinking all day, exhausted from sitting in a jarring carriage all day and with child. What did you think—"

Genevieve's eyes flew open. "*With child?*" She met his gaze, saw he was completely serious and clamped her lips shut, pressing them tightly together. "How do you know?"

"I can count," he returned dryly. "It's been nearly two months and you've not had your menses."

Silent on the matter, Genevieve reviewed her own memory and grimaced. "I didn't think, didn't know —"

"Now you do," he said abruptly. She felt him lean over, felt his nose brush her as he leaned down over her, his forearms on the bed on each side of her, holding her beneath him. Helpless to do anything but open her eyes, she struggled against the wave of dizziness, keeping her gaze focused directly on his eyes. "And if you ever do such a foolhardy thing again as you've done today, my dear Lady Devon, I will forsake one of my own vows to not treat you as a child and turn you upside down over my knee to spank you as if you were a naughty six-year-old in need of a liberal application of her nurse's hairbrush."

Genevieve closed her eyes again. She supposed she deserved his censure, but she hadn't known.

She hadn't wanted to know.

Opening her eyes, she focused on his, watching every nuance of their color and shade as she asked, "Am I truly carrying your child?"

The light in Peter's pupils flickered with telltale emotion, gifting her with how deeply he felt about the pending addition to their household. Even so, Peter levered off her, sliding one hand down her arm, brushed her hip and covered the lower portion of her stomach with his big palm. "Yes. You are."

"Does sleeping in London trigger the nightmare?" she asked. She kept her eyes on his head, satisfied when he looked up at her sharply.

He frowned, but confessed. "Yes."

It was all the answer, all the admission, she needed. "Then we won't stay there," she declared. "There's no need —"

"Sometimes," he interrupted, "you need to be in London, particularly if you intend to keep a fashionable wardrobe, see how your painting's hung or to see your mother."

"I can stay at Fielding House when your mother is there," she whispered. "I thought you liked London, that you enjoyed the nightly tour of the gaming hells."

Peter's words were rushed. Their eyes were locked now. "Never. I hate sleeping in the city at night."

"Sell the townhouse in Clarges Street, then," she whispered. "If you must have a house in London, look in Merton or Twickenham or Richmond. That's close enough for both of us."

He nodded. "So you don't wish to return for the Little Season?"

"No," she blurted. "No. I want to stay here. With you, not with you driving back and forth like a madman. I read your note."

He raised his eyebrows, looked his question.

"I love you too, Peter," she whispered.

"I knew that," he suddenly grinned. "You've loved me for years, even when you didn't know it yet."

Outraged, she smacked his shoulder with her open palm. He wore only shirtsleeves, captured her fingers easily and pushed her hand into the mattress at the side of her head. Slowly his mouth descended until their lips rested against each other. Genevieve wanted to tell him why the moment meant so much to her, but she didn't know how to explain it. She was too busy soaking up the taste of Peter to draw back and attempt words, anyway.

A knock at the door separated them.

Mrs. Inglebright and Grady together brought in a heavy tea tray laden with food and the requisite brew.

Grady, silent, tried to hide behind the housekeeper's skirts and slipped out immediately as Mrs. Inglebright began her farewells, the tea already steeping in the pot. When the door shut behind her, Genevieve rested her head against the pillow and sighed. "You'll have to forgive him, you know."

Peter growled.

"He didn't know. I didn't realize."

Peter grunted. Genevieve opened her eyes to see him spooning jam onto dry toast. Obediently, she struggled to sit up and let Peter feed her a few bites before she announced, "I came into the room ready to read you a proper scold, you know."

Peter was sitting on the edge of the bed, pouring her a cup of tea. He raised a brow, silently inviting her to continue.

"Why did you run? Why didn't you wait to tell me yourself?"

He shrugged. "I didn't go to Scotland," he pointed out.

"True." She took the cup and saucer from him and sipped, letting the warmth seep into her marrow. Genevieve drew in a long, slow breath. "But you could have woken me at dawn, explained. Asked if I wanted to come home, too." She blinked at him. "I thought you liked London, that you enjoyed prowling through the hells, the challenge of gambling—"

"No, I never did. I did it to avoid sleeping." Peter pressed his lips together, frowning.

"Good," she whispered, peering up at him as he faced her, one finger reaching out to trace her cheek. "You know I suffered through those two Seasons as the proper thing to do in the spring, but I'd rather not."

Peter grinned at that. "You've already managed that one quite beautifully," he announced, tapping her nose. "I was willing to permit two weeks during these early months, but by springtime you definitely won't be going farther than the village, and that only under my closely observant eye. The garden will be much more to your ability to manage."

"You're going to be insufferable, aren't you?" she asked.

"Completely unhinged," he agreed mildly. "I love you, you know."

Genevieve looked up at him, raised her arms and shuddered with relief when Peter drew her against his chest. "I want to sleep with you," she confessed. "It hurts that you will not allow it."

Peter's hands flattened against her spine, rubbing her through the gown, frowning at the evidence of her corset through the gown.

"Once the baby comes — "

"That's months away!"

He continued, as if she hadn't interrupted. "If I haven't had nightmares for a good long while — and I tend not to have them here — then we try it. But after last night, I wouldn't want to try it immediately."

She sighed but didn't dare pout. Genevieve knew that once made, his promise wouldn't be broken. Maybe he wouldn't agree to sleep with her tonight, but surely a declaration of love and a baby to come were enough excitement for one day? Not to mention the awful hours of rocking back and forth in the carriage.

Drawing back from his embrace, she studied his face in the lamplight then kissed him, a kiss of comfort, acceptance and love.

"You need to get out of that corset," he told her, his brows lowering. "And I don't want to find that damn thing on you again. No doubt it contributed to your swoon."

Genevieve almost — almost — found his disapproval arousing. But she admitted it was endearing. "You'll have to help me," she said. "Annabelle won't be here tonight." The words were sultry, suggestive.

He drew back and to Genevieve's surprise, frowned at her, rather more severely than she'd expected. Genevieve reached out and untied his shirt so that it gaped open at the top, slipping her hand inside to cup the hard pectoral muscle, making certain her nail scraped against his stiff nipple.

Peter sucked in a sharp breath, shaking his head. "You haven't even been out of bed since swooning. The *only* thing you're doing tonight in bed, Genevieve, is resting. I'm happy to undress you, but I'm not endangering you. Tomorrow is soon enough."

Genevieve did pout at that pronouncement, biting her lower lip. She looked at him reproachfully from beneath her lashes, an expression that brought an amused and tender expression to his lips. "Indulge me," she invited.

"Naughty," he replied, his lips flattening.

She stared at them, imagining him sucking her nipples, holding his hands against her spine up at just the right angle —

"Genevieve!"

"Fine," she grumbled. "You can undress me, slip off my stockings, pour my bath, wash me, dry me, slip a flannel nightgown over my clean, pink skin then tuck me into bed without a grumble."

Of course he couldn't do that. He couldn't help but stroke her skin as he undressed her and washed her. His hands were alternately gentle and firm, but always tender. Peter couldn't stop himself from lowering his lips to her stomach and feathering kisses over the precious stretch of skin where his future grew. He lost his shirt while he washed her, and she didn't hesitate to stroke the pads of her fingers over the muscles of his abdomen, tracing the faded scars so lovingly that he shuddered with emotion and need.

After Peter had dried her as sensuously as one could do with a flannel towel, he carried her from the bath to the rug before the fire and brushed her hair until it gleamed. He knelt behind her and bathed her shoulders with kisses while his hands stroked her sides down to her hips, then up to cup her breasts. He thumbed her nipples until they ached and she arched back against them, whimpering in shameless need.

Peter carried her to bed, sans the threatened nightgown, and pressed her back against his chest. He slipped one hand between her thighs, using his blunt middle finger to find the bud hidden there.

Genevieve was soon exclaiming aloud, almost sobbing with need, as he brought her to the edge of heaven and pulled back, then repeated the pattern until she kicked him in the shins as she fought, smacking her hand down over his to hold it in place. "Peter!" she demanded.

A husky chuckle was his verbal response. Driving her to the brink again, his finger stilled and Genevieve cried out in agony. "What do you want?" she begged.

"Tell me again," he demanded.

"I love you," she returned instantly. Peter rewarded her, his finger plunging deep within her and his thumb abrading the over-sensitized, throbbing nub until she screamed as she climaxed.

He held her tightly as she came down.

Genevieve tried to turn over but he shook his head against the top of her hair. "Just rest, angel. Close your eyes and rest. Stay here and be safe."

Genevieve yawned, realizing she was sleeping in his bed, but it was easy to obey the injunction to stay. She could feel his erection pressing against her bottom, but she was already worn and he seemed in no rush. She was certain he'd love her as soon as she recovered a bit. The thought of him filling her with that wide cock was enough to make her shiver with anticipation. She obeyed and let herself relax as she recovered.

And slept.

Chapter Eighteen

Peter stood by the bed and simply stared at her, sleeping there between his sheets. Arousal rode him heavily, both from his self-denial the night before and the hours he'd spent lying awake in her bed, imagining her asleep. He might as well have stayed with her, watching her, because he couldn't think of anything except her, asleep and naked in his bed.

She'd never slept in his bed — never before. And now the thought of her there? Now he didn't want her to sleep anywhere else. The idea of her in his bed, naked and vulnerable, was more than sensually arousing. Just her presence would be a comfort to his aching, eager body. But even more, he felt as if he were caring for her more intimately, more properly, more completely, in a setting where she was surrounded by his own belongings, his sheets, his scent.

Peter's rational mind named him a fool. He'd paid to decorate her rooms, and they adjoined his. He owned the entire house, the land, her damn bed, the sheets on it, even the bed curtains that could be drawn to make a warm cocoon that cradled her at night. But the sight of her in his bed the night before had struck his soul, and now he wanted more.

Naked, he fisted his cock and pumped it twice, holding back the urge to tumble her sleeping form deep into the mattress and take her unawares. She deserved better, better than he was, but Peter knew he'd never let her go. Maybe when she'd been seventeen, if she'd fallen madly in love with a young buck, maybe he could have contemplated an annulment and the loss of her bright smiles, but not now—not that he'd ever really given her a chance. She'd been fascinated by him from the first, and he'd done nothing to discourage her, not then. She knew his faults and forgave them. She shared his bed and carried his child. She'd openly and generously stood for him, for them, against her family. She hadn't even realized about the babe when she'd done that, he thought, smiling down at her.

Peter wiped the tender smile from his lips, knowing it was a telling expression that he'd be wise to never make anywhere except in private, when she was there to admire it.

No, Peter was keeping his angel. Forever.

He put one knee to the coverlet, reaching up to slowly slide the blankets away from her. He'd already built up a fire in the grate and locked the door against intrusions by Robin and Grady. As far as he knew, she hadn't been nauseous in the mornings, but just in case, he had a teapot sitting near the fire with hot water.

She reclined on her left side, head tipped down, one hand clutching the pillow beside her and the other wrapped around her abdomen, as if her subconscious was thinking of their child.

Peter shivered in anticipation of touching that glorious expanse of skin. Her back, side and bottom were a beacon, inviting him to curl around her and draw her against his chest. He wanted to cup the globes of her breasts in his hands, feel them swell as he fondled them. He slid beneath the sheet, reaching for her, his cock suddenly painful, before he spent another moment in consideration.

Genevieve was as intoxicating as he'd anticipated. No, even more so. His imagination could never conjure up reality. Her skin was an improvement on silk, satin and velvet, her tresses more magical than golden threads. She exhaled softly and wriggled back against him, the instinctive movement welcoming. That acceptance alone inflamed his senses. To his surprise, she turned to her back, but then she drew him down until their mouths met.

He rocked against the supple stretching of her thigh, letting his cock abrade that delicate skin, teasing them both. She thrust her tongue into his mouth, the taste of her even in the early morning a sweetness he craved. He stroked her, appreciating the early morning heat that radiated from her, ministering to her breasts and squeezing until her nipples grazed his chest.

Genevieve moaned, a hedonistic noise that sent heady streaks of pleasure thrumming through him. He loved the sensual sounds she made as he loved her body, and he set himself to drawing more of them from her. Even as he used his teeth to nip at her collarbone and beneath her ear, she thrashed about, urging him on, lovely little sighs spilling from her.

Peter chuckled huskily, sliding down her body more, and he closed his lips over one of her nipples. A jerk of her body was indication enough. He closed his teeth around the turgid tip and she squealed, her hands clutching his shoulders.

With such encouragement, Peter devoted himself to drawing more squeals, squeaks and cries from his angel. She accommodated him, perhaps not graciously, but with increasing desperation, until she moved her hands from his shoulders to his hair. To his surprise, she locked her legs around him, preventing him from moving farther down. Instead, he turned his attention to her other nipple, surprised when her cries became frantic pleas for relief.

He glanced up, saw her arching body beneath his and nearly sank into her in that very second. But her words were what he truly needed, what caused him to acquiesce to her demands. "Peter, *please*. I don't just need to come. I need you, inside me – so hard inside me." The words were hoarse, beseeching.

At one time, Peter would have been immune to feminine pleading, but Genevieve was no mere female. She was his – his to torment and his to satisfy, his to enjoy, to obsess over, to tempt, to sink into. His angel.

He dug his knees into the mattress and shifted his hands, lifting her a few inches higher, and pushed forward. Already wet and needing him, Genevieve uttered a low, throaty moan and used her feet to climb the back of his thighs, opening herself even more deeply to his penetration.

Freeing his demons to the one act she asked for and he desired beyond any other, Peter sank into her, the head of his painfully rigid cock edging past her tight opening. A great noise of pleasure came from her throat so he pushed inexorably on, encouraged and nurtured by her honest need for him. As he penetrated her, the walls of her hot tunnel scraped his flesh, inflaming him further, tightening him.

When he was as deep within her as he could possibly go, when her hips were tilted and her feet crossed over his backside, he shifted his hips and rocked back then forward.

The movement caused her to shudder in his arms, beneath him, around him. He felt the waves of pleasure coursing through her, signaling the approach of her orgasm. He thrust again, setting up a faster rhythm. Genevieve met his eyes, her own intense, tears forming at the corners. With a wild cry, she climaxed. In her womb, the small vibrations that had sent his cock into a frenzy escaped to rush through her writhing body.

Peter wasn't interested in control. He wanted her wild around him and he drove deeper, hard again and again until the final explosion hit her and she stiffened around him.

When he felt her limbs loosen as satiation spread, Peter uttered a growl of satisfaction and plunged into her a final time, letting the fire rip up through his balls and cock until his seed flooded her. The pleasure was immediate and thorough, but Peter felt and accepted the deeper emotional need that was satisfied by their lovemaking. Though she already carried his child, there was a primal satisfaction in marking her with his seed, a pride in claiming her as his and the animalistic urge to rub himself against her so that every male near her would know that she belonged to him – and not just in a legal sense.

Collapsing to her side and brushing a kiss to her temple, Peter wondered if that was perhaps why he'd been willing to ride back to London today and take her into the *ton* tonight. He hadn't simply consented to her desire to show him off. He'd wanted to stake his claim as both her husband and her lover.

He'd have to accomplish the feat some other way, although once the *ton* knew she was expecting, the implication would be somewhat clear, though not clear enough to suit him.

In the meantime? Peter frowned and looked down at her, but Genevieve was falling asleep again, her eyelids already closed and her breathing slowing.

Good. He would have time to discuss matters with Mrs. Inglebright and organize Genevieve's care for the morning.

* * * *

When Genevieve awoke, it was to discover that Peter was out with his steward. Wincing and somewhat relieved—he'd been rather more vigorous that morning than customary, though heaven knew he'd taken her to a height of pleasure she'd never refuse—she happily let the downstairs maids pour her bath. They had been drawn into service because of Annabelle's absence, so she had to focus to direct them as to her clothing and the remainder of her toilette.

One of the maids delivered a breakfast of tea and toast as another one put up her hair. She ate, greatly relieved to find that Mrs. Inglebright had thoughtfully included apple jam and chamomile for her tea. While she hadn't had any morning sickness, she agreed with Peter. She likely was pregnant, and it was best to be prepared.

She went downstairs with the stated intention of driving to Fielding Manor to see Lady Fielding and Sir John.

Her request created a ruckus. She quickly discovered that Peter had given definite orders that she was not to stir beyond the front door without an escort. Ellen had left, per her usual routine, as early as eight o'clock, driving the gig herself, and Grady himself refused absolutely to send to the stables so that Genevieve could ride. She ended in the Fielding closed carriage, with Grady on the back and the Fielding coachman — once he had been sent for — to make the mile-long trip.

While she waited for the carriage, she wrote Peter a pithy note informing him of her disapproval of her imprisonment, even if he did think it for her own good. She ended it with a pouty, "I love you anyway," and signed it with a flourish. Folding it, she left it on the table in his dressing room, fully assured that he'd find it eventually.

She found Sir John much improved, though still in pain. He'd progressed from the bedchamber to spending the day in Lady Fielding's morning room downstairs, where he could sit on the settees and watch the gardens through one window and the long lawn that separated the house from the home farm through the other. Lady Fielding had made arrangements to reschedule their tour of Italy for the following spring, but when she heard Genevieve's news, she and Sir John openly discussed delaying it again, as the lady very much wanted to be in attendance when her first grandchild was born.

Sir John, ever practical, invited her to stay to lunch. Ellen joined them. Lady Fielding regaled them with tales of Peter as a babe and his terror-inducing toddler escapades.

It was late afternoon before the Fielding carriage bore her home, Ellen at her side. Genevieve, despite Peter's coddling of her the night before and her own exhaustion from the day of physical and emotional stress, was young and hardy and had only truly needed that one night to recover. Still, she'd declined Lady Fielding's invitation to dinner and to send for Peter to join them, and instead agreed that they should come for dinner in a few days. Without asking him, she knew he'd want quiet time alone with her, and she felt the same.

Despite the weeks they'd spent together, somehow their relationship seemed suddenly precious and new. Perhaps she was reading too much into their interactions, but Peter was somehow hers now. Where before they had been lovers, keeping some part of themselves reserved from the other, this morning had been different. This morning they had been husband and wife, bonded soulmates. She wanted to nurture that, to build on it, and she thought Peter would, too.

If not, he'd assuredly want to be certain she didn't tax herself, and she could count on that.

The first intimation that not all was right in Genevieve's world came when the carriage pulled to a stop and she descended, Ellen following. Robin helped her down from the carriage and when she looked her inquiry, he gestured to the door. "You have guests, my lady. They are closeted in the library with Sir Peter." She arched a fine eyebrow and he hastily added, "The Earl of Meriden, the Marquess of Clare, His Grace the Duke of Lennox and the Honorable Mr. Colby Bentley, my lady."

Her face deliberately impassive, Genevieve nevertheless hurried up the stairs, removing her bonnet and gloves as quickly as possible. "In the library, you said?"

"Yes, my lady," Robin confirmed. He took her belongings but set them to the side, following her down the corridor and through the back parlor to where the library doors usually stood open in welcome.

They were firmly shut and, to her surprise, Grady hovered to one side, almost pacing. He straightened when Genevieve appeared, a look of relief swamping his face before he forcefully schooled it. "My lady," he greeted her, bowing slightly.

A muffled noise from behind the doors jerked Genevieve's attention from Grady. She stared at the door, saw Grady's jerk. "How long have they been in there?" she asked directly.

"Nearly a half hour, my lady," he said, almost whispering. He stared at her, almost accusing. "I believe they are relations of yours."

"My sire, an uncle and two brothers-in-law," she admitted, pursing her lips tightly in disapproval. "I suppose we should be grateful that the other three did not appear." Another thump echoed. "Why haven't you gone in?" she demanded. If Alden, Oliver and her Uncle Neil had come, that would have been seven versus Peter, instead of four.

Grady looked almost faint. "My lady, Sir Peter dismissed me." He swallowed visibly. "And the doors are locked."

"Surely there's a key," she demanded.

"I have it, my lady," Robin volunteered. "Mrs. Inglebright has a master key to all the doors."

Genevieve took it from him. "Pray they didn't leave the key in the lock on the other side," she pronounced grimly. "And be thankful they aren't able to dismiss me."

Ellen, who had joined them, looked set to stop Genevieve, but another thump and rough exclamation from beyond the doors halted even that lady. Her eyes flared briefly as she marched up beside Genevieve. Genevieve's hands trembled for a moment as she fumbled the lock, but then they were pushing the doors wide together, and marching into the fray behind them.

It was every bit as bad as Genevieve might have imagined, if she'd had time to prepare. The older men — her sire and Uncle Colby — were leaning against the doors to the rear terrace, essentially blocking any attempt at escape. They were hardly in their dotage, but Meriden and Clare were in their prime, of similar age to Peter. The pair of them had trapped Peter against a bookshelf to her immediate left.

A quick survey showed that Clare's bottom lip was busted and bleeding, while Meriden had clearly suffered a punch to his left eye. *Serves him right,* Genevieve thought angrily. Without hesitation, she came up behind Meriden and Clare. Taller than her, she was unable to reach their ears easily, so her hands — one for each — gripped the back of their collars and jerked hard.

Both were already turning at her entry. Behind her, she heard Lennox's cry of shock. Too late to stop themselves, both of her brothers-in-law turned at her interference. She was too close to them, however. Their elbows and shoulders impacted her upper body, shoving her backward.

Genevieve had a flashback of being shoved against the bedpost at her room in Winchester House. Winchester had been responsible for that debacle. This time, there was no bedpost for her to fall against. Instead, she stumbled backward, landing hard against the back of the sofa. She tried to stay on her feet, hearing Peter's agonized cry. With a wild motion he lunged for her, even as she stumbled.

To her everlasting surprise, instead of landing on the ground, she almost bounced off the back of the settee and into Peter, who pulled her hard against him.

They tumbled to the floor together, but Genevieve was on top, cradled by Peter's body and his arms, and her fall was no more of a shock to her body than if she had followed him down onto the softest bed.

Complete silence rocked the room, before Ellen lived up to the duenna she was and took charge. Silent, Genevieve stared at Peter, whose hands cupped her face. Beyond them, Ellen's frigid tones cut through the silence. "Gentlemen, I trust you will have an acceptable explanation for this atrocious behavior. And we shall hear it tomorrow morning at nine o'clock here in the library. In the meantime, I'm sure you'll all want to have dinner in your rooms while we see to Lady Devon and Sir Peter."

Lennox cleared his throat and went to overrule the woman he saw as merely a servant. "My good woman, I think not. Lady Genevieve will be accompanying me back to London. We'll leave immediately—"

"I will not." Genevieve found her voice, and used the most waspish tone she could manage, while still shaken. Beneath her, Peter was clearly hurting. "If you want to have any sort of reconciliation with me after this shameful episode, you'll do as Ellen says. Peter needs me right now, and he was already worried about me."

Cautiously, she went to move, but Peter tightened his grip on her. "Gently," he whispered. His eyes were dark with pain.

"Where are you hurt?" she asked, moving her hands off of him, so she would not press her body to his as she moved.

He gave her a lopsided smile. "I'll be fine. My stomach is going to take a few days to recover. But you?"

She closed her eyes for a second, considered. "I think everything's okay. I don't feel anything different."

"Still, you're going directly to bed," he decreed, his voice low with concern. "I'll send for the doctor. Surely the man knows more about childbearing than about burns, at least until we can send for someone from London."

She wrinkled her nose, but a sucked exclamation of shock behind her distracted them both. Peter struggled to sit up, his fingers sliding into her hair at the back of her scalp. "I hardly think that's necessary, Peter. Whatever might happen would happen before anyone could be fetched from London. And Doctor Mabry couldn't do anything except advise me to rest and wait."

"Which is exactly what you're going to do." He struggled to his feet, then looked over his shoulder to where Ellen had been trying to herd the other men out of the room. She thought, remembered Peter's words and groaned. It wouldn't have taken them five seconds, especially not Meriden and Clare, to realize the import of what Peter had said.

Indeed, the pair had already rounded the settee, their faces having transformed from guilt, for unintentionally shoving her, to incipient horror. Peter growled and manfully attempted to put himself between her and the two, who were already reaching out to throw him out of the way.

"Touch him again and I'll send you to your wives with green paint in your hair and orange curse words painted on your curricles," she hissed, coming up on her knees and wrapping her arms around Peter's hips.

Clare flinched. "But—"

"He's mine. I'm staying. He's definitely staying, and you are going home to your wives, where you belong. Tomorrow, after you offer him the most abject apology you can damn well imagine," she snapped.

"I think—" Meriden tried to interject.

"You haven't *thought* at all," Genevieve cut him off. "Now *go*."

Clare looked at Peter, a bit sheepishly. "I was going to offer to carry her upstairs, but I'm almost afraid to touch her." He cleared his throat, straightening his coat with a shrug. "And I'm not convinced she wouldn't kick me."

Peter looked at them impassively, then said straightly, "You've had your say. I've had mine. She's my wife." He glanced past the two men to Ellen. "Have Grady come in. He can carry her up, and Robin can help me."

"Of course," Ellen agreed and moved to obey.

Chapter Nineteen

Peter had agreed to let Robin clean him up and bandage his ribs, not so much because the pain was unbearable, but because he'd wanted to make his way as quickly as possible to Genevieve's side. To his dismay, the older women of the household were all present, Ellen and Mrs. Inglebright chief among them. Genevieve, like him, had been stripped of her usual clothes. She lay on the bed in the often maligned flannel nightgown. Though she was still and looked rather small among the pillows, she was smiling up at Ellen, a sight that was really the only thing that calmed him.

Mrs. Inglebright saw him half staggering, and she gestured quickly at the older maids, waving them from the room. Leading Peter off to the end of the room, she spoke quietly. "Lady Devon is perfectly well for the moment, sir. Better to be safe, though. Do you think you can keep her in bed for two or three days?"

"I'm going down to the library tomorrow, Mrs. Inglebright," Genevieve stated evenly.

"It's also best that she's not overset," the housekeeper advised. The older woman looked at him critically. "Can't do anything about your face at the moment, but try not to let her see how much your ribs ache, sir."

Peter stiffened. "I'll be fine," he stated resolutely.

The housekeeper sniffed and eyed him critically. "That's the spirit," she said. "If you could warn me the next time you plan a brawl in the library, sir, I'll be certain to have enough ice prepared."

Peter, unamused, stared at her. "You may have been here since my mother's tenure," he began, but from the opposite end of the room, Genevieve interrupted.

"Peter, won't you come and sit with me?"

Mrs. Inglebright nodded with her usual deferential air, but Peter was not fooled. Every woman in the damn house was angry, and he supposed he couldn't blame them. But what was he supposed to have done? Muttering under his breath, he crossed the room and sat beside the bed. It would be uncomfortable to spend the night in that straight-backed chair, but he had no intention of leaving Genevieve's side, not as long as she was in danger. Reaching out, he gripped her hand in his and held it tightly.

"Are your ribs broken?" she asked.

He grimaced, but thought before answering. "No. They hurt, yes. I'd be lying if I said otherwise, but they are not broken. When I was in Spain, nearly killed by the damn cannonball and my chest was injured, they were broken then. I think this is mere bruising."

Genevieve watched him carefully, so he settled without complaint on the chair. "Mrs. Inglebright is going to tell my mother about this debacle, isn't she?" he asked, wondering at her pitying look.

"Yes," Genevieve answered. "I imagine she'll be over by breakfast time to check on us both and hopefully focus on fussing over you. And she'll stay for the interview with my male relatives in the library."

Peter groaned.

"I wouldn't hope for Sir John to be with her to deflect her or comfort her either," Genevieve went on. "He's on his feet and getting around the house better than even a few days ago, but I don't think a carriage would be a pleasant experience for him."

"No, I think not," Peter agreed.

"Do you have anything you wish to tell me, tonight, before tomorrow's discussion with my family?" she inquired.

"You have every right to be angry," he admitted. "But I didn't attack them, you know. I let them each get in a first jab before I started defending myself." He glanced at her. "Although I gathered their precipitous rush up here was partially occasioned by a note you penned. Something about me keeping you up here in Suffolk for the foreseeable future?"

Genevieve winced. "Perhaps I could have phrased it better. I was in a rush. I thought I said that we were going to be in Suffolk, that you didn't want me in London alone— Oh."

The small gasp caused Peter's heart to nearly palpitate, but it was only her sudden understanding that had caused that gasp, not any discomfort.

She squeezed his hand. "You didn't have to lock the library door. That rather delayed things."

Peter glared at her. "*That* was to keep you and the others out, *so that you didn't get hurt*. Mrs. Inglebright warned me not to overset you, so I'm not going to pick you up and toss you over my lap, but for the love of

Saint Mary, Genevieve, what were you thinking? This time you didn't have the excuse of ignorance about the baby. Don't *ever* try to interfere in a fistfight."

Ellen, who had exited the room at Peter's entrance, re-entered in time to hear that injunction, her hands filled with the hot water urn. She snorted as she approached, adding precious hot water to the teapot. Taking the urn with its remaining water to sit near the fire where it would quickly boil, Ellen couldn't avoid glancing at him. Peter gave that widow the sternest stare he could manage, but the woman had been infected with whatever emotion Genevieve and Mrs. Inglebright felt. "Seems to me, sir, that it would have been more sensible to not be engaged in pugilism in one's library. Surely Gentleman Jackson's Saloon in Bond Street is a more appropriate place for such things."

Ellen returned to the low table where the tea set was sitting out. A cup of the brew had already been prepared and consumed, presumably by Genevieve, but Ellen opened the tea chest with its delicate silver key and carefully measured out the leaves from the silver spoon kept inside.

Ellen said nothing while she performed this office for Genevieve, but his wife had no such qualms. "Gentleman Jackson's Saloon is in London. They were here. But the library? There's a perfectly serviceable front lawn for brawling on the grass. Devon Place has a garden, too, where you might have scuffled. I understand there's even a curious feature called a paddock near the stables where you could have roughhoused with all the maturity of youthful swains fighting over a lass. But since you retreated to the library, where there were gas lamps and other breakables at every turn, you might have considered the options and not locked the library doors. Then Grady, Robin and the footmen could have stopped it."

"And gotten hurt," Peter commented. He watched as Ellen crossed to the fire to check on the urn. While he continued, he watched Ellen place the tea leaves in the teapot then retrieve the hot water, which was by now boiled. "Genevieve, I'm only going to say this one time. You could have stopped them without coming closer or allowed the servants to stop it. *Don't ever* do that again."

Ellen sniffed. The tea would require a few minutes to steep before Ellen could pour any. "On that point, my lady, I do agree with Sir Peter. It was foolhardy. I know you were upset, but you must think of the babe now instead of reacting to your emotions. Of course, I understand it is more difficult to think clearly and control one's emotions when carrying a child."

Genevieve struggled to sit up, still glaring at Peter. He rose immediately to assist her, savoring the gentle touch of her hand on his jaw. Despite her anger, she didn't turn away from him, and that was evidence enough for him of her regard.

To his surprise, Ellen did offer him a cup of her brew. The three of them shared the tea, then she departed with the empty urn and the wastewater. Peter helped Genevieve to recline back onto the pillows, then he settled onto the chair. Sighing, he tipped his head back against the wall and let his brain rest.

After a moment, he asked, "Do you really think you'll be perfectly all right?"

"Yes," Genevieve sighed. "We missed dinner."

"Do you need more to eat?" he asked without looking, knowing there had been a tray delivered when he had been suffering the ministrations of Grady and Robin. Now his torso ached too much to eat.

"No," she said. "I'm already tired of lying still. Won't you join me in bed?"

He paused, but admitted, "I don't think I'd be able to sit up afterward."

"Just lie beside me," she said. "I swear I'll wake you if you fall asleep."

Peter couldn't resist. He extinguished the candles and turned the wick on the lamp by the window as far down as he could. Still, lowering himself to the bed was a painful experience. As he shifted his shoulders and stilled, her hand reached out, her fingers sliding over his palm to intertwine with his. Peter felt his heart thump. He knew she wasn't inviting him to intimacy, but reaching out for comfort. "Come closer, angel. Curl up beside me."

"I was scared," she whispered. "Not about the baby. I didn't even think about the baby. I was scared that they were beating you, that they'd do irreparable harm or that you'd hate me because they did it in my name."

Peter stayed quiet for a long while, but he knew she would finally find out on the morrow what he'd known from the day their engagement had been announced. "You had nothing to do with why they were here," he finally stated. "I made a vow two years ago and I broke it. That's why they came."

Genevieve's hand on his chest tightened. "What do you mean?" she finally asked. "The vows you took two years ago... They were to love, honor and keep me. You haven't broken those."

"No, that's not the oath I was referencing." Peter stared at the ceiling and considered. "Then, they were rightly worried about me taking advantage of you — of your youth, your innocence. You were still a schoolgirl."

She sniffed. "I was two months from seventeen. Young, yes. But I would have been presented six months later. I would hardly have been the first seventeen-year-old bride in the *haut ton*, even if I wasn't an heiress."

"The bucks and bloods would have lined up to bid on you," Peter returned. "And Winchester would have sold you without compunction to the highest bidder. It was only pure luck that I was there to interfere in his deal with Malone and on a day he was fretting about money. My reputation helped, too. But as much as you trusted that my mother would protect your reputation from being tainted by marriage to me, the duke wasn't nearly as ready to depend on my mother and stepfather's faith in me. He tracked me down and had me take an oath, one sworn in my own blood where he'd busted my lip, to be frank. I promised that I would not touch you until you were nineteen and had been given the choice to stay or to annul the marriage. I broke that oath when I took you to bed in Fielding House, and they realized it out in Merton. Alden and Oliver weren't part of it. Clare wasn't in the family and Meriden was busy getting married to Abigail at the time. So today they all did mean to punish me for breaking my word. I can hardly take them to task for it or for doing what they could to keep you safe, despite the marriage."

Beside him, Genevieve had listened, but Peter didn't look at her until he'd stopped speaking. Then he turned his head and looked down at her very intense gaze. "There's still five weeks until your birthday and you're already *enceinte*."

She sniffed. "The lot of you are fools," Genevieve muttered. "If you weren't already injured, I'd punch you in the stomach myself for being such a bloody idiot."

Peter frowned. "Why?"

"Haven't you figured it out yet, Peter?" she asked, lifting her head until he turned his and their gazes met. "If they had any real interest in protecting me as a child, they would have removed me from London and hidden me, despite the engagement. It would have been easy enough for you and the family to have said I was staying in the country and that we'd decided on a longer engagement. Winchester would have looked for me, but it's obvious to me that Lennox could have hidden me in any number of places, but he didn't want to risk that much, now did he? It was easier for them," she added, "to decide to threaten you instead. So much easier than doing anything to save me from what everyone portrayed as a disaster."

"Marriage to me was a disaster?" He raised an eyebrow, staring at her.

"No, but that's not the point. They *acted* like it was — my mother especially — but also Lennox and my uncles. But none of them bothered to do anything about it — not for me, not for Abigail, not for Gloria."

"Fiona came to me and asked for my word of honor that I wouldn't harm you. And you know I gave it."

"She didn't have the power to do much else. At least she made the effort, and she tried to talk to Gloria, who refused to listen. And she went to try to talk Abigail out of the mess, only to find that Abigail actually liked Meriden —"

"Hush," he whispered, noting her growing agitation. "I needed to tell you tonight. That's what they're going to try to explain tomorrow—that I can't keep you because I broke my word. I wanted you to be prepared."

"They'll remove me from this house only if I'm cold in the grave, and even then I expect you to build me a mausoleum and keep me here," she snapped.

"That's not funny!" Peter almost shouted, rising painfully on his elbows and gripping her shoulders. "Don't *ever*—"

Regret flashed over her face. Softly, she brought her palm up to his cheek and cupped it. "I'm sorry, Peter." She pressed her lips to his and he drank in the sweetness, both from her natural taste and the tea she'd consumed earlier. He hummed happily into the kiss, accepting her apology without comment. He hadn't realized how angry she remained with her family, but her comments were revealing. Even now, Genevieve still saw him as her white knight, her rescuer. In return, she'd cast herself as his champion, his angel. He couldn't have a defender more stalwart than she.

He was in too much pain to sleep. Instead, he stayed beside Genevieve in the bed, keeping her warm, staring at the play of the lamplight on the ceiling and wrestling with a single question. Would it be better to protect her from a confrontation with Lennox the next day, or to protect her from a lifetime of anger and bitterness by letting her face him? And, either way, how did he help her heal afterward?

Peter didn't have a wide range of choices that he felt helped him manage his own demons. But there was one he might share with her, one secret of his present that helped him cope with the past. They'd see her relations off tomorrow, wait quietly a few days to be certain she was safe, then he'd see.

* * * *

Meriden began. All four men, plus Peter, filed into the library together and seated themselves in the settees and armchairs that made the seating area before the fireplace.

Genevieve was already stretched out on her side on a daybed that had been moved from the morning room. Grady had carried her downstairs after an early breakfast, Peter close at his heels but still too sore. He'd picked her up from the bed and held her close, but had said he didn't want to chance the stairs, and Genevieve could see the pain in his face as Peter followed. He sat now in an armchair that he'd turned so he was close to her head. Indeed, he'd reached out with a hand where he could comfort her with an easy touch.

"You have every right, every reason, to be angry," Meriden confessed. He was two years married to Abigail, but he still looked a disreputable ruffian dressed in the finest clothing. His gray woolen trousers were perfectly fitted, his Hoby boots were highly polished and his white morning jacket was a Schultz. He had arms of bulging muscle and large and well-groomed hands. But despite these fineries, his hair hung around his neck, his jaw was disfigured by a wartime scar that seemed excessively prominent with his fresh shave and his eyebrows were low and heavy. Still, Genevieve had heard all good things of him from Abigail. Her sister believed him to be honorable and protective and deeply devoted to her and their infant son.

She raised her eyebrows, inviting him to continue. Meriden met her eyes and grimaced, turning and pacing up the open space between the two settees that faced each other, then back to her. "I do not blame the others. I am responsible for myself. I had been told of an oath that Sir Peter swore and that he had violated that oath." His eyes flicked to Peter. "And Peter did not deny that he had not kept his vow. But it does not mean that we should have brought violence to your library. Mrs. Wyman was correct to say that there were other means by which to address the matter."

Genevieve remained sitting quietly. She inclined her head regally, eyeing him expectantly.

Meriden's lips quirked. "As it happens, when Abigail hears of this affair—and yes, I will confess that I will doubtless receive a severe scold on the matter—I'll have to accept her censure and disappointment. I apologize unreservedly for my part in the fiasco and especially for being out of control when you entered the room. Will you accept my abject apologies?"

Accepting that he'd made a perfectly reasonable apology, Genevieve nodded. She wasn't actually of a mind to forgive any of them yet, but she wouldn't have to see them much longer. "I expect you'll be leaving for Abigail, wherever she is, once this interview is finished, and that she'll write to inform me of your repentance."

Meriden grimaced. He clearly understood that her forgiveness was conditioned on his confession. Abigail would not let the matter rest easily.

Clare stood even as Meriden bowed. Like Meriden, he was married to one of Genevieve's sisters, but Clare's relationship with Gloria was less than a year old. More significantly, perhaps because it was a second marriage for them both and Clare was nearly twenty years Gloria's senior, the couple was much different from Abigail and Meriden. Where Abigail prettily deferred to Meriden or waited for his approval, Gloria would quietly make a decision *then* inform the marquess of it. With a smile, Genevieve remembered Oliver and Alden both refraining from deciding some issue regarding the wedding breakfast until they had consulted Fiona. She glanced at Peter, idly wondering how their relationship would develop. Peter obviously expected her to make good decisions. Did that mean he didn't expect to be consulted at every turn?

The stray thought distracted her, so when Clare began speaking, her head jerked up. Clare was just past forty, with a son who was only slightly younger than Genevieve herself. She suspected Clare's reaction to her was more paternal than sibling. Clare did not have any siblings but had raised a son from the cradle without the boy's mother.

He drew a deep breath and confirmed her thoughts. "I spent a great deal of the night trying to determine if I would have done the same had you been my daughter, but you are not my daughter. If you had been, you would not now be married to Devon — or rather, you wouldn't have been married to him two years ago. Nevertheless, you are his wife, and whatever happened two years ago is irrelevant. You were obviously happy when we saw you a few days ago. Whether you were — whether you are — sharing his bed or not is not my concern. It would only *be* my concern if you came to me, or to Gloria, with some complaint or crisis. I interfered unjustly. I did not take Peter's oath on any matter myself. While I have a good deal of respect for His Grace," he concluded, glancing over his shoulder to the duke, who looked suddenly tired, "this was a matter that should not have involved me, and I behaved poorly. I apologize unequivocally."

As before, Genevieve inclined her head. "You will take this matter to Gloria."

Clare tried to keep his mien impassive but he clearly wanted to grimace. "She'll rake me over the coals," he shifted uneasily.

"And yet, I know she will write and tell me about your discussion," Genevieve stated evenly.

He sighed. "Yes," he agreed.

When he returned to his seat, Genevieve looked directly at her uncle and Lennox, sitting beside each other on one of the settees. To her eye, Lennox looked belligerent, even angry, but her Uncle Neil simply looked guilty.

He rose abruptly to his feet and paced back and forth for a moment. "It was the wrong vow to force Sir Peter to make," he blurted out harshly, waving a hand at Peter.

Neil was the oldest of the men present, older than Genevieve's mother and the duke, but not yet in his dotage. Uncle Neil had given up any wild pursuits but he was a belted earl, still, and extremely active in politics. If anything, he was restricted more by the ill health of Genevieve's aunt and Uncle Neil's wife, her *Tante* Susan, who had experienced heart palpitations once too often. She was easily fatigued and subject to swoons and now spent most of her time in the country, where she could lie on a chaise or stay in bed. Genevieve wanted desperately to stand and urge him to sit, but she knew that was not the correct tack to take. She refused to stand for the duke, so she couldn't do it for her uncle, either.

Uncle Neil stopped and stared at her for a minute, before saying bluntly, "Your Aunt Susan was twenty-five when she married me, and your Aunt Jane was twenty-seven when she married your Uncle Colby." He paused and shook his head, admitted, "However, you are the same age Gloria was when we all watched her marry March without objecting." He laughed harshly. "We all thought that Gloria was old enough to know her own mind." His eyes flicked to Lennox then to Clare. "And yet we went out at the same time and tried to interfere in your life until you were even older than she, without any evidence that your husband was the same sort of lout we knew March to be."

Genevieve held her breath. The marriage of Gloria and March was rarely mentioned among the family these days, out of respect for His Grace — and for Gloria and Clare, too. But Gloria had been her age when married to March. That had been a mistake.

Except Genevieve had spent almost two years learning about Peter before she'd gone to his bed. Her marriage to Peter wasn't a mistake, and if Peter wasn't perfect, he hadn't chosen to manage that which haunted him by imbibing alcohol and making a name for himself in the brothels.

At least, not since he'd married her, she amended.

Genevieve sighed. Her Uncle Neil was skirting the real issue she had with the duke. But he had stopped and considered, as she'd asked them all to do. She nodded to him to continue.

"Looking back, I see we made the same mistake with you that I made in permitting your mother to marry Winchester. I should never have approved that match, and yet I didn't look deep enough to see that my own sister was desperately unhappy and simply acquiescing because she didn't feel she had any other options. When your marriage was announced, I reacted the same way. I felt hamstrung by Winchester's manipulations of you and sought to manage the outcome from behind the scenes, instead of bucking society for your greater good. I failed both you and your mother, your mother twice now. So no, I won't be confessing and asking for forgiveness from Susan, but from your mother."

Genevieve actually felt the tears well at these words. Her Uncle Neil actually looked old now, wearier than she'd ever seen him. After a long moment, she managed to ask, "What vow should you have extracted from Peter?"

Uncle Neil clenched his jaw. A tic twitched above his right temple. Eventually, he said softly, "We asked him to swear that you would have the choice of marriage or annulment when you turned nineteen. I should not have settled for such a vow. He should have sworn that you would always have the choice of leaving him — that it would always *be* your choice, that you could, at any time, sue him for separation."

The words hung in the air. "I would have taken that oath without a second thought," Peter offered quietly. "Because it always is the truth of our marriage. Genevieve is always the one who can choose to leave. I will never abandon her, but I would accede to her wishes if she wished to dismiss me."

Genevieve sighed. "I'm not giving him up, not for any of you," she said dryly. "It took me too long to convince him to keep me!"

"Yes." Her uncle nodded gravely. He glanced at the others, then stared at the duke for a moment. "I do believe, dear niece, that your final interview with His Grace might be better concluded without the three of us present. Would you kindly excuse me — us — to pack, while you and the duke pursue the discussion?"

Agreeing, Genevieve accepted kisses on the cheek from all three and watched them depart, their shoulders drooping in relief as they passed out the library door. She knew such men did not apologize well or easily. The interview had to have been difficult for their temperaments and consciences.

The Duke of Lennox remained seated on the settee, deep in thought.

Genevieve looked at him and waited.

Chapter Twenty

When the duke did not speak, Genevieve braced herself and spoke. "Now, I would not change my marriage for any reason. But why? Why did you not prevent it?"

It was the point she had never understood. Gloria's first marriage, as distasteful as it had been, had made a twisted sort of sense. Gloria had been encouraged, eventually pushed, by Winchester to wed Lennox's eldest son, Lord March, a mean drunk who had been at odds with Lennox since the schoolroom. But the marriage meant that Lennox would eventually be succeeded by a grandson of his own blood and her mother's, as well as Lennox's special friend Lord Robert Twicken, Gloria's natural sire. Despite Lennox's stated opposition to the match of March and Gloria, Lennox had not prevented that marriage either

Lennox sighed, standing and walking aimlessly about the room. When he spoke, it wasn't about Genevieve at all, at least not immediately. "I've wielded an immense amount of political and social power over the years. And yet, it seems that, despite any good intentions, I've failed my own children more than anyone." At the end of the room, he stopped to stare out of the long window before looking at Genevieve. "Alden, of course, was my first great failure as a parent. You might know of it. I couldn't protect him, not from Oliver's family, not from March, his own brother. I let him leave England instead of protecting him, instead of defending him. I called that protection, letting him run away."

Genevieve frowned. She'd known the story. But how did it apply to her?

"March was the greatest failure, or maybe Gloria. How does one fail a son, an heir? I allowed his nannies to raise a spoiled brat of a boy, left him to their tender indulgences with the full knowledge that I did more for England and my own prominence here in London than I could have mired in Wales, where I virtually abandoned my sons." He glanced at her, at her and Peter. "If you felt smothered in your mother's household, my sons were the exact opposite. They ran wild and always at odds. But I did not once seek to stop it. I won't excuse myself. Alden was blunt enough when he finally took me to task for it. My only excuse is that I was consumed by grief — guilt over the death of my wife in childbirth, for a babe I had insisted upon despite having two sons. And later, grief for not keeping Robert — Gloria's sire, you know — from going off to France and getting himself killed in the war, to no good purpose. And there was your mother, too. God help me, I thought her to have more of a claim on my life than my own sons." He stepped closer, and Genevieve, who did not know him enough to read his facial expressions, nevertheless could see the torment written there. "She needed me. I could see it. I didn't see that the boys did, and I thought they would be better served in the country than in London's streets. Then your brother died, and Johna needed even more from me."

Lennox sighed. He paced around the room, speaking as he did. "March was already a mean drunk before he came down from Oxford. I never understood why, never thought to ask, to try to interfere. I assumed he'd pull himself together. Of course he didn't. I saw him sniffing at Gloria's skirts, hoped she would be his salvation." His face blanched. "I should have stopped it. She should never have been forced to suffer him in bed. She never complained, but I can't help but believe he was a petty bully there, too. Only after Gloria was with child did I see how much she feared him, how guilty and complicit I was in permitting such atrocities in my own house."

The older man sank to the daybed beside Genevieve. "I should have taken March to task when he was fourteen and terrorizing Alden. Or when he was sixteen and first in trouble with drinking and…and…"

"Light-skirts," Peter supplied.

Lennox grimaced but nodded. "It wasn't until Eynon was born that I thought to seek out March's ladybirds. What I learned about him… That's when everything made sense. I failed him, and my failure with him has had lasting impacts on you, on Alden, on Gloria, even Eynon."

His face firmed and he straightened, clasping her hands in his. "I will not apologize for believing you safer with Devon than under any other's roof. What else could I do? Send you to Europe for five years?

America? Your uncle was right. We extracted the wrong vow from Devon, to leave you untouched until you were nineteen. I didn't understand then. It took Gloria and March to see where we — where I — had gone wrong. But we were not wrong in allowing the marriage — at least in name only — to go forward. The only safety you could have truly known was in the legal care of someone other than Winchester, and the only way to trump his legal guardianship of you, at least then, was to make you someone else's legal responsibility. How else could we wrest control of you from Winchester, except through marriage? It would have been Devon here or someone else."

Genevieve stared at him. She'd always felt betrayed by this man, but she could see his point. If he had stopped her marriage to Peter, Winchester would have gone about arranging another marriage. Devon had already rescued her from an even worse match. So why was she so angry with Lennox? Because he was her sire but had never been her father?

She pulled her hands from his then looked down at her lap. Beside her, Peter remained quiet, refraining from agreeing with Lennox or promoting his own agenda. She was grateful for that. Genevieve suspected she knew what Peter wanted. He wanted her at Devon Place with him as much as possible. Such a life, a life she too wanted, would necessarily prevent any close relationship with Lennox and Genevieve's mother, who primarily resided in London. Lennox had any number of country houses, but none in Suffolk.

There was no reason, she realized, to fuel her irrational anger. Not now. Except —

"Peter, do you forgive him?" she asked. "Not for browbeating you into any ridiculous vow, but for taking part—no, leading, this utterly unnecessary campaign to leave you battered and bruised yesterday." While Meriden and Clare had done most of the damage, she had no doubt that they had only participated at the behest of Lennox and her uncle. They would not have come after Peter of their own accord.

Lennox's surprised look was all Genevieve required to know she had asked the right question. Like the others, she didn't intend to simply grant him absolution. She had no wish for Peter, or for herself, to repeat the experience.

"Yesterday," Peter drawled, "I didn't do much fighting back, not until all of them had taken a few jabs. I knew perfectly well that I'd broken my promise to wait until your birthday. However, if they come after me again, I won't be so acquiescent."

The duke's consideration was almost amusing. Genevieve could see his arrogance seeping back into his face, his masculine self-importance rearing. She moved to quash it, quickly. "That seems reasonable. Just as importantly, should His Grace forget himself and interfere in my marriage again, I believe he will find himself immortalized in perhaps the worst painting I've ever executed, and I'm sure your mother would be happy to exhibit it at Fielding House for me. I'm imagining something utterly humiliating. Perhaps hanging by his coattails over the side of a bridge, or struggling to keep a child's rowboat afloat?"

The duke's face remained steadfastly impassive, though Peter stirred behind her. After a long moment, Lennox murmured, "You have my word. I will not interfere in your marriage again. You are patently mature enough, old enough and able enough to manage your husband."

Genevieve raised her eyebrows, but agreed.

Once the four men had departed, still markedly deferential to her, Genevieve spent the remainder of the morning abed, at Peter's insistence. After luncheon was served on a tray in her chamber, however, Genevieve made her way back into her studio.

* * * *

Peter stood in the studio doorway and watched her closely. For two full days she had painted, with the easel arranged so that the light from the French doors hit the canvas at a precise angle. She hadn't discussed the subject of the painting and Peter hadn't asked. Instead, he'd let her climb into his arms at night, holding her tightly.

They hadn't made love. Refraining hadn't been a conscious decision that first night. He'd been too sore, too pained and too worried. The second night he'd held her and worried about jarring her too much. Last night she had been exhausted from the long hours at her easel. Dinner had been consumed in virtual silence. He'd carried her upstairs and she had been asleep almost before he could remove her gown.

Peter knew all about trauma — battlefield trauma. Emotional trauma couldn't be too terribly different, he imagined. Since their wedding, he had done his best to support her and ease her fears, but clearly the abrupt dissolution of her family two years earlier had left some deep scars, scars that hadn't healed.

After a few minutes of watching her, Genevieve spoke. "You might as well come in and sit" — she

nodded to the daybed but didn't look away from her
work—"instead of standing there."

Peter strolled in. "I didn't wish to disturb you," he
said, watching her hand work furiously with the brush.
He considered trying to approach from behind but
suspected she wouldn't appreciate any lover-like
caresses, at least not at the moment.

Genevieve didn't reply, so he seated himself and
settled to watch her, wondering. He had watched her
paint before, but not these roiling, dramatic
brushstrokes. He tried to contemplate the subject of her
frenzy but couldn't guess. He needed to hear her voice.
He was nearly going mad from the unusual silence.

"Who do you talk to, Genevieve, when you are upset?
My mother? Ellen? One of the maids?"

She tipped her head, acknowledging she'd heard
him. But she didn't answer.

"Thinking back, I realize it couldn't be your mother
or your sisters, not with being separated from them.
And while we were married, we were hardly intimate,
not at the beginning."

At that, she nodded. "Who do *you* talk to? Certainly
not me. When you are upset, you hie off to Scotland,"
she accused.

Peter didn't bristle. He knew her anger was a façade,
part of how she was finally coping with long-ago loss.
As much as he'd thought of her as grown, he realized,
Peter had still been protecting the girl Genevieve. Her
question was legitimate. She didn't just deserve an
answer as his bride, she had earned an answer as his
partner, his helpmate, his soulmate. She'd remained
loyal and steadfast when he'd been an idiot, when he'd
pushed her away, when he'd continually built a barrier

between them by refusing to share her bed at night. He knew well that sleeping beside her settled both of them.

"Correct. I haven't spoken to you about the incidents that haunt me. Do you want to know?" Peter asked. "It's not a pretty story. I was no hero in it. But you are my wife, and not just in name or in the eyes of the law or the church. You are the wife of my heart now."

Genevieve turned fully to him, blinked. Her gown was covered by a stained painter's smock. Her hair was pulled back and bundled atop her head. In one hand she gripped a long-handled heavy brush, a dark color staining the bristles. In the other, her palette was balanced. He watched it tip to the side, unsurprised when she jerked her gaze to it, corrected her grasp and set it on the bench behind her. Adding the brush, she wiped her hands on a rag and slipped off the smock.

Beneath, she wore a fetching gown of thin muslin. It was rounded at the collar and tied with a wide satin ribbon below her glorious breasts. The fabric fell unfettered from there to the floor, leaving her form unconfined.

With nothing but a chemise beneath the gown, her nipples were faintly outlined in muslin.

Peter's mouth watered.

Still, he couldn't get distracted. The conversation was too important. He waited. Genevieve walked to him, and he smiled. Her face was slightly flushed, her lips full and pouty. Drops of oil paint dotted her upper cheekbones, nose and chin. He'd wager she had no idea that her face was speckled.

"Angel," he murmured huskily. Her breath hitched at his voice, her eyes sparking. "After," he whispered. "Do you want me to tell you?"

She considered him, her fingertips reaching out to brush his jaw, then trail down his chest along the path where he knew the evidence of his own scars remained. They were in his mind as well as his body. "I want to know," she said softly, shifting closer so she was looking up at him through her lashes, "Why Scotland? What do you get from going there?" Her voice wasn't beseeching or coy. She was being direct. "I presume the memories, the nightmares… Those are from the war."

He nodded. "Mostly Toulouse," he confirmed.

Genevieve waited. When Peter realized she wasn't going to expand her request, he bent his head and kissed her, drinking in the exquisite taste of her lips. "Come," he invited, taking her arm. "Let's stroll. It's difficult for me to sit still when I think of the war, but it's chilly outside, so perhaps the conservatory?"

She nodded, accepting his arm and they made their way through the house. When they had gained the long room that jutted from the back of the house, with its windows on three sides and skylights, he closed the doors behind them and took her arm again.

"Scotland," he said, "isn't about the place, though I do own the hunting box there. It's a pleasant enough house, just big enough for the caretaker, Robin — when I go up — myself and two guests, not that I ever take anyone. There are only three bedrooms in the main part of the house and a small dining parlor. When I'm there, a local woman named Mrs. MacCray comes in to do the housekeeping. My father bought the property and renamed the house and acreage Glen Devon, which I considered pretentious. Some years ago, I re-titled the estate Glenfields."

Genevieve hadn't commented, but he knew she was concentrating and felt confident she would glean all she could, even from such mundane details. Genevieve, he believed, knew him rather better than anyone had expected. She'd paid attention, even as a girl, and taken the time and energy to study his actions and reactions—not just to understand his behavior but to understand the motivations behind them.

"The nightmares," he explained, plunging into the heart of the matter, "come in part from Toulouse. On the first day, before we knew Napoleon surrendered, we took soldiers and wagons across the western side of the city. Other regiments were assigned to weaken the French from other directions. By attacking on all fronts, we hoped to divide their troops enough that we'd break through on one side." He glanced at her. "The troops I led attacked an entrenched, well-defended force. We really had no hope of overcoming them, only in keeping them busy, so it became a game. Our job was to avoid the cannonballs and musket shots and whatever else they launched from their defensive positions, but stay close enough so that we were actually threatening." Peter shrugged. "I lost the game and nearly got caught by a cannonball. I jumped to the side, twisted my damn ankle and was hit by a ball of burning rags. One of my corporals dragged me behind the defensive lines. He was hit in the back by musket shot while saving my life. But some days afterward, he died from an infection while we were both in the field hospital."

"Oh no," Genevieve gasped. His gaze had drifted away during the end of the tale, but now he jerked his eyes back to her. She looked horrified. "So you feel guilty too."

"The damn thing was, Napoleon had already surrendered," Peter said quietly. "The entire battle was a fucking waste. We didn't know that, yet, and it had finally stopped raining. We didn't want to give them even more time to settle into position than they'd already had."

Genevieve nodded beside him, her hand clasping his forearm where she had tucked her arm beneath his. Such trust, he thought, savoring it. Her horror was for the ongoing weight of his guilt. She wasn't disgusted. "When I came back from Spain, one of the first things I did was look up the man's family. He hadn't married and had no children, but I found his parents living in near destitution here in London. He'd sent them a pittance income from his wages, and they had no other steady income beyond what his mother could earn taking in sewing. His father had no business living in London. He had a bad set of lungs and wheezed constantly. I took them up to Glenfields and built them a small cottage overlooking the loch where they are quite content as my pensioners."

"How very generous of you," she smiled up at him. "But just what I would have expected you to do."

"Over the years, I found that when the memories were the worst, calling on Mr. and Mrs. Banning was precisely what I needed to remind myself that I am not responsible for Banning's death. I know that sounds backward. He made the decision to save me, and I am grateful for it, but it was his decision. I am responsible for how I keep living. While the Bannings are grateful for me and miss their son, they are happy knowing that he was my personal hero, that he died bravely and that it was me he saved. That's what I remember when I go there. And I'm happy to take you with me, angel, though it will mean Robin has to bunk on the kitchen floor so your maid has some privacy."

Genevieve leaned close against him, though they continued to stroll slowly. He was quite sure neither were looking at the profusion of plants that grew around them, as both were lost in their own worlds, but eventually he offered, "I don't know if anything will ever completely rid me of my nightmares, if I will ever be completely well enough to trust that I won't act out in violence in the middle of the night. But what I do know is this, angel. Being with you, near you, that dulls the pain, the paralyzing fear. Being here in the country helped, but these last few months... I know how often circumstances triggered my nightmares and terrified me. I know I was—I am—scared of hurting you by mistake in my sleep. But having you with me has helped in so many ways, so far beyond your understanding. I can't even describe it. So now, I ask you again, how do you cope? What do you need to purge that anger that I realize you've been nursing since we wed? Is it painting?"

Genevieve considered, stopped, turned to face him. "Yes, I think it is. But as has been clear the last few days, painting hasn't been enough, has it?" She sighed, twisting her lips a bit. "I'm not going to rant and throw things, but there's this *passion* inside of me that's just demanding justice, insisting it be allowed to simply rage. I know it's not something I can let out. I have to control it, direct it—but I have never been able to purge it."

"I don't know if you'll ever completely purge it," Peter murmured. "I'm glad that you've found painting to help, but I hope you'll find other ways to exculpate your mother, sisters and even Lennox. The responsibility for our marriage lies on my shoulders and Winchester's."

"No," she objected, grasping his hands in hers and lifting them to kiss the back of his fingers, one hand at a time. It was a loving gesture, one he felt rock him to his heels. "No, you saved me from something worse than an unwanted marriage. In my head, I know the blame is solely Winchester's."

Chapter Twenty-One

Peter couldn't help it. He pulled his hands from hers and cupped her face, cradling her jaw as tenderly as possible as he bent to take her lips.

Genevieve responded as he prayed she always would. Ardently, without hesitation, she moved closer to him, inciting his desire with her lush femininity. He was suddenly, achingly, erect after she opened her mouth to him. She swayed back and forth, obviously teasing his cock. The few days they had gone without making love had been too long. Desperately, he wanted her under him. He wanted to cover her and experience the supple strength of her beneath him, urging his passion to hotter, higher pinnacles until they were both lost.

Peter didn't know if he could wait until they made the long walk back to their rooms. He wondered if perhaps the chaise in the library might do, or the table in the anteroom at the top of the main stairs. He could sit her on it and flip up her skirts.

Genevieve, as if she could read his thoughts, broke the kiss on a gasp. "The bench by the herb bed at the back."

Peter moaned and took her mouth again. He knew she was directing him deeper into the conservatory, at the far end where a high-back wooden bench provided a comfortable resting place for those who could not walk the entire conservatory without sitting. It was shaded from the glaring sun by stunning fruit trees that grew in large pots as high as Genevieve's hips and overhung the oak bench with its thickly padded, tufted gold velvet cushions.

Genevieve would be, could be, comfortable there, laid upon it. They had locked the conservatory door, so he could strip her naked in the dappled sunlight and sink into her with agonizing, scintillating slowness.

This time he pulled back through the rushing in his ears. He had to blink to focus then discovered that he had moved his hands while they kissed. Peter found Genevieve's breasts through the thin muslin and squeezed them, as if he would never have another opportunity to fondle them.

She didn't seem to mind. Even without his mouth on hers, Genevieve's eyes had glazed. She tipped her head back, lifting her breasts in silent offering, a gift he could hardly refuse.

Peter tugged at the collar of her bodice. Instead of stretching, the thin fabric ripped, exposing her chemise beneath. Genevieve gasped and looked down, but Peter determinedly jerked harder, freeing the material at the seam under her arm and pulling it fully away.

"Peter," she objected, but the word was breathy, more encouraging than not. She reached up and tugged at the ribbon that kept her gown in place, then at the one tied over her breasts on the delicate chemise. Peter watched, his body stiff from his face to his ankles, as she released the remaining fabric that covered her. He clenched her hips, and when the last barrier fell away and her plump, beckoning nipples were free, he encircled her waist, picked her up and held her against his chest.

She gasped and gripped his shoulders, arching back in flagrant entreaty. He could do nothing other than oblige and set himself to licking and sucking at the buds she'd presented him.

Genevieve struggled to think, to remember where they were. He couldn't slide inside her in the middle of the path, with nothing to brace her on. "The bench," she managed to utter, desolate at the thought of his mouth parting from her skin for the few minutes it would take them to relocate.

Peter mumbled something incomprehensible and set her to the ground, but instead of moving them along the path, he began to strip her of the remains of her gown and chemise right there. She blinked, frowned, gasped, but before she could formulate any coherent thought, she was nude.

Blinking, she reached out for Peter's jacket, but he shook his head, working at the buttons of his trousers. She licked her lips. He fixed his eyes on her tongue and he faltered. Still, it took only a minute to free his staff from its confines. He jutted outward, curving and long and engorged with his seed.

Genevieve had no other response but to open her arms to him.

The angle was difficult. He had to hold her bottom in his palms as she gripped his hips with her thighs and circled his lower back with her legs. Even so, his cock slid smoothly home, filling her. She bucked and he took a step back, shifting her so that she was a counterbalance to his weight.

"How?" she managed, licking her lips again. He stared down at her, desire written on the planes of his face as much as in the heavy grip of his fingers.

"Put your lips to my skin," he demanded. She tipped her head forward, her mouth finding his collarbone and nipping lightly.

Peter's hips jerked once and thrust. She rocked against him, welcoming him, encouraging him. He repeated the motion and she responded again.

Soon, almost too soon, they had created a rhythm, cradled together under the glass of the conservatory roof. Completely dependent on his movement for the rollicking sensation, Genevieve tried to encourage him, sucking on the skin that was pulled tightly over his neck, nibbling there when it seemed he might slow.

The climax caught her, flung her mind into oblivion. She screamed against his neck, shuddering violently as he held onto her in a death grip. Only when the ecstasy faded did she even realize that he'd come inside her too, releasing his seed.

To her surprise, he turned and staggered forward a few steps, his cock still buried inside her. "Peter!" She tried to stop him, but he simply let go of one bottom cheek and smacked it lightly, then continued walking.

The pulsing movement created by his steps ignited her again. Instead of struggling, she whimpered and clung to him more tightly, small convulsions tensing her muscles as the motion of his worsted wool trousers over his hips abraded her inner thighs. Genevieve could already feel her nerves spiraling toward the explosive end she so desperately desired. He was hard, growing inside her, signaling that his arousal was awakening as hers did. Compulsively, she scraped his shoulders, her fingernails sharp.

She hardly noticed when he paused, not until he bent her backward, lowering them both to the bench. He went to draw back, but she struggled to hold him close, gripping his shoulders and tightening her thighs.

"One moment, angel," he growled, disentangling himself. "I want to feel your velvet skin against mine." The low words reminded her of his clothing, now rumpled from her movements on him. He was already stripping off his waistcoat. Then he drew the shirt over his head. She moaned at the magnificent sight of his muscles gleaming in the sun. Lower, his cock was jutting forward from the placket of his trousers. He quickly finished unbuttoning himself and shoved down the garment, taking his stockings to the floor with him.

Peter bent down, and she reached out to brush her fingers over his hair, his temples. But he was quickly on his feet again and bowing over her, nudging her thighs far apart. The bench was accommodatingly wide. Genevieve reclined against its back and propped her foot on the far armrest. When Peter slid home, lifting her hips a bit to deepen his penetration, she raised her right thigh and encircled his again, holding him close.

He growled against her forehead, shifting his upper body to hold himself a bare inch above her as he fucked her. She whimpered at the separation, pushing her hands into the cushions so that she rubbed against him, sliding her nipples over his chest as they rocked together. The expression on his face, drawn and tight but with his gaze fixated on her, stilled Genevieve's heart. She felt tears form in her eyes, pressed harder against him and felt him slam deeply inside her.

All control evaporated. She screamed, clung, burst into flames and dug her fingernails into his shoulders as the vibrations washed over her. And still he drove her on, unrelenting, his cock throbbing within her even as he withdrew and buried himself inside her sheath again and again.

When he came deep within her, his face contorted into twisted relief and his mouth covered hers, his tongue driving deep.

Genevieve lay back on the bench, utterly worn.

Peter picked up his shirt and gently wiped the sheen of perspiration from her face, then sat back on the bench, Genevieve's feet in his lap.

They remained like that for a moment or two, until Genevieve asked wearily, "How am I to get back to our rooms, then, with my gown half shredded?"

Peter blinked at her. "It's my damn house. If I want to carry you through it with you bare to the skin and in the midst of your release, no servant had better make themselves seen or heard."

Genevieve rolled her eyes. "It's also Ellen's home now, and soon there will be nursemaids and nannies and a small one to call the place home too."

He smiled at that, cupping the lower curve of her stomach. She knew she was attractive to him, but now Peter looked as if he were mentally measuring, looking for any evidence of change.

"I suspect it's a little early for that, Peter," she chided gently.

His gaze moved up her body, pausing well below her chin, before meeting her gaze. "You, my dear, are utterly distracting." He sighed, tapped her chin and moved her legs so he could stand.

He strode off through the maze of plants, a sight which Genevieve happily admired from behind him. She hummed, smiling in welcome when he returned, her garments in hand. The chemise was easy to don, then the remains of her gown. Over it, Peter buttoned his waistcoat, grumbling as he dressed himself in his shoes, trousers and shirt.

"I'll ring for a bath once we go up," Genevieve promised. "It's a bit early, but not irredeemable, especially as I've been painting."

Peter smiled down at her. "Yes, and it's adorable."

Genevieve frowned at him then looked around, but there were no mirrors in the conservatory.

No one appeared as they exited and climbed the main stairs. In the anteroom Peter took Genevieve into his arms and carried her through the corridors to their rooms. She noticed he was loath to leave her, staying to strip her of her clothing again and helping her to don her dressing gown. She groaned when she finally examined herself in the mirror, wiping ineffectually at the tiny spots of paint dried on her face. The rainbow of colors on her cheeks demonstrated how energetically she'd been painting.

Peter only grinned engagingly and kissed the flecks before he tugged the bell-pull for her and retreated.

Genevieve was well aware that he'd left her without insisting on an answer to the question he'd posed before she'd distracted him with their lovemaking. He wouldn't have forgotten, and he would expect her to remember. He'd ask her again how she coped with the remaining anger and grief left from the implosion of her family, and the next time he'd expect a response.

She thought about his question as she bathed and dressed for dinner, insisting on a particularly attractive evening gown she knew Peter would appreciate. It displayed her décolletage to advantage. Beneath it, she simply wore slippers and went without stockings and corset.

Her maid promised to lay a fire in the dining room to keep her warm.

Genevieve leaned contentedly on Peter's arm when he appeared in her rooms and escorted her downstairs. They dined in pleasant companionship, speaking of their plans for the autumn and of the holidays. After dinner, they retreated together to the library, where Genevieve wandered until Peter lit the fire and approached her.

"You asked earlier," she began idly, staring up at one of her own paintings, hung over the fireplace, "about how I handled my anger, what I did to cope. I didn't know how to answer, except painting." Behind her, Peter stilled, then moved to her side, leaning against the bookcase next to her. She glanced at him, then looked back at the painting. "But later, I realized the answer, and I thought you deserved to know."

Peter eyed her, raising an eyebrow as he waited.

She shrugged, then grinned. "You… It's you."

Peter narrowed his eyes, looking puzzled and questioning her without a word.

"At first, early, you were my white knight. You'd rescued me. You'd saved me. You were my salvation. Whenever the anger bubbled up inside me, I forced myself to wait for you to call at Fielding House, to remind myself that you cared. I used you to distract me. Later, there was the excitement of having you escort me to events, to waltz with me. This year, I think the crisis with Gloria brought it back to me. Remember how His Grace helped Gloria escape Winchester, something he didn't do for me. I mean, I realize he probably did it because of little Eynon, not because of Gloria herself, but that's what started it."

She drew a deep breath. "There I was, married nearly two years to you, and something inside of me was slowly getting desperate. Maybe I thought it was a need for you," she confessed. "I don't think I had been nursing a heartache for Lennox, for a parent, not at all. I had Ellen and your mother and Sir John. Without them, I-I-I don't know what I would have done since we married."

"But they weren't enough of a salve, were they?" Peter asked, prompting her when she stopped.

Genevieve shrugged. "There you were. I wanted you. I freely admit it. Your mother and Ellen encouraged me. I suppose neither of them knew about your vow to stay out of my bed until I was nineteen."

"No, they wouldn't have known," Peter confirmed.

"So I plotted and planned and manipulated to see if I could attract you. And, in paying attention to you, I distracted myself from what I was feeling." She smiled at him quickly, then her lips wobbled and she looked away. "Through all of this, I discovered so much about me, about you, about us together. I learned about love, about trust, about intimacy. I *crave* being with you—and not as a distraction. But I will say that after this afternoon in the conservatory, I no longer feel as if I'm going to explode."

"Interesting." Peter grazed her figure with lust-filled eyes. She suppressed a laugh and glared at him. "If that's what you require, I'm happy to volunteer."

Genevieve humphed. "I also plan to burn that canvas I was sacrificing." She wrinkled her nose at him. "Let me paint you," she proposed in the sultriest voice she could manage, patting her hand against his chest.

"Not tonight, angel." Peter's amused expression filled her with a soul-deep happiness she couldn't explain. "Tonight I have other plans."

Genevieve opened her eyes wide. "Indeed?" she purred. "What plans would those be?"

Peter reached up and locked his hand around her wrist, fastening with iron-clad tightness.

"You, naked except for yards of satin ribbon, and my bed. Maybe by morning you will get to sleep. For tonight, I suggest we use each other to put everything from our minds except...us."

Joy exploded in Genevieve's heart. "Yes, yes," she agreed, and Peter drew her into his arms.

About the Author

Elle writes stories to entertain her friends and amuse herself. Over time, the stories have got better, and she hopes romance lovers everywhere will love them as much as she does.

Elle lives among the redwoods in the very great state of California with a devoted Mr. Sabine, one golden-headed daughter and one loving, eternally young pup. Yes, those are her curls and part of her study bookshelves!

In her spare time, she loves to explore fairy circles, climb to high places to see the Pacific and look at the bottom of the Golden Gate Bridge.

Elle loves to hear from readers. You can find her contact information, website details and author profile page at http://www.totallybound.com.

TOTALLY
BOUND

Home of Erotic Romance